LINES OF LOVE

What Reviewers Say About
Brey Willows's Work

Song of Serenity

"This was a fun introduction to a new series in a world I already love to bits, and I'm looking forward to meeting the other eight muses in upcoming books."—*The Good, the Bad, and the Unread*

"*Song of Serenity* is an all-around fun read. ...Willows is an auto buy author with me because she consistently puts out original stories that stay vivid in my mind long after I've finished the book." —*Lesbian Review*

"The story was filled with passion, tension, and a wonderful sense of a believable kind of magic."—*Lesbireviewed*

"A contented smile graced my lips when I closed the back cover of this book. Willows' latest work (as always) was a joy to read and it filled me with a peaceful happiness from the first word to the very last. Words are inadequate when it comes to describing the calibre of Willows' storytelling ability; it has to be felt. And that is where the core of Willows' talents lie—so beautifully displayed within *Song of Serenity*—the gift to elicit a readers thoughts, feelings and imagination."—*Queer Literary Loft*

"...it's a journey that feels familiar to anyone who's ever tried to make a relationship work. How comforting is it to think that gods and goddesses face the same questions?"—*Jude in the Stars*

Changing Course

"Cosmos dust and prowler balls, this was good. The romance is exactly what a good love story should be like. …This was an exciting adventure with a satisfying romance. A quick read that kept me turning pages. A story with a lot of heart."—*Bookvark*

"*Changing Course* is a wonderful book about intergalactic love between two people who were never supposed to meet and how a once chance meeting changed the course of both their lives forever."—*Les Rêveur*

"Ms. Willows has done an excellent job of world building which is essential for a story like this. The alien world and the different types of people are so vividly drawn that they seem real to the reader. The characters, both main and secondary are very well developed. The story begins with a bang and never lets up. …This is a fantastic novel and is going into my favorites category. It has my highest recommendation." —*Rainbow Reflections*

"No matter what genre Brey Willows turns her hand to we can count on meeting incredible characters, falling into a mind-blowing world and being swept away by a wonderful story."—*Beyond the Crime Scene Tape*

"[A] beautifully crafted sci-fi story with exquisite world-building. …The romantic element was touching and the sex was so hot—but it takes something special to blend that with a fantastic story. *Changing Course* does all of that. I loved it."—*Kitty Kat's Book Review Blog*

"Imagine if you will, the pairing of a lesbian Jenna Stanis (from *Blake's 7*) and the lesbian answer to a young Han Solo. Throw in a thrilling crash landing and a whole host of dangers on the planet itself and you have the makings of something quite, quite special. …I really, really enjoyed this book. It had all the elements I loved in the books I loved as a teenager and then some."—*The Good, The Bad and The Unread*

Spinning Tales

"I love what the author has done with traditional fairy tales, and I appreciate the originality of the new characters and elements to classic stories."—*Kissing Backwards*

"This was a charming read! I liked the main character and the way the fairy tale realm works. I also found some of the problems and solutions to be quite funny and fun to read. This is a good read for those who like fairy tales and retellings."—*Fierce Female Reads*

"The story was wonderfully, magically imaginative. And you know, I didn't doubt for a minute that the cottage existed exactly where she said it did! ...I loved the story and the imagination behind it but most of all I was enthralled by the use of language. It was beautiful and poetic and lyrical. ...*Spinning Tales* is excellent and I highly recommend it."—*Kitty Kat's Book Review Blog*

Fury's Bridge

"[*Fury's Bridge*] is a paranormal read that's not like any other. The premise is unique with some intriguing ideas. The main character is witty, strong and interesting."—Melina Bickard, Librarian (Waterloo Library, London)

Fury's Death

"This series has been getting steadily better as it's progressed."—*The Good, the Bad, and the Unread*

"The whole [Afterlife Inc. series] is an intriguing concept, light and playfully done but well researched and constructed, with enough ancient and mythological detail to make it work without ever becoming a theology lesson. If you believe in a higher being how would you react to God or Jesus, Jehovah or Mohammed, being available by email? If you don't believe, how would you feel if the gods—all of them—materialised? ...The romances are well done, unusual issues when eternal forces fall for mortal humans and mental concepts collide. But while the romances are central, the stories are far bigger, dealing, albeit lightly, with the constant battle between good and evil, forces of Chaos and destruction wanting humanity to destroy itself while the gods make a stand for peace, love and ecological sanity."—*Lesbian Reading Room*

Fury's Choice

"As with the first in the series, this book is part romance, part paranormal adventure, with a lot of humor and thought-provoking words on religion, belief, and self-determination thrown in. ...It is real page-turning stuff."—*Rainbow Reading Room*

"*Fury's Choice* is a refreshing and creative endeavor. The story is populated with flawed and retired gods, vengeful Furies, delightful and thought-provoking characters who give our perspective of religion a little tweak. As tension builds, the story becomes an action-packed adventure. The love affair between Tis and Kera is enchanting. The bad guys are rotten to the core as one might expect. Willows uses well placed wit and humor to enhance the story and break the tension, which masterfully increases as the story progresses."—*Lambda Literary*

Chosen

"If I had a checklist with all the elements that I want to see in a book, *Chosen* could satisfy each item. The characters are so completely relatable, the action scenes are cinematic, the plot kept me on my toes, the dystopian theme is entirely relevant, and the romance is sweet and sexy."—*Lesbian Review*

Visit us at www.boldstrokesbooks.com

By the Author

Memory's Muses Novels:

Vision of Virtue

Song of Serenity

Lines of Love

Changing Course

Spinning Tales

Chosen

Afterlife, Inc Trilogy:

Fury's Death

Fury's Choice

Fury's Bridge

LINES OF LOVE

by

Brey Willows

2022

LINES OF LOVE
© 2022 BY BREY WILLOWS. ALL RIGHTS RESERVED.

ISBN 13: 978-1-63555-458-8

THIS TRADE PAPERBACK ORIGINAL IS PUBLISHED BY
BOLD STROKES BOOKS, INC.
P.O. BOX 249
VALLEY FALLS, NY 12185

FIRST EDITION: DECEMBER 2022

CREDITS
EDITOR: CINDY CRESAP
PRODUCTION DESIGN: SUSAN RAMUNDO
COVER DESIGN BY TAMMY SEIDICK

Acknowledgments

Forks in the road are difficult things. They're spiky and the tines have gaps between them where all the world can slip through. They're not nearly as dependable as, say, a spoon. And the people who help you navigate those spiky, holey forks are worth their weight in gold spoons. Sandy at BSB, you have been my friend for many, many years. We have discussed countless odd and often publicly inappropriate topics, and I'm lucky to have you in my life. To Rad, who has been a guide and mentor for nearly fifteen years, I'm eternally grateful. Cindy Cresap, you've been a mentor, a sounding board, and a perfectly positioned guide. Your words of encouragement have been more valuable than I can ever say. And to the rest of the team at BSB, thank you for everything you've done with and for me. To the readers who keep coming back, you're amazing and I hope you continue to play in the worlds I submerge myself in. And last, to my wife, who waits at the forks with all other available cutlery in hand, who helps me conserve my spoons, and who cuts through my self-doubt with carving knives: I love you.

Dedication

Love is bedside roses, talky time, car karaoke,
morning hugs, cuddle time, date night, eye contact
across the room, sexy dancing, and a million
more things that will never be enough.

For my wife, who teaches me every day
what love looks like.

CHAPTER ONE

Eris Ardalides ducked under the spray of champagne from a newly uncorked bottle as she gracefully slid past the table of celebrating folks still in suits from the day's work. She held aloft her drink so she didn't spill it on any of the grinding, pulsing bodies crowding the dance floor under the sensual blue lights. Sweat beaded on her neck, and she grinned at a woman who caught her eye and moved in a way that left no question as to what she was offering if Eris wanted to take her up on it.

Another time, she might have stopped. But tonight, the Infinite Club was packed and needed more than a club owner enjoying the fruits of her labor, however luscious those fruits might seem. She said hello and smiled at many of the regulars she'd come to know, albeit on an extremely surface level. More than one woman pressed against her, stoking the flame that always burned at the core of who she was. The line at the bar was acceptable, not too long so people gave up waiting for drinks, but not so short that it looked like no one was drinking.

Eventually she made it to the front entrance where her bouncers, both Polynesian pre-fader gods with the Afterlife, Inc. wings embroidered on one side of their black polo shirts, the Infinite Club logo, complete with arrow and dove, on the other side, were keeping things in order.

"Everything good?" Eris asked as she looked outside to see the line of people hoping to get in. Saturday night in Malibu Bluffs, California, meant no one cared about sleeping and everyone cared about getting into the hottest club in the state.

"Yeah, good. Cupid tried to get in again but we turned him away."
There was no mistaking the disdain in the bouncer's tone and Eris clapped him on the shoulder. "All fun and games in the love world, eh?"

He simply shook his head and went back to watching the crowd. Cupid was a smarmy little shit who had overplayed the cute card and was most often so drunk on ambrosia he could barely stand. He lost his godly appeal in a drum beat when he leered and slobbered on the various dancers, and Eris had long ago banned him. She didn't mind the gods coming along for a good night out among the mortals, but she preferred to keep it mostly human. The groups coming together usually complicated things in unpredictable ways. Not so long ago, she'd found a strange face in the wall and realized one of the gods had made some poor human a permanent part of her establishment. They used her nose as a coat hanger now.

"Your brothers in boots are here." Kayla, one of the waitresses, moved to Eris's side. "I've put them at your usual table."

Eris pulled her into a hug and kissed her cheek. "You're the best."

"In ways you haven't even figured out yet," Kayla said, returning the squeeze and then moving away.

Eris gradually made her way to the table occupied by her small group of friends, dubbed the brothers in boots by her team. All butch women who rode Harleys, they were the best group of friends Eris had hung out with in three thousand years. After she'd checked the bar and kitchen once more, she finally got to the table and flung herself into a seat opposite DK.

"Just in time. I was about to hit the floor." DK raised her bottle and looked toward the dance floor. Even at fifty, DK's broad shoulders and huge smile meant she took center stage when she began to move.

"Good luck. There's barely room to breathe." Eris picked up DK's beer and took a swig, earning her a glare.

"Just means you can have sex while practically standing still. Simply turn in a circle and enjoy the buffet." Deb gave her trademark sexy grin and smoothed back her thick, dark hair that sat just above her collar. "Although nothing beats Latin night."

"There's too many steps to learn on Latin night," Ebie said, her muscles bunching under her white button-down shirt as she leaned on the table. "At least here you can just move."

Eris laughed. "The last time I saw you on the dance floor must have been a decade ago. Why would you care about how the dancing is done when you don't do it?"

"She means she's too white for Latin night." Deb dodged the shoulder punch Ebie threw at her.

"Yeah, well, my set starts in about ten minutes." Eris stretched, letting her friends' banter ease the tension in her neck. She loved the frenetic atmosphere of the club, and having her friends around made it even better when it began to get stressful.

"I didn't think you were doing sets on busy nights anymore," DK said, still watching the dance floor.

"Not normally, but my usual DJ got married last week, so I'm stepping in tonight while she's on her honeymoon." Eris nodded at a staff member who caught her eye and pointed to his watch.

"Ah, the honeymoon. The last great week she'll ever have." Deb shook her head and put her hand over her heart. "You have to feel for the ones who fall for it."

DK finally looked away from the dance floor. "You've fallen for it repeatedly. Sometimes with more than one woman at a time."

"Nah. Not really." Deb looked serious for a moment. "I mean, when it happens, I think she'll be the one. But then, another one comes along. Forever is a word that should be struck from the English language. For now is always better."

The group laughed, but Eris felt the statement in her bones, like an old ache from breaks that hadn't healed perfectly.

"Women aren't worth the trouble. You never know what they want, and even if they tell you, you're bound to get it wrong." Ebie, who hadn't been with anyone in more than ten years, had long since decided she'd be better off single. She flirted and dated once in a while, but she wasn't about to get with anyone again.

"What do you think, Muse of Love?" DK said, kicking at Eris's boot. "Is it all for nothing? Are we doomed to have it all end at some point?"

Eris took another long swig of DK's beer, finishing it and giving her a cheeky apologetic smile. "You're all Darwinian meat bags who overthink things until you wreck them. You could have real love, but you wouldn't know what to do with it in the long run."

The group groaned and waved her off as she headed for the DJ booth. They'd often had long talks about love and what it meant and why it mattered, but she'd given up trying to get humans to understand the nature of love and creation and how important it was. Even the ones who proclaimed they were in love didn't seem to really understand what it was. Divorce rates during the pandemic years had soared, increasing by ninety-five percent. When things were bad, when couples were forced to be with one another more than they were at work, the relationships had broken down.

She jumped into the DJ booth and put on the headphones. No, the Muse of Love wasn't necessary anymore. Her old job was outmoded. She pushed the keys and let herself fall into the music. This was her world now.

Slats of sunshine and shadow kept the morning cool as Eris hiked up the trail near the house. One of the things she loved about her job was that it left her the days to enjoy the quiet of the canyon around her home. Though it was only a fifteen-minute drive to the club, her place in Dark Canyon felt a million miles away. Oaks and sycamores provided shade and the pines gave off a heady scent as they baked under the California sun.

She stopped on the bluff where she caught a glimpse of the vast ocean in the distance and she turned her face to the sky, her eyes closed, as she breathed the silence and simplicity into her soul. Something pushed against her leg, and she grinned without opening her eyes, knowing full well who it would be.

"Wondered if you'd show up today." A soft head pushed against her hand, and she opened it to let the mountain lion's head press against her palm. The rumble of its purr vibrated up her arm. After she gave it a good scratch behind its ears, it flopped to the ground beside her in a patch of sunshine and rolled lazily onto its back. "You're such a little hussy."

Eris sat cross-legged on the rock beside it and rubbed the soft, warm belly as her thoughts drifted to the night before. The club had closed around four in the morning, though her group of friends were gone by then. DK and Deb had predictably left with someone, and equally predictably, Ebie hadn't. Plenty of offers had been thrown Eris's way, but after their conversation about love, she'd lost her appetite for some fleeting company.

The giant cat's ears perked up and she rolled over, listening. Soon, Eris heard it too. The telltale sound of a Harley headed up the winding canyon road. Eris stood and the cat did too. "Looks like I've got company. You coming to the house?"

Unsurprisingly, the mountain lion didn't respond. Rather, she sat looking into the distance as though Eris wasn't there. A cat was a cat, after all. "Okay, then. See you."

Eris turned and headed back down the mountain trail toward her house. Butted up against the cliffside and surrounded by trees, it was the farthest from the road, and the last one before the forest took over completely. It was her sanctuary, her place away from the world, and with its proximity to the beach, it gave her the best of everything.

She arrived just as not one, but two Harleys pulled into her long drive. One, custom made for the enormous god who rode it, blinked translucent purple in the shafts of light. The other, red and sleek, looked like a toy beside it.

She waved as she passed them and headed up into the house. "Leaded or unleaded?" she asked.

"Unleaded for me. I'm on a health kick," Sian said, taking off her helmet and running her hand through her short blond hair.

"Me too. Not for a health kick. I just want some iced tea." Prometheus, looking every inch the biker with his thick gray beard and massive arms, also took off his helmet.

Eris went to the kitchen and poured three tall glasses of iced tea, adding a slice of orange to hers and Prometheus's, and a bit of sweetener to Sian's. By the time she was carrying them out to the deck, both were already relaxing at the table.

"Thanks," Sian said, taking a long drink. "It's hot today, especially in full gear."

Eris stretched her legs out in front of her. "Prom, why do you wear a helmet? We could whack your head off with a sword and you wouldn't die. We'd just reattach your head. What's the point?"

He laughed, the sound bouncing off the trees and canyon rock around them. "We're supposed to set a good example, aren't we? If we tell humans to do things that we won't do, then how can they keep believing in us? In what we say?"

Eris shook her head, smiling in return. "I'm pretty sure you're the only god to think that way. Too bad you're not one of the primary gods. It would be a better place."

He shrugged his massive shoulders. "The world is what it's always been since I brought humans fire against the wishes of Zeus." Lightly, he pushed at Sian's shoulder. "Like this little human here. They're really an awful lot of fun, even when they do refuse to share your bed."

Sian rolled her eyes but didn't respond. The conversation had been had many times since Eris and Prometheus had saved her from a plane crash she'd been in with Eris's sister Clio. When they'd returned and she'd been nursing her broken heart, Eris had taken her under her wing and shown her how easy it was to turn heartbreak into something more fruitful. Love, after all, was fleeting and there were plenty of women to pretend at it for a night or two.

"What brings you guys to my little piece of paradise?"

Sian's eyes were closed as she tilted her face to the sun. "Prom suggested a ride, and I haven't seen you for a while. Wanted to make sure you weren't wallowing in your sucky love pit."

"I don't wallow. Ever. And I've just been busy." It wasn't entirely true, and they all knew it.

"What's on your mind?" Prom asked.

Bird calls and the rustling of little animals in the underbrush were the only sounds as Eris considered her answer. Silence was never an issue with these two, something she appreciated immensely. "Honestly? Nothing. And I guess that's what's bothering me. There's nothing to think about. I work and I come home. I sleep, fuck, eat. I'm just—"

"Existing." Prometheus nodded knowingly, his old eyes wise in his kind face. "You can't think you're the only immortal to do so? We all fall into a slump at some point."

Sian snorted. "What you've described is life, buddy. It's just life. That's what we do."

Eris wasn't sure how to respond without offending her by saying that's what *humans* did.

Prometheus had no such compunction. "For humans, yes. That's very much what many of you do, mostly thanks to your short lifespans and occasionally shorter attention spans. But not all of you. Electricity, the internet, burning coal for fire, sending telescopes into space… thinkers, people who were always thinking about something, have moved your kind forward in amazing ways."

Sian shifted to look at Eris. "Yeah, but that's not everyone, is it? That's just a handful of people. So can't you cloud fairies be like us? Some who think or do more than others?"

Prometheus's laugh once again boomed off the canyon, sending birds squawking into the air. "To some degree, yes." He gestured at Eris with his glass of iced tea. "But Muses weren't built that way. Their whole purpose is to inspire, to get people to think and feel and create. If a Muse isn't doing that, then the lack of thinking about it will bother her."

Eris simply nodded. There wasn't anything more to add to it.

"So you're having a midlife crisis of some kind. What is midlife for someone who doesn't die? Or do you just crash into some kind of ennui tar pit until someone kicks your ass out of it?" Sian's tone made it clear she wasn't feeling all that sympathetic.

"Fuck off." Eris laughed, the feeling lightened. "Until the world learns to love again, I'm just taking a back seat. When things change, I'll get back into the game. No big deal." She stood and stretched. "Let's go get lunch."

Prometheus stood and waved her off. "I have lunch in my saddle bags. Got it from the cafeteria at Afterlife. Thought you might like a bit of home."

He went out to his bike, and Sian bumped Eris with her shoulder. "Seriously, you okay?"

Eris bumped her back. "Yeah. I'm good. Existence can just feel a little long sometimes."

Sian watched a squirrel hopping through the brush below the deck. "I can't imagine living forever and not knowing what to do with myself. I hope you figure things out."

Eris warmed at Sian's genuine concern. "Love between friends can mean a hell of a lot, you know."

Sian glanced at her and away again. "Sap."

The rest of the afternoon was spent eating food from Afterlife, and Prometheus was right. The dolmades and moussaka were a beautiful taste of home that made her remember a world that was simpler and where she knew she belonged. Like everything, the feeling would be fleeting, but she could enjoy it for now.

Chapter Two

G race Gordon rested her head on the cold glass conference table. There wasn't enough aspirin in the world to take care of the headache her last clients had given her. The woman, wearing a real fur coat even though it was eighty degrees outside, had been determined that her husband owed her and her adult children the life to which they'd been accustomed. She seemed stuck on the fact that he made a strange wheezing sound when he snored, as though that alone required some kind of financial penance on his part. The fact that he was filing for divorce, and that she'd signed a prenup, made no difference, no matter how many times Grace tried to explain it.

The door opened and Grace turned her head, not bothering to lift it from the table.

"Thought you'd need this." Her assistant, Brad, set a large glass of water and two pain pills beside it.

"Please tell me she's gone." Grace forced herself to raise her head and quickly swallowed the pills and water.

"Her little rat dog pissed on Carol's money tree plant, and her son shoved a security guard, but yeah, the whole posse of posers is gone." He sat next to her and pulled the file forward to look it over. "The husband put up with a lot. Can you imagine having to hear about her daughter's Botox lawsuit one more time? Or about the son's latest big production?"

Grace looked at the photos Brad was flipping through. Not only had the wife had affairs, but she'd also posted photos on every social media platform of her with every man she'd cheated on him with. Why it had taken him so long to begin divorce proceedings she couldn't fathom. "People will put up with a lot when they're hoping something is real."

"Let's walk down to Javier's and get lunch. You've hardly been out of the office this week." He stood and pulled her to her feet.

At the thought of Mexican food, her stomach rumbled loudly and they laughed. "Perfect." She grabbed her bag and they walked out into the hot afternoon. As always, the intersection of Santa Monica Boulevard and Avenue of the Stars was bustling with people, mostly from the many office towers, but plenty of tourists roamed the area too.

"Those are killer boots, by the way," Brad said, dodging a street hawker selling sunglasses emblazoned with LA's Gods are Hotter than Yours in silver rhinestones.

She flexed her toes in the tight leather. "I didn't need another pair, but Macy's was having a sale. And I do love a pair of knee-high boots."

"Many a butch would love to have them over their shoulders, I'm sure." He shot her a mischievous grin. "Speaking of which, when are you going to start dating again?"

She sighed and managed to avoid answering as they arrived at Javier's, a fancy, overpriced but good Mexican restaurant that they often had margaritas at after long days at the office. They ordered quickly, both knowing what they wanted, and he sat there looking at her quizzically.

"What?"

"Answer the question." He dug into the basket of artisan tortilla chips, which meant they were usually spiced with something odd.

"I don't have time. You, of all people, know what my schedule looks like. And if I'm going to make partner next year, I definitely don't have time to waste on nights out with women who only want a fling, or who want to marry me the next day. There doesn't seem to be an in-between." She sighed happily at the spice of the salsa coating her tongue.

"Oh please. The 'I don't have time' excuse is so weak. Plenty of people manage to date and climb the social ladder. You have occasional weekends and evenings off. You can't tell me you couldn't fit in a date or two per month, even if it was just to scratch your itch. And you must be itchy as a dog covered in fleas in summertime."

Between the iced tea, chips, and salsa, her headache was beginning to ease, but Brad's teasing was a little irksome, even when he let his Southern accent pop out. Probably because she didn't have a good answer. "Why are you so interested in my love life, anyway? Don't you and Craig have enough going on?"

He sat back so the waiter could put down the enchiladas and tacos, and then set to swapping one of her tacos for one of his enchiladas, the way he always did. "That's the thing. We're so deliriously happy that I want everyone in my psychic sphere to be too."

She groaned at the delicious flavor of the beef as it practically melted on her tongue. "The moment I find the woman who meets at least seven out of ten things on my list, I'll make all the time in the world."

"The list." He rolled his eyes and dabbed at his mouth with his napkin. "You can't make a list of things you want another human being to have. Sometimes the right person isn't the one you think you wanted. I never would have imagined myself with a little pot-bellied bald man, but now I can't imagine myself with anyone else, ever."

"They don't have to be perfect. But if I know ahead of time that they meet at least some criteria, then I know they'll have a chance of being right for me, and that we could have something that would last. It's logical."

They ate in silence for a moment, devouring their food way too fast. Grace continued to ponder their conversation. "Every day we see couples who didn't make sure they were compatible before they committed to one another. This way, I can be sure there's a chance of us being sympatico. Like I said. It's logical."

"And utterly unromantic." He finished his meal and sat back with a happy sigh and checked his watch. "We've got half an hour before the Smythe couple come in. Let's get Starbucks on the way."

They paid and made their way onto the quieter back street leading to the coffee house. Two of the senior partners were coming out when they got to the door.

"Grace, good to see you getting some air." Rob Kline, of Kline and Associates, always looked austere.

"Don't get too much, though. Wouldn't want that partnership spot going to someone else." Rob's son, Richard, laughed too loudly and it didn't reach his eyes.

It was no secret Grace and Richard had never gotten along. He was petty, misogynistic, and so full of his own entitlement it was a wonder he didn't explode into a mess of torn money and narcissism. He'd asked Grace out several times, even after she'd told him she was gay, and he seemed to take it personally that she'd said no. Or maybe it was when she'd told him to keep his slimy octopus hands off her at the last office party. Loudly and publicly.

She smiled sweetly. "No worries there, guys. Just getting caffeinated for the rest of the day."

They ambled off, leaving her like a mote of dust in their wake, and the relaxed feeling she'd developed from her lunch with Brad dissipated.

Brad put his hand on her shoulder. "Don't let the bastards get you down. You'll get that damn partner position and Richard can stuff it up his tight, waxed ass."

"That's an image I didn't need in my head." She laughed and squeezed his shoulder. "Thanks, though."

Back at her desk, she sipped her coffee Frappuccino and sorted through the files for the rest of her caseload that day. She just had to stay focused, and everything else would fall into place.

Grace walked through the empty parking lot. She'd traded her gorgeous boots for a simple pair of sneakers after the rest of the office had gone dark. Even so, lifting her feet to get to her car took monumental effort. She was so exhausted she wanted to crawl into the back of her car and sleep right there. But then, she couldn't show up at the office the next day looking like she'd slept in her car. In this city, image mattered a little more than skill.

There was a shout, and the ground shook beneath her. But it wasn't a rolling or shaking like an earthquake. She leaned against the car and looked around, and then promptly dropped her keys and pressed herself against the cold metal.

A beast came out of the darkness. Glowing ruby red eyes showed on each of the three heads. The huge body lumbered at her, and the head in the middle dropped a tree trunk at her feet.

It waited. Its thick tail, so dark it could be the entrance to a black hole, thumped against the ground, rattling the windows of Grace's car. The middle head dipped toward the tree, while the other two heads appeared to be looking for something.

There was another shout, and the middle head picked up the tree trunk in its giant, sharp-toothed maw, before the beast ran off down Santa Monica Boulevard.

Grace took in a shuddering breath and caught it again when a tall, handsome woman ran out of the darkness from the same direction the nightmare had come from.

"Have you seen my...dog?" she asked breathlessly, glancing at Grace and then away at the street around them.

"You mean the giant monster with three heads?" Grace asked, crossing her arms.

"Cerb is *not* a monster. How rude. Which way did he go?" she asked, glaring at Grace. There were screams and shouts, and the woman groaned. "Hades is going to kill me. Never mind." She set off running in the direction of the commotion.

Her hands trembling, Grace picked up her keys, opened her car door and slid into the seat, her legs shaking. The world had changed so much since the Merge several years ago. Gods were seen ordering pancakes at diners as easily as in churches and on TV. Violence, for the most part, had diminished massively, although as part of human nature, it still took place.

But monsters running the streets, that was new. Those eyes and teeth would haunt her dreams tonight, that was certain. And who the hell was the woman who'd chased after it? She'd looked normal enough, but normal people didn't chase three-headed dogs down the streets of Century City or reference the god of the underworld.

Still shaky, she got on the road and headed the opposite direction of the surreal situation.

Her home, a little one-bedroom in a quiet neighborhood in Altadena, was only thirty minutes away, but it was far enough to feel like she could really get away from work. Some of the other lawyers lived much closer, especially the associates like her who wanted to spend as little time as possible away from their desks. But she liked the cottage type house with its tiny backyard within walking distance to the park full of wild parrots. It wasn't fancy, and it certainly wouldn't have passed muster among her colleagues, but that made it even better. She never felt the need to have people over.

She tumbled into bed after a cursory brush of her teeth, too exhausted to lie awake thinking about the bizarre experience in the parking lot.

In the morning, however, she woke from dreams of being chased through empty streets by a monster. Sweat soaked her tank top and she was queasy with anxiety. She got out of bed and went straight to a hot shower, which made her feel better almost immediately. By the time she got out, the dream was nothing more than a wisp of memory and she was ravenous for breakfast.

She checked her phone while her coffee brewed and saw a missed message from Brad.

Going to a club tonight. I'm picking you up at eight and dragging you out no matter what you're wearing. Xo.

She set the phone down without replying and poured her coffee. Surely an assistant wasn't supposed to tell you what to do. Wasn't it supposed to be the other way around? Sipping, she sent a reply with nothing but an emoji sticking out its tongue.

In truth, it would be good to get out. He was right, she'd been burning the midnight oil and it wasn't going to last. A little bit of fun to refuel wouldn't hurt, and she could leave the office well before it would be time to go out so she could come back and figure out what to wear. She got ready at a leisurely pace and ordered an extra-large latte on her drive in. The office was fairly quiet, with only a handful of other lawyers already at their desks. Working six days a week wasn't unusual in this business, and she liked the quiet hum on the weekends when she could really concentrate.

The rest of the day flew past, and before she knew it, she needed to head home to get ready for the night out she now wanted to avoid entirely. All she really wanted was to snuggle down with a book and a glass of wine.

She laughed when she picked up her phone and saw a text from Brad.

Don't even think about telling me you're not coming. I'll be there at eight.

She didn't reply. If she really didn't want to go, he'd have accepted it. But life was about balance, and she needed some.

At eight exactly, Brad pulled up in his convertible KIA and hopped out. "We're taking your car. They wouldn't let us within fifty feet of the door if we pulled up in mine." He looked her over. "Nice. Not Boston nice, but LA nice."

She smoothed down the crosscut blouse that draped over her breasts, leaving a thin, long line of cleavage but not so much it was crass. Her jeans, bootcut and slimming so she wasn't self-conscious about the slight tummy she never seemed able to get rid of, felt good. The chunky metal heels on her boots were the finishing touch.

"I hated going out in Boston. Everyone had to be so dressed up. It made the entire night uncomfortable." They got into her Audi and she followed the GPS directions he punched into the console.

"Yeah, but they look classy out there. And taking a suit jacket off a guy is hot." He pressed buttons until he got to a station he liked. "Anyway, a few of my friends are going to meet us there too."

She'd met some of his friends before, and they were much like him. Fun, intelligent, witty, and ready to have a good time. They chatted about work, gossiped about their co-workers, and even talked a little about his family, who adored him and wished he'd come back to Georgia one day.

Her eyes widened when they pulled up to the club. They got out and handed the keys to the valet, and she frowned at the line that reached all the way down the side of the building. "I'm not standing in that in the hopes we get in."

He took her hand and led her to the door. "Hi. We're on the list." He gave his name, the bouncer ticked it off and then lifted the rope to let them in.

"That's impressive," she shouted as they were instantly slammed with a heavy bass beat.

"Marcus knows the owner," he shouted back, looking at his phone. "They're at the back."

She followed him past the bar, through the heaving, bouncing crowd, to the deck area, where tables were arranged along the sides with views of the ocean below. Brad's friends waved them over, and she was glad to see there were already drinks waiting for them.

The banter and fun were instant, and her shoulders began to relax. The drink was sweet and cold, and the air was warm and sultry. She hadn't been to Malibu in a while, and she didn't think this club had been here when she'd last been on the beach. Gold hearts, arrows, and doves were the theme throughout, dangling from the ceiling here and there as well as painted onto the tables. Quotes about love were scrawled in bold script on walls and printed on the little paper napkins. While it could have been over-the-top and cheesy, it managed to maintain a classy, chic vibe instead.

Brad grabbed her hand and led her to the dance floor, where she let herself fall into the music. She moved, not caring what she looked like or what other people thought. The music slowed and there were whistles and calls through the crowd, and she looked around to see what was going on.

There, on stage, was the woman from the parking lot last night. The tall, sexy butch wearing a T-shirt with the sleeves cut off, a thick silver necklace that glinted in the strobe lights, and an American eagle belt buckle looked completely at home wearing the DJ headphones, one hand raised in the air as she bounced, the other doing whatever it was DJs did with the array of electronics in front of her.

"What's wrong?" Brad leaned forward and shouted.

She shook her head. "I ran into that woman last night. The DJ!" she shouted back.

He looked surprised but didn't say anything else until they got back to their table. "Where exactly did you run into the muse of love?" he asked as he gulped down half a bottle of water.

She frowned, unsure she'd heard right. "What?"

He motioned at the hearts and arrows on the table. "The muse of love. Eris owns this place and she's a hell of a DJ. She's also one of the Afterlife crew. You know, immortal, unattainable, and too hot for human consumption. Where did you see her?"

The group at the table waited for her to answer, and finally, she shrugged. "She was chasing a monstrous three-headed dog through our parking lot."

There was a moment of silence before they erupted in laughter. Like Grace, they all wondered what the story behind that was, but she didn't have any answers. She let herself relax into the surreal evening of dancing at a club owned by a muse, surrounded by other people who just wanted a good time.

She was at the bar, waiting on a drink, when someone came to the bar in front of her. It was the muse, sweaty, sexy, and looking edible.

Booze-addled and happy, Grace tapped her on the shoulder. "Did you find your dog? Dogs? Is it one or three if it shares one body?"

She turned and looked down at Grace. She must have been at least five foot ten, and her light blue eyes sparkled with humor. Traces of sweat beaded on her collar bone, which Grace very much wanted to lick.

"I did, thanks. We were playing fetch, and I threw his toy just when someone else was coming in the door. He managed to escape, but I got him home before he ate anyone." She held out her hand. "Eris."

Grace took her hand, noticing how large and strong it felt in her own. Her stomach flipped. "Grace."

Instead of letting go, Eris held her hand and led her to the dance floor, where a thrumming sexy beat set the tone. Grace followed Eris's lead into a sensual, almost frenetic dance that made her head spin. The feel of Eris's hard, jean clad thigh between her legs made her throw her head back and simply feel the way their bodies were moving together.

One song morphed into the next, and Grace was on fire. It had been far too long since she'd been with someone and her breasts ached, her nipples were too hard, and her clit hurt against her jeans. Barely a breath of space existed between their bodies and the lust in Eris's eyes was unmistakable. She lifted her chin and Eris crushed her lips to hers, tangling her hands in Grace's hair.

They broke the kiss and Eris turned abruptly, guiding Grace through the throng of bodies to a corridor at the back. She punched a key code into a panel by an unmarked door and shoved it open, pulling Grace in behind her.

The sex against the door was hard and fast. Eris opened Grace's jeans in a heartbeat, and then her hand was inside Grace's panties, her fingers thrusting into her drenched pussy. Grace wrapped her leg around Eris's hip, pulling her close, one hand on the back of Eris's neck as the other clawed at the wall while she moaned and rode Eris's hand.

Whatever it was Eris was doing with her fingers, it was driving Grace insane. She came hard, her body quaking as she pushed down on Eris's fingers. "God, don't stop. Please don't stop." She didn't care that she was begging, and it seemed to light Eris's fire. She yanked Grace's top down to reveal the white lace bra and then sucked her nipple hard through the lace, her fingers never stopping as she fucked Grace into a sweet oblivion that wasn't about to end.

After the third, or maybe fourth, orgasm, Grace sagged against the wall and Eris slowly slid out of her. Eris rested her head against the door beside Grace's, her hands loose on Grace's hips.

A crackle, a voice, and someone calling for Eris made her raise her head. "Sorry," she said softly, and turned to pick up a radio off the desk. "Go ahead," she said into it.

"We need you up front for a customer issue," someone said. "Quick."

"On my way." Eris set the radio down and gave Grace an apologetic smile. "Sorry, again. I need to run." She lifted Grace's hand and kissed it. "Maybe we can continue this another time."

Grace, befuddled and fucked incoherent, simply nodded. What did you say? Thank you for fucking me stupid? Eris gently moved Grace to the side and then opened the door.

"Feel free to use the bathroom in here. It's at the back, over there." She leaned down and kissed Grace's lips with the tenderness of a lover. "See you soon."

And then she was gone, and Grace was alone.

CHAPTER THREE

The morning light cast long shadows through the floor to ceiling bedroom window of the beach house. Eris stretched and yawned. The sheets were cool and the air was already warm, meaning she'd probably head to the pool at some point. Voices floated up from outside and she kicked aside the sheets. She padded barefoot onto the balcony and saw a group of people already lounging outside. She rested her arms on the balcony railing, scanning the group. Nope. She didn't actually know any of them, but that wasn't unusual. After a crazy night at the club, she often invited random people she'd been dancing with over to the beach house next door. This place was nice, but it was purely practical, unlike her home in the canyon where her heart resided.

A woman by the pool saw her and waved, and Eris gave a half-hearted wave back before going back inside. The hot shower helped clear her head, and she grinned at the memory of the woman she'd enjoyed in the back office the night before. Grace, if she remembered correctly.

With her long hair, perfect breasts, and perky butt, she'd been exactly what Eris had needed last night, and she'd been irritated at having to cut their night short. Another ten minutes and she might have brought Grace back to the beach house for a marathon night.

But instead, she'd had to deal with a group of protesters, of all things. They were crowding the front door, holding placards that read stupid things about immorality and indecency, and she recognized more than a couple of them as people she'd had to kick out of the club at one time or another for behaving like entitled pricks. Fortunately, more than a few members of the Malibu PD were in the club, and they were happy to wade in and get the protesters moved across the street.

By the time Eris had freed herself from the irritating debacle, she'd been unable to spot Grace in the crowd. It wasn't like she was feeling all that sexy, though, so she'd grabbed a strong drink and poured herself back onto the dance floor.

There was a light tap on her door. "Come in," she said, toweling her hair and thinking that she needed it cut. Short and sharp was her style in this era, and she didn't like it touching her collar.

"Just checking to see if you wanted breakfast?" Chris, her house manager, ducked their head into the room.

"Nah, I'll grab something on my way home, thanks. Everything good here?"

Chris tilted their head back and forth. "You've got a few down there who seem to think this is their new hangout pad. Want me to do anything about that?"

Eris grinned. Chris weighed about as much as a wet sack of potatoes and had arms like string beans, but their tongue was sharp enough to send people scuttling away in a hurry. It was rare Chris had the time or patience for the club goers Eris brought around, and it was amazing their patience never faltered when it came to Eris herself.

"Yeah, if you could do a sweep, that would be great. Just let them know I'm leaving so they have to as well."

Chris nodded. "There are apple Danish and bagels in the kitchen, along with fresh OJ, if you change your mind before you go." With that, they closed the door softly behind them.

Eris sat on the edge of the bed and stared at her feet. Hollowness, like the kind found in a long-lost cave, filled her. It wasn't the first time. She'd felt it often in the hundred or so years since the Industrial Revolution. But lately it was deeper, darker. As hard as she tried to keep it at bay, there were mornings like this when it flowed through her like a rising tide.

She jerked, startled by the phone vibrating on the nightstand. She leaned over to pick it up and instantly held it away from her ear.

"Fuck. Fucking fuck. What the hell, man!"

"Sian, those words won't allow me to help you. What's wrong?" She lay back on the bed and tucked her arm under her head.

"There's a fucking mountain lion refusing to let me out of my car. It keeps screaming at me like I'm lunch. Come out and scare it off!"

Eris heard the lion's eerie scream and laughed at the tsunami of swear words that followed. "I'm not home. I'm down at the Malibu place, but I can be there in twenty."

"And what am I supposed to do in the meantime?" Sian's words were coming out like gunfire.

"Well, I don't suggest you get out of the car. Females only scream like that when they're looking to mate." She hung up as more swearing filled the air.

Once again, the hollowness could be pushed aside for a while and filled with the company of good friends and nature. It would do, for now.

She pulled up in front of the house and burst out laughing. Sian was in her car, arms folded across her chest, clearly talking to the mountain lion who was lying in the sunshine on the hood of her car.

Eris got out and walked up beside Sian's window. Sian lowered it a fraction. "Most people have guard dogs they keep inside, you know."

Eris went to the mountain lion, who rolled over and presented her belly. "I appreciate your help, but eating my friends isn't a good idea."

The cat's rumbling purr stopped when Sian's car door opened. Sian froze.

"Come on, now. Play nice." Eris motioned and Sian got out slowly, her expression one of distrust.

"Come pet her so she knows you're family."

Sian looked at her in disbelief. "She's spent the last hour screaming at me. I'm very fond of my hands, thank you."

"She'd go for your jugular, not your hands. Come on, chicken butt."

Sian grumbled but moved forward, her hand stretched out. The mountain lion twitched, sniffed her, and then rolled onto her back. Sian gave her a good tickle and then stepped away. "I need a drink."

Eris led the way inside, and the mountain lion remained sunbathing on the car.

They got their drinks and sat in the shade on the deck. It was already getting too hot to sit in the sun. "What's up, buttercup?" Eris asked.

"I wanted to make sure you were okay. What with everything going on."

Eris looked up, confused. "What do you mean?" The phone rang and she held up her hand. "Hold on." She looked at the screen but didn't recognize the number, though the number that started with three sixes indicated it was Afterlife. "Hello?"

"Eris? It's Hermes, over at Afterlife. How are you, darling woman? You're good, aren't you? You're always good. So hot and handsome, strutting all your stuff like a good LA muse should."

Eris started to respond, but he kept talking.

"Anyway, darling woman, I'm doing a little back lot work, if you know what I mean. I've started talking to this streaming service who want to do a revamp of those old dating shows, you know, where someone goes on a date with three different people? Only now we'd include every color of the rainbow, mortal and immortal, in one glorious cluster bang of an orgasm. And who better to be the face of the show than the sexiest butch of love in the world? Can I count you in? I know I can. When can we meet to talk specs?"

Eris waited, but he seemed to be giving her response time now. "Sorry, Herm. I'm not your woman."

There was a moment of silence. "Eris, darling, you're the muse of love. You'd inspire all these people to find the matches of their dreams. How can you turn that down? And think how good it would be for Afterlife. It would show us doing something fun, something sexy and now."

She'd always found Hermes a little over-the-top, and this conversation was already draining her. "I'm retired, Herm. I haven't been in the business for a long time now, and I don't have any intention to get back in the game. Sorry. Maybe try Cupid."

He huffed. "Cupid would be disastrous." He hesitated. "Although, I suppose that would add some spice. You'd never know what the hell would happen. Okay, fine. If you change your mind, let me know. It might be good for you to get some good press too, you know. Ciao."

He hung up before she could say anything else. What did he mean, she needed good press? She shook her head and put the phone down. Before she could resume the conversation with Sian, the doorbell rang.

"For the sake of all the fucks. What's going on?" She made her way to the front door, where a woman was pressed up against the window. "Can I help you?" Eris asked.

The woman, who continued to stare at the mountain lion getting a tan on Sian's car, handed Eris an envelope. She took it, and the woman said, "You've been served." Skittishly, she slipped off the porch and walked, crab-like, back to her car as she watched the lion watch her.

Eris looked at the envelope with her name typed on the front. "What the hell?" She opened it and scanned the legal document as she made her way back to the deck.

"What was that about?" Sian asked.

"I'm being sued." Eris continued to read, her incredulity building with every entitled, irritating sentence.

"For what? Someone get hurt at the club or something?"

Eris threw the stack of paperwork on the table, her disbelief quickly turning to anger. "It's a class action lawsuit by people who got together in my club and then tried to have a relationship. Those relationships failed, and they're blaming me as the muse of love. They're also suggesting that they could have had the relationships they'd wanted to find in my club if I'd been doing what I should have. They're saying I've been derelict in my duties."

Sian burst out laughing. "Dude. That's amazing. Suing a goddess of love because your love life is shitty. Beyond insane." When she saw that Eris wasn't laughing, she sobered. "They can't really sue you, can they?"

Eris picked up her phone and found the contact number for the attorney she used for the club. "No immortal has been sued. It isn't done." The attorney answered on the third ring, and even though he was on the golf course, he listened to Eris's issue.

"Christ. Eris, I'm sorry, but that's so far out of my field that I can't help. In fact, I have no idea who might be able to. No one has had to defend a god against a mortal lawsuit. Frankly, I can't imagine anyone wanting to represent the people suing you, and defending you is going to be the weirdest challenge ever. I can make some calls, but no promises."

She hung up and looked at Sian. "What were you saying before the doorbell rang? What did you mean, 'with everything going on?'"

Sian pulled out her phone and typed something in, then handed it to Eris. "See for yourself."

It was a video on CNN that showed the protesters from the club the night before. A debate then ensued among the commentators about the responsibility of the immortals to live to higher standards. Eris was mentioned as an example of one who was behaving like a rich human instead.

And then they questioned the need for her existence.

She blanched and her stomach dropped. "You can't debate whether or not someone should exist."

Sian got up, went inside, and came out with a fresh cold glass of iced tea. "No, you can't. But the world is crazy and entitled people will always find someone to blame for their downfalls." Her phone chirped and she looked at it. "Look, Clio is heading out today, so I have to go get the plane ready. Are you going to be okay?"

Eris nodded absently. "I'll call Afterlife. Their legal department will handle things."

Sian nodded and gave her a quick punch on the arm. "Let me know what happens." She stopped at the door. "Actually, you need to come with me and help me get my car back from your guard lion."

Eris hefted herself from the chair and followed Sian outside. She made a sound and the mountain lion stretched, then leapt from the hood of Sian's car and trotted off into the trees.

"You okay?" she asked as she unlocked her car.

"Yeah. I will be. Just a lot to think about." Eris gave her a quick smile. "Nothing I can't handle."

As Sian drove off, Eris wondered if that were true.

CHAPTER FOUR

Grace sat across from her brother at Wild Thyme, her favorite place for breakfast. She mopped up the last of the maple syrup on her banana walnut waffle and sighed happily.

"I wish our parents had given us tall, skinny genes instead of hobbit genes." John finished the last of his bacon and pushed his plate away. "I'm going to have to kill myself at the gym every night this week."

Like Grace, John was on the short side, and he too was curvier than he'd like to be. He'd always envied the other boys in school who were tall and muscular, and they'd both had their share of bullies thanks to their pubescent chubbiness.

"I'll just stick to my diet of crackers and coffee for most of the week, and real food on weekends. I'm sure that's healthy." She grinned at him, and he gave her a sympathetic smile in return.

"I have a date, by the way," he said, stirring his coffee.

Her heart jumped at the thought. "Really? That's wonderful."

He shrugged. "We'll see. Probably just another flash fry, but it'll be fun while it lasts."

"You know we're not our parents, right?" She held his hand across the table. "You deserve more than you let yourself have."

"Who says I want more?" He squeezed her hand and went back to his coffee. "After what Mom and Dad put us through, I can't imagine being with someone long-term. I honestly don't think love is a real thing. It's meant for Hallmark cards and country songs."

Grace shook her head. "Not true. There are a lot of couples out there who are happy as can be. Couples who have been together for years and years and still love each other."

"How can you possibly be so sure of that when you do the job you do?" He smiled at the waitress who set down his usual piece of pecan pie. It didn't matter that it was ten in the morning. It was his thing. "You see nothing but the misery our parents caused every single day."

That was true, of course, and she wasn't about to admit that it got her down sometimes. "But those are people in the midst of misery, not people who are happy. We don't get to see those. I really believe that there's someone right for everyone. The couples who divorce are getting a second chance. They can decide not to be with the person they're with, who is wrong for them, and then go on and find someone who's right. Staying together when you're miserable is way worse. What if Mom and Dad had stayed together?"

He whistled and grimaced. "That would have been way worse." He stabbed at the pie like it was a memory he could slay. "What about you? Anything on the romance front?"

She played with a coffee spoon, debating how much to tell him. They'd always been close, but maybe it was too much? What the hell. "I had sex in a dance club with the muse of love."

He choked on his pie and pounded on his chest until he took a gasping breath. "Sorry," he said breathlessly. "Come again?"

She proceeded to tell him the story and mentioned that it might have been the greatest quick sex of her life. The story sounded as surreal as it had felt, and they were soon laughing.

"Damn." He wiped at his eyes. "The world is so crazy now, isn't it? You can go to a club and have sex with an immortal who likes to play fetch with the guardian of Hell." He quickly finished his pie. "Are you going to see her again?"

"I doubt it. It isn't like I have the time for that kind of thing, and I doubt she's into relationships, given the way she took charge like it's something she does all the time." Grace had replayed what was probably the hottest moment of her life over and over again. "Not to mention, could you imagine the pressure you'd be under? I mean, Valentine's Day with the muse of love? A card and flowers probably wouldn't be enough."

He laughed. "Okay, I'll give you that. Doesn't she tick any of the boxes on your list, though?"

"Just because she ticks a few boxes doesn't mean I'm willing to go for someone so outrageously out of my league." In truth, she ticked several of the more superficial boxes, but there were a few she couldn't tick off without actually knowing someone, and there was about as much likelihood of her getting to know Eris as there was a unicorn arriving to take her to the grocery store tomorrow. Although, these days, that might even be more likely.

They paid their bill and headed into the small parking lot. He gave her a hug and held her at arm's length. "I know we joke, and neither one of us is likely to settle down. But call me if you need me, okay? Going it alone in this world sucks."

She scanned his face, looking for any worrying signs. When they were teenagers, he'd gone through a particularly bad time, and she'd sat through many nights with him as he cried and struggled to find a reason to keep going. "Do I need to worry?"

He smiled, his understanding clear. "No. I'm just saying that we're both prone to falling into emotional sludge thanks to our overwhelmingly shit parents, and feeling alone can make that a lot worse."

As she drove home, she considered what he'd said. Was it true that neither of them were likely to settle down? Granted, she wasn't about to settle for anything less than perfect, but surely if she held out, she'd find it? The thought of spending the rest of her life alone was depressing. Her own company was nice, but ultimately she wanted someone to come home to, to laugh with and who brought her flowers for no reason. She wanted to be able to curl up against someone on the couch and have strong arms around her.

That led her back to thoughts of Eris, and she immediately changed tack. She wasn't about to spend any more time on that dead end.

She spent the rest of the afternoon in her little garden, pulling weeds and paying attention to the pepper and zucchini plants. She didn't really cook, and she didn't have any idea what she'd do with them if she actually managed to grow any, but she liked the idea of having fresh veggies she'd grown herself.

Pleasantly worn out at the end of the day, she flopped onto her couch and opened her latest romance novel. But before she could get into it, her phone rang.

"Why on earth are you calling me on a Sunday night? We need to set boundaries."

"Turn on CNN. Quick." Brad sounded breathless.

She did as she was told and her heart stuttered when she saw a photo of Eris on the screen, her arms around two scantily clad women. Below it, the banner proclaimed *Immortals on Trial*.

"What the hell?" she said, leaning forward as though it would give her an answer.

"Right? She's been named the defendant in a class action lawsuit. A group of people are pissed off that she retired, and they're blaming her for their faulty relationships."

Grace settled back into the sofa, thoughts whirling. "You can't sue an immortal. That has never been done. Who is counsel?" A new face came on the screen, and she scoffed. "Never mind. Fucking Zane Shaw."

"Look at his hair. How much oil do you think he has to use to get it that slick?"

"I don't think he has to use any. It oozes from his disgusting soul." Just the sight of him made her feel ill. He was well known for representing the shady side of humanity as well as for taking on cases with high profiles, no matter how disreputable the client. He was also far right and lauded the right-wing agenda openly. The problem was, he was damn good at his job, and he often won his cases.

"Gotta go. See you in the morning." Brad hung up without waiting for her to reply.

She turned up the volume and listened to the debates. The case against Eris wasn't important just because of her case alone; it could set a precedent for suing other immortals who were thought to be derelict in their duties. The world would explode into lawsuits brought by disgruntled humans.

For the briefest of moments, she considered calling the club to see if she could talk to Eris, to support her. But why? They didn't know each other, and there was a good chance she wouldn't remember Grace at all. Not to mention she probably had the backing of the entire Afterlife compound, which took up an extensive section of Santa Monica.

The following morning at the office, the primary topic of conversation was Eris's case, which had been dubbed People vs. Love.

Speculation raged over who would be willing to defend her, and best guesses were that the legal team at Afterlife would be behind her. Who better to defend an immortal than an immortal, after all?

But at lunch, which Brad brought into her office, they pondered the theoretical options.

"She'd be better off with a human defense team," Grace said, having given it a lot of thought. "It would make a jury more sympathetic than if she had some huge god standing beside her."

Brad nodded as he crunched through his salad. "I agree. But a human would have to be crazy to take a case like this. The pressure from every side would be immense. And what if you lost? Would you be turned into a frog or kale or something by a pissed off god?" He speared a piece of cucumber and then glanced at her. "But I feel sorry for her, you know? She retired and tried to just live her life."

She narrowed her eyes at him. "What are you saying?"

"I'm saying I feel bad for her. And I'm sure, as someone with intimate knowledge of her, that you do too." He leaned down and picked up a file he'd put on the floor next to his chair, and then slid it across the desk to her with his fork. "And I'm saying that the lawyer handling the case would be in the spotlight. And if said lawyer did an outstanding job, whatever the verdict, they'd probably be in partner territory by the end of it."

She stared at the closed file, her appetite abating at the Pandora's box in front of her. "It's a gamble. Like you said, the pressure will come from every side. Gods will be pissed if I lose, the partners will need me to win, humans will be against the person defending the gods…"

"But the romantic in you will fight till your dramatic dying breath to defend the embodiment of love." He flipped the file open, again with his fork. "You know I'm right."

She pushed her sandwich aside and started flipping through the initial filing. Though the news had said it was a class action lawsuit, it wasn't. It was actually a mass tort lawsuit, which was far more complicated. It meant that every individual involved in suing Eris had filed their own lawsuit against her, and then those cases had been compiled into one massive suit. Various claimants meant various claims of injury and loss, all of which were being blamed on Eris's lack of diligence in her role.

She closed the file, which was too thick to read through over lunch. "Why go after Eris? Why not go after Aphrodite or Cupid? They're really in charge of love, aren't they? Isn't a muse all about the arts?"

"Maybe you should ask Eris and see what she thinks." He got up, cleared their lunch debris, and headed for the door. "Her number is on the inside of the file," he said over his shoulder.

Grace pushed the ticking time bomb aside so she could concentrate on the rest of her client work earmarked for the afternoon. No matter how hard she tried, though, her focus kept shifting to the file that might as well have had a blinking red light on it.

Chapter Five

In the old days, we would have burned a city to the ground or killed the whole village. That would have kept them in order." Hades looked only vaguely interested in the conversation, although blue and white flashes sparked in his clothing, suggesting he was more irritated than he was showing.

Eris played with her food. The Styx restaurant on Level Minus Two of the Afterlife compound was Hades's baby, and the food was usually extraordinary, but she couldn't seem to find her appetite right now. "I'm pretty sure the gods aren't allowed to do that kind of thing anymore. But thanks for having my back."

He waved away her gratitude. "We've been friends for many years, Eris. Though I've never fully understood your desire to spend time here when your counterparts prefer the clouds of Olympus with my pretentious oaf of a brother."

Hearing Hades speak of Zeus that way always made her smile, even though she knew full well letting anyone other than Hades see that would get her a lightning bolt in the ass. When it came down to it, Zeus, Hades, and Poseidon had stood together when the Merge had taken place, shoulder to shoulder, and their differences were set aside.

Six years on, though, they were back to their ancient rivalries, but they kept their squabbles out of the mortal realm. Only other immortals knew how they goaded and pissed each other off. "I don't know if I understand my desire to hang out in the monochrome darkness with you, either. But I'm glad you let me."

He shrugged his massive shoulders, his long, narrow face the epitome of the grim world he ruled over. "Cerberus doesn't like playing with anyone else. He always tries to eat anyone who tries."

She'd avoided telling him about Cerb's escape. He'd been away in Russia at the time and seemed to have missed the news reports about the three-headed dog trampling cars and taking out streetlamps in Santa Monica. "He's a cuddly thing, really." Her phone pinged and she checked the readout. "Legal is ready to talk to me. See you later."

He motioned to the waiter. "Box this up for Eris."

The ghostly apparition with blank eyes picked up Eris's plate and floated away. She shivered. Why *did* she like coming down here, where the lack of all emotion, let alone love, was carved into the nature of the place?

The server came back and set the white box with the simple black river logo in front of her. At least she wouldn't have to make anything later.

She took the elevator to the main floor and then headed toward the legal offices. Her sister Calliope had been in charge of the department but had left to return to being a muse. Tisera, the fury who oversaw many of the corporate and legal matters, was away at an Ecology and Evolution conference. Themis, goddess of Justice, was currently in charge but had been vocal about wanting someone to take her place.

Eris tapped on the door and opened it. Themis came around the desk and gave her a tight hug. Her long, flowing brown hair tickled Eris's arm, and she couldn't help but notice that Themis's eyes looked tired.

"Have a seat, handsome." Themis sat in the chair beside the one Eris took. "I'll get straight to the point. We have a problem."

Eris sighed. "I figured as much. But I was thinking, what if I don't respond? What if I ignore it altogether? It's not like they can arrest me for not paying attention to their stupid case, right? Immortals can't be arrested."

Themis's frown deepened. "The problem is, you're not a god. You're a lesser immortal, one who appears more human and works more closely with them. You live among them, whereas most of us keep a separate residence. Your reason for *being* is tied to them." She raised her hands. "It creates a gray area that hasn't been explored. Sure, you could fail to respond, and we could put forward something to say that immortals can't be sued. But…" She motioned, as if to the world outside Afterlife. "That might open up a whole other barrel of rotten fish that we'd have to deal with anyway."

"Okay." Eris had a sinking feeling, given Themis's expression. "So what do we do, assuming I have to respond in some way?"

Themis flinched. "Honestly? I need to find someone to work with who knows human law."

"You're telling me that we, a multinational corporation of deities both ancient and more modern, need humans' help on a legal matter? That you, the goddess of justice, doesn't know human laws?" She didn't bother to temper the incredulity in her tone.

"Human laws have changed dramatically since the Merge, and they're constantly in flux. Since I've been here at Afterlife, I've lost touch with much of what's happening in the human systems. I've left a message for Calliope to call me, but she's in Scotland. She'll have a better hand on human law than I do, given how much time she spent helping them make the laws in the first place. My concern has always been about wisdom and giving good counsel, not in actual written law. And we're in new territory. It isn't surprising that the humans have the temerity to sue god; it's more surprising that it's taken this long for it to happen."

Eris's shoulders dropped. She was the ultimate example of lover rather than fighter, but right now, she really wanted to hit something. "Again, what do I do?"

Themis pulled her into a hug. "Hang tight. Let us try to figure out everything on our end. In the meantime, maybe stay out of the limelight. Hell, go to Olympus and relax with some nymphs. I'm sure there are some who miss you." Her smile was kind, her understanding of Eris's frustration clear in her eyes.

"Yeah. Okay. Thanks." She shoved her hands in her pockets and made her way back to the lobby. She passed cubicles with gods answering emails, assistants rerouting prayer requests, and more than one or two gods who glanced at her and away again.

In the parking lot, she hesitated. Where to go now? Running off to Olympus didn't feel right. And dammed if she'd hide like she'd done anything wrong. Loads of gods had retired. Why should she be treated any differently than they were?

The sound of clicking wings filtered in before she could turn away, and she nearly groaned in his face as Hermes fluttered down in front of her, his garish gold-winged shoes landing him gently. While they'd been all the rage in Athens in the year 1000 BC, now they just looked like something out of a budget music video made in someone's living room by their five-year-old.

"Hey, Herm." She did her best to sound cordial.

As usual, he seemed oblivious. "Eris, darling. You're just the person I was looking for. And here you are. It's fate, right? Total fate. Walk with me." He hooked his arm through hers, his lanky hair falling over his eyes as he led her toward the open green space behind the compound. "I've heard about your little problem with the humans. And you know what? Totally fixable. It's all about reputation and what the public see, right? About image. And we can fix your tainted image by having you do the dating show, babes. It'll make people see that you're still engaged with the whole love thing, right? They're saying it's because you decided not to play nice with the humans anymore that their love lives are in the tank. But you can show that you're still out there making people swoon and fall head over heels, and that will suck the joy right out of their case, just like that." He snapped his fingers. "When can I tell them we'll start, babes? Should we go to the studio now?"

She gently disengaged her arm from his. "I don't make people fall in love. You know that. And legal has told me to do the opposite of what you're asking, Herm. They want me to disappear for a while."

He shook his head so hard, his hair flew about. "No, no, no. Totally wrong thing to do. Totally. You disappear and it will give them more reason to doubt you, babes."

She shrugged and backed away, heading toward her car. His overuse of the term *babes* made her want to press the heel of her palm to his nose. Hard. "Maybe you should go talk to Themis about it, Herm."

He looked at the building and shifted from foot to foot so that he floated slightly off the ground, his sandals flapping gently. "She's been supremo pissed at me for a few hundred years. She holds a grudge, you know? But maybe."

She turned and walked quickly away. "Let me know how it goes." She was fully aware of how Themis felt toward the messenger god. Hermes had "accidentally" messed up an important message from Themis to the Counsil of Nicaea, which had then failed to incorporate any of the ideas from female followers of the new Christian order. She had yet to forgive him for what she saw as a serious misjustice which had then determined much of the way women were treated for the next several centuries.

She got into her truck and headed onto PCH to begin the drive home. What should take about half an hour would take closer to ninety minutes this time of day, but she didn't care. It wasn't like she had anywhere she needed to be.

❖

The night was a messy, chaotic blur of alcohol, sweaty bodies, and the release of bottled-up frustration let loose on the multitude like a tsunami after an earthquake.

Eris danced until she couldn't breathe and sweat soaked through her top, making it cling to her. She lost herself in the DJ box and threw herself into the persona, bouncing, waving, and calling to the audience. After, there were women. Several at once, mouths and hands everywhere, her fingers wet, and her lips bruised.

All night long, she repeated the refrain pounding in her head. "Fuck love, you beautiful meat bags!" The crowd roared their approval, even though they obviously didn't understand where the hell she was coming from.

Rolling over, she groaned as the morning sunlight pierced her eyelids like needles and she rolled back, only to bump into something. She cracked one eye open and saw blond hair covering a pillow. Wincing, she slowly sat up and rubbed the grit from her eyes before she focused again on the woman in her bed.

Women. Three, by the looks of the shapes and varying shades of hair splayed over the sheets and pillows. She tried to remember the night, but nothing came to her. Shame. It had probably been a good one.

Silently, she left the women sleeping and slipped out of the room, wearing her boxers and a white tank top that still smelled of the night before. Chris was in the kitchen plating piles of pastries beside a ceramic coffee pot. They glanced at Eris, gave her a quick grin, and pointed with the tongs. "Water, orange juice, coffee. Bagel with butter, no cream cheese."

Eris slumped into the chair at the table with her breakfast and feasted in the order Chris had dictated. She ate in silence, strangely comforted by Chris's quiet, steadfast presence. She was sipping coffee, feeling miles better, when a text came through.

Hi, it's Grace. You may not remember me, but I'm a lawyer, and I wondered if you needed help with your dilemma? No pressure.

It wasn't always the case that Eris remembered the women she enjoyed. But Grace had made an impression. It had been too quick, but there'd been something about her, about the fire in her eyes and the way she'd given herself over to Eris's touch without pretense or self-consciousness that was rare, especially in LA.

She reread the text and a flicker of light lit her soul. She knew the Fates well. She'd been part of their plans for thousands of years. The fact that Grace had shown up in her life just when it had hit the bricks couldn't be a coincidence.

Of course I remember you. Don't know if you can really help, but it would be good to talk. She hit send and had barely taken her coffee cup to the sink before there was a reply.

Today?

Why would Grace want to meet to talk about work on a Sunday? It didn't matter. She needed the help. She had no idea where Grace lived or worked and wasn't sure where to suggest that wouldn't make it look like she expected Grace to come to her. Fortunately, she was saved from her indecision.

Marmalade Café in an hour?

She sighed with relief. That wasn't even fifteen minutes from the beach house.

Perfect. See you there.

At least she wouldn't have to worry about recognizing her. She could still picture that thick hair that had cascaded over her fingers and feel Grace's soft curves under her hands. But this was going to be a very different meeting from the one she'd enjoyed before.

"Everything okay, boss?" Chris asked while polishing a glass that didn't need it.

Sometimes, love meant not burdening people you cared about with things they had no control over. She was tempted to say everything was fine, but that wasn't fair. "The press might come around, Chris. I'm sorry if they bug you." It was lame and too simple, but she didn't know what else to say.

Chris nodded and finally set down the glass, only to pick up another. "I watch the news." They tilted their head toward Eris's bedroom. "Not sure that kind of thing will help, though. Or this." They pushed their phone over and Eris hit play on the video.

"Oh, for the love of Zeus." She grimaced as she watched the viral video of her in the DJ booth yelling, "Fuck love!" in time to an electronic beat. She sneered at the camera focused on her when she said, "You aren't my responsibility, you entitled apes." Even though the crowd laughed, it wasn't funny. "No. That probably isn't going to help."

Chris pulled their phone back. "How can I help?"

Eris shook her head and held up her phone. "I've just had an offer of help from a lawyer I know. Kind of know. Anyway," she said, shaking her head at Chris's knowing smirk. "I'll be sure to tell you if there's anything coming your way. For now, I need to clean up."

Chris set down their glass and motioned for Eris to follow. In the back guest bedroom that also overlooked the sea, Chris opened the closet to reveal a selection of Eris's clothing. "I had a feeling that at some point you'd need a kind of escape route, so I made sure you had everything you needed in here. Your shower stuff is in the bathroom."

Eris's eyes watered at Chris's thoughtfulness. "Wow. Thank you."

Chris shrugged. "Just remember to give me a good recommendation if you disappear off to Olympus or whatever."

Overwhelmed, Eris pulled Chris into a tight hug. "If I go to Olympus, you'll just have to go with me."

Chris hugged her back. "How about you just stick around instead?" They slipped out of her embrace. "And you really need a shower."

Eris laughed and wiped at her eyes. "I really do."

"You smell like an alcoholic locker room." Chris gave a quick wave before they left the room.

Eris sat on the bed for a moment to get her bearings. She'd long been convinced that love was something lost in the last hundred or so years. But every once in a while, the genuine generosity of spirit of those people in her close orbit served to surprise her. She hefted herself from the bed and got in the shower. The hot water washed the night's foibles from her skin and helped clear her head. Maybe Grace could help her, maybe she couldn't. But at least she was in motion.

CHAPTER SIX

G race sat at a corner table on the patio, farthest from the front, and with only one table nearby. It was a small café, and that helped too. The last thing she wanted was for anyone to overhear the conversation she and Eris were going to have. But she also hadn't wanted to meet in her office where any overzealous co-workers might see them talking. She wasn't sure how her bosses would feel about her taking the case. She was a divorce lawyer, after all. But when it was love itself being sued, surely that fell into her purview?

She met with clients all the time. She argued in front of judges and faced down angry spouses arguing over millions of dollars. But as she sat there waiting for Eris, her palms were sweaty, and her leg bounced. Was this a mistake? Was it a bad idea to represent not just an immortal, but one she'd had mind-blowing sex with? Probably.

Eris walked in and looked around, and when she spotted Grace, she raised her chin in acknowledgement and made her way over.

Grace wiped her palms on her shorts. In a simple white tank top and long cargo shorts, Eris looked like the ultimate butch California beach candy. Tall and lean, she moved gracefully, her dark hair cut short but just long enough to fall over eyes the color of a morning summer sky. But that wasn't all Grace noticed. The sensual, sexual god who'd pressed against her on the dance floor was gone. In her place was a woman with hunched shoulders and circles under her eyes. When she got to the table, Grace saw that her eyes were also a little bloodshot. Was it from crying? Or alcohol? Or both?

She stood and held out her hand. "Nice to see you again."

Eris took it, and then leaned over and kissed her cheek. "Likewise. I was surprised to get your message."

The server came over, and Grace ordered a Cobb salad and a cold brew coffee. Eris ordered a banana nut muffin and black tea.

"I hope you don't mind. I just…" She'd practiced this speech all the way here, but now the words wouldn't come. "I'll start at the beginning. I'm a divorce lawyer with Kline and Associates. I've been with them for seven years, and I'm up for partner next year."

Eris nodded and played with a stir stick. "Congratulations."

"Thank you. So my question is, do you have representation yet? If you do, then we can just have a great breakfast together. If you don't, then maybe I can help."

"Hopefully, we'll still have a good meal together." She gave her a quick smile. "As for whether or not I have representation…" She shrugged and broke the stir stick, which she threw aside. "I don't know, honestly. I've talked to the Afterlife legal department, but this has thrown them. At least one of the gods wants to remind humans in a very specific way that they're not our equals."

Grace blanched and started in on her salad. "Let's save that as a last resort, shall we?"

Eris laughed, and her shoulders seemed to ease. "I think I talked him out of it. But as you know, this is new territory."

The fact that Eris didn't technically have counsel already was good news. "Would the lawyers at Afterlife be willing to be part of a team working on your behalf? It would be good to show a united front, humans and gods working together type thing."

Eris seemed to consider that as she picked at her muffin. "I don't know, really. The person in charge there is temporary. She doesn't even want the position, but when my sister Calliope left it open, she stepped in."

Grace speared another piece of chicken. "And would your sister be on the team?"

Eris sighed. "Maybe. But she travels back and forth to Scotland, and she and her partner live up north."

Grace frowned and set down her fork. "Eris, I have to admit, I thought you'd have a whole heap of people rallying around you. But it sounds like you're kind of on your own." Seeing the look of sorrow flash across Eris's expression made Grace's heart ache. How did the muse of love end up with one no one on her side?

"Yeah, I guess I am. I mean, I have friends, and if I asked, every god at Afterlife would bring a hammer down. Obviously, we don't want that. Not to mention, this is scary, and I don't think any of the gods want to be tarred with the brush I'm about to be painted with. Followers lodging complaints is one thing. Followers bringing lawsuits would create doubt in the gods, and doubt can spread like fire through dry brush."

Grace began eating again, but her thoughts were in a whirl. "I understand that. I think it's the same on the human side of things. Everyone is going to want your case, but it may be that no one is willing to face something that's going to be globally high profile, or something that could mean a very short life here and a very long one in a place no one wants to be after they're dead."

"So why would you?"

It was a simple question, asked without judgment. It deserved an honest answer. She kept her eyes on her food. "There are a few reasons. One is that we have some history, and I feel compelled to be involved because of it."

Eris's eyebrow quirked ever so slightly.

Grace hurried on. Eris had probably slept with plenty of lawyers in the course of her lifetime, and they weren't scrambling over one another to help. "Another reason is that, like I said, I'm up for partner next year. I think taking a high-profile case like yours could be good for my career."

"Couldn't it also tank your career? If you lose?" There was no missing the hurt in her voice.

"I've given it a lot of thought and talked it over with my paralegal. I don't think it could. Taking on a case where I'm bound to win is a good thing, and on the off chance I lose, I'll still have made a damn good showing." She lightly touched Eris's hand. "Because I'll do everything I can to defend you."

They sat in silence, Grace enjoying her salad immensely as Eris continued to pick at her muffin.

Finally, Eris looked up again. "And what if you find me at fault? What if you think I'm in the wrong? Can you still defend me wholeheartedly?"

"Well," she said, moving the empty bowl aside, "a lawyer doesn't always have to agree with their clients. As it happens, I've read the motion on your case, and I don't think it has any merit. I don't think you're in the wrong and that's another reason I want to be involved."

"And if you decide otherwise at some point?" Eris sat back, her arms crossed, her light eyes unreadable.

"Then I'll still do my job to the best of my abilities." She leaned forward, meeting Eris's gaze. "But there's something I'll need from you, and that's complete honesty. No matter what, you have to tell me the truth, and if there's anything relevant to your case, I have to know. Because if we get blindsided, I can't do my job."

Eris's lips pursed and she stared at some point beyond Grace for a long, tense moment. "Okay. I can be honest. But are you sure you can handle the immortal world?"

Grace relaxed. Eris was as good as saying that she'd accept Grace's help. "Honestly? I guess we'll see. I handled your three-headed dog without running around screaming my head off, didn't I?"

Eris finally laughed. "Yeah, you did."

Grace smiled. "And as much as I enjoyed our encounter at Infinite, our relationship from now on needs to remain strictly professional. I don't want any claim of bias or losing my professionalism."

Eris looked vaguely disappointed, which was nice. "I get it." She finally uncrossed her arms and reached across the table to take Grace's hand. "Thank you. Really. I can't tell you how good it feels to have someone in my corner."

Once again, Grace hurt for her. What would it be like to live so long and be so alone? "You may not be thanking me when I'm putting you through your paces and asking you lots of intrusive questions. But always remember that we're on the same team."

The waiter put the bill down and Eris picked it up. "On me, as a thank you."

Grace tilted her head in appreciation. "Now, we'll set up a real meeting at my office. Can you put me in touch with the legal team at Afterlife? And your sister?"

"I'll call them when we're done and give them your number, if that's okay? People at Afterlife are a little wary about giving their number out to humans. I should check with them first."

Grace nodded, impressed at Eris's quick thoughtfulness, even in the face of her own dilemma. "Of course. Why don't you come to my office on Thursday? It's a light day for me, so I can square away plenty of time, and if anyone wants to come with you, they're welcome. Would two in the afternoon work for you?"

Eris looked a little distracted as she nodded. "Um, in the interest of being totally honest?"

Grace raised her eyebrows when Eris tapped something into her phone and then handed it over. Grace hit play and watched the viral video of an obviously inebriated Eris looking almighty sexy and shouting rather negative things about love to her adoring crowd. She handed it back. "Well, let's not do that again, shall we?"

Eris laughed when Grace grinned at her. "Yeah. I'll behave."

They walked out of the little café into the blazing hot day. "Eris, I can't make promises. As you said before, we're in crazy new territory. We're probably going to have a long road ahead of us, assuming I can't get the case thrown out in prelims." She wrapped her hand around Eris's strong bicep. It was meant to comfort Eris, but it made parts of Grace twitch which were definitely not welcome to the party. "But I'll give you my best."

Eris wrapped her hand over Grace's and once again leaned in to kiss her cheek. "That will be enough."

On Monday morning, Grace accepted the files from Brad, who looked as nervous as she felt. She made her way to the top floor and asked Rob Kline's paralegal, a woman whose pinched face always reminded her of a bag folded too tightly, if he was available.

She buzzed him, and Grace was allowed into the temple that was the head partner's office. Sun blazed through the floor to ceiling windows, but the automatic tint kept it from being too much. The office was larger than a big portion of her home, and the heavy leather furniture spoke of wealth and taste.

"Grace. This is a surprise. What can I do for you?" he asked, looking over his glasses at her.

She motioned to the chair across from his desk, and he waved her into it. "I wanted to talk to you about a new client I'm taking on."

His brow furrowed. "You know all associates have general discretion over the cases they take. Is there a reason you need to pass this by me?"

She handed him the file, steeling herself and only barely able to keep her hand from shaking. She didn't know what she'd do if he told her she couldn't take the case.

He scanned it quickly and then set the file down on his desk like it could explode. "That's unexpected. Tell me why."

"It's going to set legal precedent. If people are allowed to sue the immortals, the entire legal system is going to get bombarded. It will require new areas of expertise, and the knots it will cause will be detrimental to the world in so many ways."

He steepled his fingers under his chin. "And if you lose?"

"Then we've still been involved in the case that changed the world. The sociological, political, and even religious ramifications are immense, no matter what direction it goes. And I want to be part of that."

"But you want to defend rather than prosecute?"

"There's already a prosecutor, and I doubt they're looking for more co-counsel." She hesitated, unsure how much she should divulge. "And I think it's wrong, frankly. I don't think you can blame a deity, especially a minor one, for having a less than stellar love life. She isn't in charge of relationships, she's in charge of creative expression." She took a deep breath. In for a penny... "Entitlement is one of my bugbears. I hate when people feel like they're owed something just because they want it. And that's what this is: an entitled group of people who want someone to blame for their shortcomings."

Rob looked at her for a long moment, and she wondered what he was seeing or searching for.

"Okay. You have my blessing. But assemble a team, because you're going to need it. You're not defending one person. You're defending the right of gods to not behave the way people want them to. The paperwork and press are going to bury you. Make sure you have enough people to handle it."

And now the next part of her bombshell. "I'm already on it. In fact, I'm expecting to hear from the legal department at Afterlife today."

His eyebrows rose. "That's quite the coup. Getting through to anyone in that compound is practically impossible." He laughed. "But then, I guess you have a very clear way in now."

Relief flooded her, making her light-headed. She'd expected pushback, bringing in outsiders. But then, it wasn't like she was working with a rival firm. "I do, and I'll keep you appraised."

He sat back in his seat, his fingers once again steepled beneath his chin. "If you start to get in over your head, you need to come to me quickly so we can get others involved. Frankly," he said, moving his hands from his chin to his desk, "this seems more like a case for a senior partner with more courtroom experience. It's tempting to assign you second chair and allow one of the partners to take the lead."

Her heart plummeted right to the tips of her red heels. The possibility he'd think that way had occurred to her, but they'd seemed to move beyond it. "But—"

"But I'm not going to do that. I know you're going for the next partner opening, and I'm going to let you ride this out to prove yourself."

"And so you don't besmirch a partner's reputation if it goes to hell," she said, with no inflection in her voice whatsoever.

"There is that, yes." His eyes glinted at her statement. "But we'll put someone in if it comes to that."

She stood and extended her hand for the folder, which he handed over. "I'll file us as counsel for the defendant today."

He looked out the window toward the ocean, which could just be seen over the opposite building. "This will get messy, Grace. Let's have a weekly catch-up so I'm in the loop, okay?"

She hugged the file to her as she moved toward the door. "I'll let your assistant know dates." Closing the door behind her, she finally let out a deep breath and leaned against it for a moment.

Rob's assistant looked sideways at her. "Are you going to faint? I'm afraid I can't catch you."

She pushed off the door. "No, I'm good. Thanks." As she made her way back to her office, she started running through the many steps to come. Brad, obviously waiting for her, straightened when she came around the corner.

"Well?" he asked.

"We have a lot to do." She smiled when he punched the air and then looked around, mortified that someone might have seen him do it. "Let's draft up the docs I need to take to the courthouse right now. I want to get there before the clerk's office closes. Then we'll begin an Excel sheet to start getting organized."

He looked as excited as she felt. One of the things she loved about her job was the challenge of winning not just for the sake of it, but to make her clients happy. And there was no question at all that she wanted to make Eris very, very happy.

Chapter Seven

Eris waited outside the front door of Afterlife, Inc. The logo, gold wings in a circle, winked in the sunlight, and she wished she had her camera to capture the way the shadow of the palm tree fell over it.

A black sedan pulled up to the curb, and she tugged her shirt down to make sure she looked okay. Not that Grace cared about how she looked, but it didn't hurt to make a good impression. It had been a week since their conversation at Grace's office, but Grace had been diligent about sending her messages to keep her up to date with even the smallest details.

When Grace got out of the car, Eris's breath caught. She was in a simple pantsuit, but it hugged everything perfectly. She looked elegant and confident, a combination Eris had always found attractive. A man got out of the car too, and he looked vaguely familiar.

He held out his hand right away. "Brad Billingsly. I'm Grace's paralegal, assistant, the cricket on her shoulder, and the devil behind some of her decisions."

She grasped his hand, already liking him. "Nice to meet you. You're a regular at the club, aren't you?" He nodded, and she turned to Grace, who was looking up at the Afterlife wings. "Are you sure you're ready for this?"

Grace looked away from the logo and into Eris's eyes. Far from looking uncertain, she looked excited. "How many humans get to cross this threshold? I can't wait." She hooked her arm through Eris's and turned them toward the door. "And after talking to Themis, I really do need to know more about things in your world. It makes more sense for us to do this here than in my office."

Eris understood the idea but bringing a human into Afterlife was only done if absolutely necessary. Although this was certainly necessary. She opened the door, which only unlocked for immortals, and waved Grace and Brad in ahead of her.

They stopped short, and she nearly crashed into them.

"Ah. Sorry." She scooted around them to the receptionist, a lesser pre-fader goddess who still had eerie red eyes and very sharp teeth. "Vila, can you buzz us through? We've got an appointment with Themis."

She looked past Eris, her eyes narrowed. "Make certain they stay beside you, and don't take them anywhere but Themis's office." She turned her attention back to Eris and gave her a sultry, if somewhat terrifying, smile. "And should you need to wipe their human stink from your body, you know where to find me."

Eris kissed her cheek. "You never know." It wouldn't do to insult her. Eris had been on the receiving end of those teeth several centuries ago, during her more wild phase, and she wasn't likely to repeat it. The puncture wounds took a long time to heal.

The door buzzed and Eris pushed it open, motioning the other two to go through. Brad scuttled through quickly, but Grace kept to a stately pace, although she'd gone pale.

Once the door closed behind them, she put her hand on both their shoulders. "You're sure you want to do this?" She tilted her head to indicate Vila. "Having someone more unusual looking is good at the desk. It keeps people who want to complain, or whatever, away. Not that anyone can get through the door, but it makes us feel better anyway."

Brad gave a shaky laugh. "It would definitely keep me away."

Grace moved Eris's hand from her shoulder and squeezed it. "We're good. Lead the way."

Eris liked the feel of Grace's hand in hers, and she didn't want to let go. But that would be crossing a line Grace had clearly put in place. She let Grace's hand slide slowly from hers and turned toward Themis's office.

They passed all the cubicles Eris had grown used to, but she was hyper alert to Brad and Grace behind her, who would be seeing the gods and their envoys at work. It was a view of the religious sectors that no one was ever allowed if they didn't belong to the immortal world in some way. The exceptions were Selene and Kera, although now, Selene occupied immortal territory, and Kera...well, the fury sister she was married to kept her in line.

She knocked on Themis's door and pushed it open. Themis stood and came around the desk covered in files. She pulled Grace into a hug, and Eris laughed at the surprised look on her face.

"You are a little gem," Themis said, holding Grace at arm's length. "It was so good of you to get involved."

"It's the right thing to do," Grace said. "This is my paralegal, Brad."

Themis let go of Grace and pulled Brad into a hug as well. "Welcome." She let him go and led the way through another door into a larger conference room.

Grace looked around. "Are we early?"

Themis pulled out a chair and sat down. "No, not at all. It's just us."

The three of them sat down. "You don't have a team? How do you handle everything by yourself?"

Themis pointed at the desk in the other room. "What we do here is almost entirely arbitration and mediation. Humans send in complaints and those get passed to the gods of the department in question, who then deal with it. There isn't anything legal, per se, to do." She sighed. "No one has ever sued an immortal, and it isn't like we sue each other. Our interdepartmental issues are usually settled by someone like me or by them having back-alley fights like you've seen in *Westside Story*. Only ours might be actual sharks."

Grace and Brad both looked a little baffled, and Eris was strangely embarrassed by the lack of a team there to meet them. It was irrational, but she couldn't help it. "I'm going to ask again. Why do I have to respond at all?" Eris said. "It's not like they can force me to appear in court. I could just stay here or go to Olympus."

Grace tapped her pen on her leather portfolio. "But how long would you stay in hiding? By not showing up, you essentially lose by default. There'd be a summary judgment against you. You'd be legally forced to resume your post..." She shook her head. "Although I can't imagine how they'd enforce that."

Themis seemed to grow larger in the room. "They wouldn't dare."

Grace sat back in her seat a little and turned to Eris. "Let me ask you this. Do you have specific powers, like the gods do? Can you turn people into not-people? Throw lightning bolts?" When Eris frowned, she continued. "I'm essentially asking if there's anything you could do that would keep them from being able to treat you like you're human."

Understanding hit. "No. I'm extra perceptive and open to what the Fates have in store for people. I inspire people to express themselves more deeply about what they're feeling, particularly with regard to love. Artists, poets, writers, musicians, they all benefit from my guidance to help them create. But obviously, they can still do it without me. I haven't been around for a while, and people are still writing soppy love songs and bad poetry. They're still telling each other how they feel and managing to fall in love. I could just help the creative ones do it a little better." She slumped in her seat, inadequacy filling her. "That's it, really."

"And that's beautiful," Themis said. "There's no true justice without the feelings of love and compassion and the ability to express them." She turned to Grace. "But along the lines of your thinking, this won't open a floodgate because you wouldn't sue Zeus, or Allah, or the Christian God. They'd simply ignore the threat, or they'd burn everything down."

"Which leaves those of you without the powers of those big timers in jeopardy. They could go after the ones who are closest to human." Grace opened her folio and began writing. "How many of those would there be? I imagine you're an anomaly?"

Eris flushed. "I'm not an *anomaly*. I was born of Zeus and Mnemosyne, one of nine children dedicated to helping inspire humanity toward greatness. You make it sound like I'm some kind of weird leftover, like something left in the fridge too long that starts to talk."

Grace held her hands up. "Hey now, I didn't mean to offend. I'm sorry. That was the wrong choice of words. I should have said that maybe you hold an unusual position?"

Themis tilted her head. "There are the pre-faders. Their powers are almost nonexistent, for the most part. And there are your sisters."

"Wait. Pre-faders?" Brad asked. He'd hardly stopped writing since they'd sat down.

"Ancient gods that people stopped praying to. When that happens, the god has a choice. Fade away into stardust and memory or give up their powers and choose a physical life among the humans. They remain immortal, but they become like the people around them." Themis reached across and touched Brad's pen. "That is sacred knowledge and can't leave this room."

"How many people know about pre-fader gods?" Grace asked. "Would this actually endanger them?"

Eris shook her head slowly. "I don't think so. That knowledge has been kept inside Afterlife, so unless some god or another has gotten mouthy, most people shouldn't know it."

"That leaves your sisters."

Eris's grip tightened on her knees. "I'll protect my sisters with my life."

"You won't need to." Themis waved in the light-blue-skinned woman with three eyes. "Thank you, Kani."

The woman set down the tray of drinks and left as silently as she'd come in. Brad and Grace stared, wide-eyed, until the door closed behind her.

Themis passed out the coffee mugs and set the carafe in the middle. "Kani is a good example of a pre-fader god. She was a minor Hindu deity thousands of years ago, but she fell out of favor. Instead of fading away, she began living a regular life but always stayed in places she couldn't be found. When we started Afterlife, she was able to be among her own kind again."

"She lived in hiding for thousands of years?" Grace sounded horrified.

"Not entirely. She can make herself look human, but it takes effort. So she mostly stayed on her own and only went among people for supplies and such."

Eris rubbed her temples. "And if we can't settle this, then my sisters and I will have to leave the human world and retreat behind the Afterlife walls too. Or abandon the physical world and go back to Olympus."

"Which would be disastrous for humans," Themis explained. "The muses are responsible for creativity, for thinking beyond the familiar so that new discoveries are made. Science, art, theater, writing, music…if the world loses the muses, the world loses what makes humans vibrant."

Brad had been writing like a demon. He finally stopped and shook out his hand. "That sounds like a hell of a summation."

"I've helped write a few in my time," Themis said and smiled gently.

Grace put her pen down and looked at Themis. "It's really just occurred to me who I'm sitting across from. *The* goddess of justice. We owe you everything. Statues of you are in every courthouse in the world. You taught us that justice is blind and how to weigh our arguments of right and wrong." Grace's words came out in a rush and tears welled in her eyes. "I'm sitting with the goddess of justice."

Themis covered Grace's hand with her own. "And I'm lucky to be sitting across from someone who appreciates the beauty of the law and how it helps people." She sat back and sipped her coffee.

Eris studied the awe in Grace's expression. It was pure and real, and it was beautiful to see. She'd seen the same look in plenty of other believers' eyes when they'd first been in attendance of the god they worshipped, but to be so close to such an intimate emotional outpouring was different. She zoned out a little as they began to write down a plan of action. She found herself looking at Grace's soft hands and how they moved as she spoke. Her little upturned nose was cute, and her eyes flashed as she asked questions and wrote down the answers. She was small, probably only five three, and was curvier than this era's typical beauty standards. In fact, she reminded Eris of one of her first loves back in Greece, when curves were a sign of health and wealth.

"Eris?"

She blinked and forced away the feeling of Grace's curves under her hands. "Sorry, I was somewhere else. What?"

"Can you give me your official title?" Grace looked like she might have an idea where Eris's thoughts had been.

"I'm the muse of love and lyric poetry, specifically erotic poetry." She grimaced. "Love poetry now tends to deal more with the loss or lack of it than telling someone how they feel about them though. And erotic poetry tends more toward porn than anything sensual."

"And how is what you are different from the other deities involved in love? Like Aphrodite, for instance."

"She gets involved in actual relationships. She helps people fall in or out of love. She deals in jealousy, and insecurity, and love bombing." It wasn't the nicest description, granted, but Eris hadn't been interested in Aphrodite's work in a long time.

"And she's responsible for people finding their soul mates, for people sticking it out when things are hard, and for people who care for others even when there's nothing in it for them. She's about selfless love too." Themis looked at Eris pointedly.

Eris didn't say anything. She didn't need to. Themis knew where she stood.

"Wait," Brad said. "So, Eris, you're responsible for creativity, for inspiring artists. You don't have anything to do with relationships, right? That's Aphrodite's area."

Eris tilted her head, thinking. She hadn't had to explain her purpose in a long time. "You're right, but there's a gray area. I'm not responsible for people getting together, that's true. But I could help them express themselves better, share their feelings with each other so that things are clear. If they're artists, then even more so, but it works on everyone around me if they're my focus. If they're simply not meant to be together, then my influence wouldn't help them, no matter what. But if there's wiggle room, then my influence might help."

The room was silent as everyone seemed to take that in.

"Okay." Grace closed her notebook after scribbling more notes. "We've got a plan, and I understand far better now what we can argue and what we're up against. Will Calliope be joining us at some point?"

"She's available by phone and has given us permission to give you her number." Themis slid it across the table.

"Eris, do you think you and I could meet to discuss some things?"

Eris stretched and felt the way Grace's gaze caressed her like a physical thing. "I'm free whenever you are. The protesters at the club have doubled so I'm staying away. My attorney told me to stay out of trouble." She gave Grace a wry grin.

Brad pulled out his phone. "I'll call for a ride back to the office and get things in motion."

Themis stood, indicating the meeting was over. "I'm here if you need me. I can clarify information on our end, although Eris can probably do that nearly as well."

Grace and Eris stood, and Eris could tell that Grace was hesitating about something. "Everything okay?" she asked.

Grace seemed to steady herself. "And can I list you as co-counsel, Themis?"

"Of course, and I'd be happy to sit beside you in the courtroom. It will be a novelty, debating the laws instead of helping make them."

Eris came close to snapping something about being both an anomaly and a novelty, but she held her tongue. They were on her side, she reminded herself.

"Great. Sitting at the table with the goddess of justice on our side is bound to help our case exponentially." Grace's smile was wide, her eyes bright. She turned to Eris. "Now. How about we grab lunch and get to know each other?"

Again, Eris had to bite back the retort that they already knew each other pretty well in the biblical sense, but it didn't seem like the right place for that. "Yeah, okay."

The three of them made their way back outside, passing gods from various sectors. Proteus, with his blue-green scales glinting under the harsh fluorescent lighting, was having a heated conversation with an Ethiopian werehyena, who was waving his silver blacksmith hammer at him. The smell coming from the werehyena was truly awful and seemed to be the primary issue Proteus had with him.

Grace and Brad both pressed closer to Eris, and she put her hands on their shoulders as she guided them forward.

The receptionist let out a soft hiss that followed them out the front door. Outside, Grace shivered dramatically. "That was an interesting experience."

The car Brad had called pulled up, and he blew them an air kiss as he got in and left.

"Pizza?" Eris asked, turning toward Venice Beach.

"My go-to."

They strolled along the boardwalk beneath the palm trees, the ocean crashing against the beach on one side, cafés and chic restaurants on the other. Eris breathed in deeply and felt her shoulders start to drop. It was nice that Grace allowed her to be silent, to gather her thoughts and let the agitation of the day fall behind them like so many grains of sand.

By the time they'd passed the roller skaters, the palm readers, the sellers of incense, jewelry, and art, she could breathe again. When they got to Rey's Pizza, they ordered two giant slices each and took the heavy, greasy pile onto the beach.

Grace kicked off her red heels and plopped down, only just managing to keep her pizza from hitting the sand. She laughed. "I think my parents named me Grace ironically. I'm the least graceful person in the world."

Eris, in contrast, managed to sit beside her easily. "You seemed pretty graceful on the dance floor. And after."

Grace's mischievous grin made Eris laugh. "Yeah, well, it helps when you have a damn smooth partner to follow."

They ate their first slices before Grace took a deep breath. "So, can we talk?"

"Do we have to? Words mess things up."

Grace snagged Eris's piece of pizza and held it away from her. "You don't get this back until you agree to spill your soul."

"Hey, no fair!" Eris leaned over to take it back, and her arm brushed against Grace's breasts. "Sorry." She jerked back, her arm on fire.

"No complaints here." Grace handed the pizza back. "I'd like to know why you retired."

Eris ate slowly, thinking. "I stopped believing."

Grace nodded. "Okay. Go on."

How could she say it without sounding like a jaded jerk? Perhaps there wasn't any other way. As Grace said, she simply had to spill her soul. "I was born to be the muse of love, to inspire people to create beautiful works, to help them express themselves to each other. From Homer to Shakespeare, I was there with them. Sonnet 18? 'Shall I compare thee to a summer's day?' That was me. I mean, it was William, but we spent a lot of time together, and he adored exploring the permutations of love. It was incredible, and I don't mind telling you that his sister was a wonderful lover and poet in her own right." She grinned when Grace rolled her eyes. "And although marriages for love weren't really an option among the wealthy, regular people almost always married for love, because there wasn't anything else, except maybe the number of goats or the piece of land. The emotions were *real*."

Grace wadded up her greasy paper, took Eris's, and clumsily got to her feet to go throw them in the trash. She came back and sat closer to Eris than was probably professional, but Eris was glad for the contact.

"Okay. So you and Shakespeare are writing things like Romeo and Juliet while you bonk his sister in your free time. How do you go from that to retiring because you don't believe anymore?"

"Bonk? Very erotic. I'll use it in my next poem." Eris drew hearts in the sand as she thought. "In the seventeen and eighteen hundreds, the Industrial Revolution happened. People were suddenly surrounding themselves with machines. Trains, electricity, factories. Once it started, it exploded, taking humans into a whole new state of being. The problem with that was that it started to distance them from each other. Work hours got longer, families got more stressed. Children were pressed into work they had no business doing."

"Surely they didn't stop loving each other?" Grace dug her feet into the sand. "The desire to express the way they felt didn't end?"

Eris stared out at the ocean, remembering. "Creation became less about the arts and more about advancement. About steel and making more, more, more. My sister Uri and the goddess Minerva were run off their feet, always around to help with inventions and new concepts. But love? It was an emotion, and emotions began to be seen as a weakness." She shivered and hugged herself. "I felt it. Like a kind of slowly receding tide. There was a little burst in the nineteen sixties, when people started talking about love and saying how important it was that we care for one another, even in the midst of another senseless war. For a second, I had hope."

"And then?" Grace asked softly.

"And then we hit the electronic era. And humans separated from each other even more. The word love was used without any real meaning. People love their phones, their computers. They love their houses, their pools. But they stopped understanding what it really means. They stopped looking into each other's eyes so they could really see each other. Everything is in passing now. The divorce rate, as you know, is more than half. *More than half.* People get married, then decide it's over. They walk away. And that number quadrupled when people who were supposed to love each other were forced into constant proximity with the pandemic. Love withered like grapes in a drought."

Some children ran past, tiny tan bodies flinging up sand as they swung their brightly colored buckets ahead of them. Eris took a deep breath. There was no need to go into detail about the more personal aspect of what she'd gone through. It wasn't relevant. "And so I retired, although I did it before the pandemic, thankfully, so I didn't have to spend my efforts on rotting emotions. I'm not needed. You hear plenty of love songs on the radio. You read romance novels, you have dating apps and shows with plenty of drama when it comes to choosing someone to be with. People are still out there talking about love, expressing it creatively in their own ways. I'm unnecessary." She glanced at Grace, whose brow was furrowed, her eyes narrowed.

"And for those same people to blame me because they can't make it work? It's ludicrous. They wouldn't have made it work regardless. Even if I'd somehow inspired them to say the right things, they wouldn't have *felt* them." She finally looked at Grace. "It isn't my fault. If they want someone to blame, they should be looking at Aphrodite or even the Fates, people actually responsible for who humans end up with."

Grace continued to look at the ocean, her expression unreadable. And as Eris, too, looked at the expanse of ocean, she ignored the tiny whisper in the back of her mind that said maybe it wasn't entirely true.

CHAPTER EIGHT

Grace rose and dusted off her suit. She looked down at Eris, who hadn't risen yet. "I can't even pretend to imagine what you've been through, or what that felt like. What you immortals see and feel is so far beyond my understanding that if I think too hard on it, I start to get anxious." She touched Eris's shoulder. "But I will say this. I think there's something monstrously sad about you feeling the way you do. That someone built for love and creativity has turned her back on it is just short of criminal, if you don't mind my saying so."

Eris shook her head but didn't look up. "How can you say that? I did my research on you. Don't you come from a damaged family?"

Grace winced at the choice of word. "No more than many families, as you pointed out." She wasn't about to divulge her personal history. No good would come of it, and there were professional boundaries to maintain. "But everything you've said today, from Themis's office to here on the beach, has given us the argument we need. They'll try to poke plenty of holes in it, but at the end of the day, they can't hold you to it." She hesitated and started to back away. "Even if they probably should."

She walked back to the boardwalk and put her heels on. When she looked over her shoulder, she saw that Eris was still sitting in the sand, unmoving. She pulled out her phone and called for an Uber, then went to pick up a smoothie in the time she had to wait.

The next step would be depositions. The people in the lawsuit would answer Grace's questions with their attorney present. She'd get to find out exactly why the people complaining felt they had a right to expect Eris's help or involvement, and it was a good chance to get the attorney, jerk that he was, to see he didn't have a case.

The car picked her up and took her the short drive to her office. Brad was sitting in her office, ready and waiting.

"How'd it go?" he asked, not looking up from his phone.

"Tell me something. Do you believe in love? As in the real thing. Sweep you off your feet, forever love?" She slid into her chair and kicked off her heels. There was still sand between her toes, and she wondered if Eris was still sitting where she'd left her.

Brad squinted at her. "Don't you?"

"I don't know." She shrugged at his look of surprise. "I want to. And despite all the shit we see here, and despite my parents, I think the real thing is possible. That's why I'm holding out. You make fun of my list, but when I fall for someone, I want it to last. And I've always believed it's out there."

"But?"

"But." She took out the small tape recorder she'd had in her pocket while talking to Eris. "This." She played the recording, and he sat back and listened, his hands behind his head.

When it was over, he blew out a hard breath. "Well, that certainly makes you doubt everything, doesn't it?"

She threw the recorder in a drawer. It wasn't ever going to be used, she just needed to be able to go back to Eris's exact words as she went about preparing their defense. "I want to say she's wrong, that she's just jaded. But how do you argue with an immortal woman whose sole province has been love? Surely that means she's right."

He grabbed her smoothie and took a sip, then winced. "You and kale. That's so disgusting." He wiped at his mouth with the back of his hand. "How do we quantify or qualify if a god, or an immortal in this case, is *right*? It has to be a matter of opinion, right? And that's how we'll win the case. There can't possibly be any definitive proof that their love lives wouldn't have been any better if she'd been involved. They're just hoping, and that's not a credible case. Like Eris said at Afterlife, ultimately, they should have asked an actual goddess of love for help, not a muse whose sole province seems to be creativity. Maybe Aphrodite feels that love is as beautiful and pervasive as it always was."

She felt only slightly more hopeful at his view of the case. "You're right. But for them to file, Zane Shaw must have something he thinks will get him a win. He'd take the case based on the notoriety, for sure, but he doesn't like to lose."

"I'll file for discovery on Monday." Brad stood and stretched, his back popping audibly. "In the meantime, what do you want to do about the Infinite club and the protesters there? Does it need to be closed while we go through the process?"

She considered the idea, but quickly shut it down. "No. That would look like we were admitting that there might be some connection between the case and the club, and we want to avoid that. Eris promised she'd stay away from it for a while, so I'm not worried she'll get caught up in anything."

He went to the door but stopped before he opened it. "You know what's a real bummer?"

"Beyond the obvious? What's that?"

"She was born to be the harbinger of love. To get people to feel and create. But if she's not doing that, then what's her purpose here?" He tilted his head, looking sad. "I can't imagine living forever with no purpose and having nothing to wake up for."

He left, and Grace stared out the window in thought. He was right, that would be awful. Human lives were driven by purpose much of the time. Work was a part of your identity for most of your life, and what you did could say something about you. She'd chosen her line of work for very personal reasons, and she rarely regretted her choice. Being true to who you were, to your passion, was something she believed in fervently, and it was a question she often put to clients when they were wondering what to do with the new chapters in their lives. She asked them what their passion was, what they wanted to do that would make them happy. Often, they didn't have an answer, but they set about finding one.

Eris no longer had a purpose. Grace pictured her, alone on the beach, lost in the darkness of her thoughts, and her heart ached. Professional boundary be damned, she wished she could hold her tight and convince her that love still existed in the world.

But did it?

❖

Grace rubbed her eyes and looked away from the computer. It had taken hours to go through the Wiki page detailing the various gods of love and lust, of which there were many. Far more than she'd realized, but she'd come to understand her viewpoint was skewed by her culture. There were love deities all over the place. Given what she'd learned at Afterlife, how many were still in existence? How many were pre-faders walking around among humans who had no idea the person on the subway or in the car next to them had once been worshipped and adored?

Brad stuck his head into her office. "Zane Shaw is here."

She barely managed to keep the swear words from painting the air. "We didn't have an appointment, did we?"

Brad shook his head, keeping his professional persona securely in place. "He said he was in the neighborhood."

"His building is a block away. He's always in the neighborhood." She shifted the files off her desk and into a drawer. "Go ahead."

Brad left and was quickly back with Zane following behind him.

"Grace! So good to see you again." He sat primly in her guest chair without being asked to.

She took the seat behind her desk. Normally she'd have sat in the chair beside someone in her office, but she didn't want to get that close to him and his oil slick hair. "What brings you to my office, Zane?"

"Just a friendly chat with opposing counsel." He examined his fingernails and then bit at one, tearing it off and letting it fall to the carpet. "You're awfully brave, taking on a case like this when you haven't really cut your teeth with the big boys yet."

"And you're awfully brave to come in here and tell me that I need to play with the boys at all." She shook her head a fraction when Brad held up a coffee carafe outside the door, behind Zane's field of vision. He wouldn't be staying that long if she could help it. "Did you need something?"

He made eye contact, his smarmy charm not hiding the shark beneath. "I saw that you listed the goddess Themis as co-counsel."

"I did. And?"

"And it isn't allowed. She's not legal counsel. She doesn't have a right to try cases in the State of California." He dragged his jagged fingernail along her desk. "I wanted to let you know I'm asking that she be struck as counsel."

Grace laughed and leaned forward. "You're going to tell the goddess of justice that she's not good enough to sit at the table?" She shook her head and sat back. "You're more of a fool than I thought you were."

"The gods might be around now, but they're still useless. You saw that mess in Moscow last year. They won't come down on me. Know why? Because they're all about image, nothing else."

"And what if by coming down on you and turning you into, say, a warthog, helps their image by showing that they mean business? How will you feel about your case then?"

He shook his head, his smug smile in place. "But they won't do it. They want to be loved and adored. They're out there advertising their religions like Apple and Microsoft advertise their products. If they punish someone for stepping up and saying they're not doing their jobs, then it makes them look bad. Followers turn against them, go somewhere else."

There was a certain twisted logic to what he was saying, but she'd never admit it. "And you don't think Eris's father, Zeus, is going to have something to say to you? You think he cares what people think?"

He scoffed, spittle landing on her glass top desk. "He's probably the worst of them. He preens in front of the cameras, all gold and glowy. He knows he can't mess with humans now and get away with it." He stood and brushed at his pants. "Anyway, I just wanted to say hi and let you know about Themis, because I like you. I always have. You nearly handed me my ass in that San Clemente case a few years ago." He went to the door and tugged it open. "Almost."

Once he was gone, Grace pulled the hand towel from the bottom drawer of her desk. She wrapped it around her hands and tugged hard, releasing her frustration and tension into it. Three more times and she could breathe past her anger. When she turned around, Brad was sitting where Zane had been, scrolling through his phone. There was a latte on her desk and a maple pecan Danish beside it.

"I'm sorely tempted to see if I can get someone at Afterlife to turn him into the weasel he is."

"More like a mosquito. Or a wasp. Some blood-sucking, stinging thing that serves no goddamn purpose." Brad nudged the coffee toward her with his pen.

"That's what he *is*. I want him to be something without the power to do anything. Like…mud. Or a tree branch." She took a sip and murmured her thanks. "He's going to try to have Themis struck as co-counsel."

He nodded. "I heard. I've already called and told her. I think there may be a chunk of wall missing in her office if her shouting is anything to go by, but she said she'd work it out."

Grace brushed crumbs from the pastry off her blouse. "You're my soul mate."

He grimaced and got up. "God forbid. You have all the wrong parts and you're way too high-maintenance." He waved as he left the office.

Grace went to her couch with her coffee and the remainder of her pastry. She kicked off her heels and tucked her feet under her as she contemplated Zane's visit. It was well known he liked to play mind games, and she really had come close to beating him on that case years ago. The husband had been a true asshat who'd been abusive and controlling, and when the wife had finally gotten the nerve to divorce him, Grace had found her a safe house to stay in until the proceedings were over. The case had been going Grace's way until the wife showed up in court with a bruise on her cheek and said she was dropping the case. She wanted nothing from him other than her freedom.

Zane's expression had been less than surprised, and when she'd met his eyes across the courtroom, she'd known full well he'd had something to do with the situation.

The question was, what kind of stunts would he pull with a case like this? She needed to get a bigger team together, and she needed to do it quickly.

Chapter Nine

E ris wasn't one for paperwork. She never had been. Unlike several of her sisters, her passion didn't lie in spreadsheets or strategies. Of all of them, she was probably the most emotional, the most desire based. The least organized.

Hence, the stack of paperwork on her table being largely ignored. Grace had sent her copies of the formal lawsuit filing so that Eris could understand what she was up against, but wasn't that what Eris was paying Grace for? She ran her hand through the mountain lion's warm fur and smiled at the resulting purr. The day was warm and quiet, and her sanctuary was exactly where she needed to be.

Her phone buzzed and she picked it up. "Hey, Callie."

"How are you holding up?"

Callie rarely minced words, and Eris was glad it was her and not one of her more voluble sisters, like Clio, who'd called. "I'm irritated as fuck. You know when we left and spent a few decades on Olympus, and it gave way to the Dark Ages? I'm sorely tempted to suggest we do it again."

"I understand, and a few years ago I probably would have agreed with you. But what you're going through is part of a learning curve, I think. There were bound to be new issues brought on by the Merge, and I think this is simply the next one."

Eris sighed and closed her eyes. "Why me?"

"Because of all of us, you're the only universal muse. People only care about justice when it affects them. Science, history, art…the people who are interested in those are specific. But love is something every human desires. You're the low-hanging fruit, sister dear."

"Fucking fantastic. I've been called an anomaly and now I'm fruit. This isn't helping my self-esteem." She glanced down when the mountain lion roughly licked her arm. At least someone wanted her company.

"We'll deal with your self-esteem after the case. I've been in touch with Grace and Themis, and we're building the team we need for your defense. I don't have to tell you how serious this is, do I?"

"No, I get it. It could open the floodgates to holding the gods responsible in a more direct, tangible way. Or, if not the gods, then the rest of us low-hanging fruit. Right?"

"Right." Callie sounded relieved. "We'll be back from Scotland next month, but Grace and Themis know they can reach me anytime. And, Eris?" Her tone softened. "You can call whenever you need to, okay? Even if it's just to talk things through. I know you've been struggling."

Inexplicably, tears welled in Eris's eyes, and she brushed them away. "I'm good, thanks. But I'll keep it in mind for the existential dread nights." She hesitated for a second, then said, "Question, though. You were struggling too, right? When you worked at Afterlife? How did you move beyond it?"

"I didn't really know I was struggling until I took a vacation. It was only when I got away that I could see how off things were. But you've been on vacation for a while now, so maybe that's not going to work for you."

Eris winced at the slight reprimand in Callie's tone. "Yeah. Guess not."

"You'll find your way, Eris. We all have over the centuries. What are you doing in your free time?"

Eris groaned. "It's all free time right now. I had my club, but Grace has told me to stay away from it while this is going on. But how long will that be?"

"These cases can take years, but yours won't. It's too high profile, and it will get pushed through quickly. I've heard there was a big prayer meeting among the Christian judges who were asking for guidance on how to try a case against a pagan deity."

"Fucking monkey tits. Like the Christian God gives a flying fuck about the muses. And who do they think inspired a big chunk of the Bible? The good parts, about loving thy neighbor and all that defunct garbage?" Eris stood abruptly, making the mountain lion hiss and roll over.

"While it concerns me that you call it garbage, you're right, and I'm sure Grace will include that in her defense strategy." There was noise in the background. "Look, I need to run. The river nymphs playing in the grotto have gone into heat. We're trying to keep them contained so they don't get off while drowning some poor human."

That made Eris laugh, and she felt a little better when she hung up. But she was still at loose ends. Maybe she should go to Scotland and play with the river nymphs. That would certainly distract her. But again, they had sharp teeth, and she wasn't about to deal with that again. It made her think of Grace and how perfectly they'd fit together.

The barbecue caught her eye, and she picked up her phone. Wallowing wasn't good for anyone, and she didn't want to feel any worse than she already did.

The smell of grilling meat filled the air, along with laughter and the clink of glasses. Ebie, DK, Deb, and Sian sat around the table, cold beer and plates of food being enjoyed in full. Eris's shoulders had relaxed, and her headache had eased as soon as they'd arrived, and she was reminded once again how important friendship was. While she might not be relationship material anymore, having friends like these who dropped everything to come hang out with her, was worth its weight in Cupid's stupid arrows.

She brought a plate of barbecue chicken to the table and slid into her seat. A long swig of beer made her sigh happily.

"Why the hell does your guard lion like my car? Why won't it lie on someone else's?" Sian pointed with her fork at the mountain lion who was once again sprawled on the hood.

"It must like the way you smell. They're sensitive to pheromones." Eris stabbed at her chicken and grinned at Sian as she chewed.

The group laughed, and Sian puffed up. "Hey, at least I'm attractive to a mountain lion. The rest of you can barely get a date, let alone attract something with that much power."

"You're saying you're better than us because an overgrown cat wants to do you?"

"It doesn't want to *do* her. It wants to hump her car. Big difference."

"It's *sleeping* on her car. It doesn't want anything to do with her at all. Like the women in her bed, I imagine."

The banter kept on, and Eris let herself fall into the easy familiarity and genuine love they had for one another. They might never say it and admitting it out loud would bring plenty of scoffing, but it was true.

The sun set behind the hills, casting a sherbet orange glow to the cloudless sky. It was still warm, but when it dropped below seventy in California, sweatshirts came out. Still, they relaxed outside. Eris threw a leftover steak to the mountain lion, who stretched and yawned widely before jumping down from Sian's car to sniff the steak. She picked it up and carried it off into the woods.

"Well, at least I can go home tonight." Sian raised up to check her car. "At some point she's going to dent it."

"Have you named her yet?" Deb asked. "She's adopted you, so you might as well."

Eris shook her head, wondering where the mountain lion actually called home. "Nah. You name things and you get attached, then they move on. She'll probably be gone by autumn."

There was quiet for a moment, before DK said, "You know, for a love goddess, you're a real downer sometimes."

Everyone laughed and Eris shrugged it off. "Just truth, my friend."

Ebie propped her feet on a chair. "What are you being sued for anyway?"

"Dereliction of duty resulting in pain and suffering." The words were salty on Eris's tongue.

"And what do they want from you?" Deb asked.

"They're asking for a million dollars each, all thirty of them, and that I be held accountable and required to return to my duties."

It was quiet as they processed that, and then DK began to laugh. "If you couldn't hook us up with true love and we're your best friends, then no one else has a fucking chance."

It lightened the moment, and Eris could breathe again. "Remind me not to add you to the witness list."

"Hey, why *haven't* we found our soul mates, since we put up with all your moaning about how this era doesn't know what love is?" Deb asked.

"Because you *don't* know what love is," Eris answered, her eyebrow up. "You have to *want* more than a one night or temporary relationship. I can't make you want more than the shallow, sexual, sheet-stealing nights than you do."

Deb tipped her beer to Eris in cheers. "And just like that, their case is in the toilet."

They tapped their bottles together.

"When I talked to Gill that first time, and I had no clue how to approach her. Did you help me?" Ebie asked, looking off into the distance.

Eris thought back to the night Ebie had met the one person she'd felt a connection with in a long time. "Yeah, I guess I did. I felt how much it meant to you, so I helped out a little."

"But it didn't work because Gill...well." Ebie shrugged and chugged her beer.

"Right. I can get things moving, help you say the right things, express what's in your heart. But the rest is up to you demented apes. And you never fail to make an absolute shit basket out of it."

"So, the people suing you are saying they haven't been able to express themselves well enough to make real connections. That they would have had a chance to meet someone in your club if only you'd done your witchy woo thing."

"Yeah, basically."

"What bullshit." Sian stretched and zipped her hoodie higher. "People just want someone to blame. Plenty of people fall in love all the time without a muse to help them say the right thing."

The others agreed, and Eris warmed at the feeling of their support. This was exactly what she'd needed. They laughed and talked for the rest of the night, and by the time they all stumbled inside a little worse for wear, Eris was less inclined to run off to Olympus.

At one point, the conversation had gravitated, as it often did, to the women who were or weren't in their lives. Eris had thought of Grace, and now, as she slipped between the sheets, she could almost feel the soft, long hair over her fingers, the swell of her breasts against her chest, and the way she'd opened so fully to her.

She grabbed the vibrator from her drawer and got off quickly, the memory of Grace's gasps and moans pushing her over the edge. Love might not be a real thing anymore, but lust certainly hadn't diminished.

❖

Eris woke to the sounds of low conversation coming from the front of the house. Her head pounded like someone was breaking rocks in it, and her mouth was as dry as Sahara sand. Groaning, she pulled herself from bed and threw on a tank top and boxers, then made her way to the kitchen.

"Chris? What are you doing here?" Mugs sat on the counter, along with pastries, and eggs were cooking on the stovetop.

"Hey, boss. I had a feeling you wouldn't remember. You texted me around one this morning telling me how much you loved me and asking if I'd come over to feed you and the friends you loved so much." Chris's small smile made it clear they weren't perturbed by the request.

"Aw," Deb said around a mouthful of bagel. "She loves us."

Eris shot her a look and poured herself a cup of coffee. "I'm really sorry, Chris. We got a little carried away last night."

Sian slouched into the kitchen, also dressed in a tank top and boxers, though hers were tight, showing off her muscular legs. "Something has died in my skull."

"If it were dead, it wouldn't hurt." Deb didn't seem as affected as the rest of them.

Eris continued to sip her coffee and accepted the plate of huevos rancheros Chris set in front of her. She didn't miss the way Chris's gaze lingered on Sian, taking her in, before they looked away and went back to cooking.

Sian was oblivious and slumped into the chair beside Deb, then rested her head on the countertop. "I don't know why I hang out with you people."

"Butch brothers forever." Deb pushed a glass of orange juice against Sian's arm.

Eris nodded her approval of the sentiment, and once again caught Chris looking at Sian. Chris turned and Eris caught their eye, raising her eyebrow slightly in question. Chris blushed a cute pink and turned away. Chris and Sian had met a number of times when they'd used the beach house after a night at the club, but she'd never seen them interact. Had she grown so oblivious that she didn't even notice attraction in those around her anymore? The thought made her soul itch, and it wasn't something she could scratch.

Ebie eventually joined them, and like Deb, didn't look as bad as the others. Chris was quiet and unobtrusive as always, but Eris could tell they were paying close attention to the conversation going on around them.

"Let's go on a ride today," Eris said. "Get lunch at the Rock House."

There was general agreement, and a time was set to meet up at their starting point.

"Chris? Want to join us? You could ride with any one of us."

Chris's eyes went wide, and they didn't seem to know how to respond.

"You can ride with me," Sian said, finishing off her breakfast burrito. "I'm the only one with a real bitch seat."

"Bitch seat?" Chris said, looking more flustered than Eris had ever seen.

"Just a jargon term for the passenger seat. Sian's has a backrest, and it makes it a hell of a lot more comfortable for a long ride." Eris felt the flutter she hadn't noticed in ages. Something tickling that part of her born to the gods, the something that told her to pay attention.

Chris slowly nodded. "Um, sure. Yeah, that'd be great." They looked at Eris. "I was going to oversee some work at the beach house today though."

Eris rolled her eyes. "And I appreciate your dedication. But this is way more important and more fun. You can ride with me to the meeting point and then switch over to Sian's bike. I've got some extra riding gear that should fit you." She didn't mention that she had lots of different sized riding clothes because she'd often taken women for long, romantic rides that ended with very little clothing at all.

As usual, the thought of a woman in very little clothing made her think of Grace. They'd set boundaries, and she needed to abide by them. But something deep inside wouldn't let go of the desire to spend more time at Grace's side. If there was one thing she'd learned in three thousand years of existence, it was to listen when that little voice inside started whispering sweet nothings. At least temporarily.

Chapter Ten

Grace picked up the phone without looking at the screen, her attention on the files spread out in front of her. "Hello?"

"Hey there."

Her attention immediately shifted to the caller, whose smooth, husky voice made her ache inside. "Eris. This is a nice surprise." She could hear the roar of motorcycles and voices in the background.

"This is really last minute, but I don't suppose you'd want to take a ride with me and my friends today? We're heading up Angeles Crest Highway to one of our favorite restaurants."

Grace bit her lip. Was it crossing a professional boundary?

"We could get to know each other a little more and you could talk to my friends. Off the record, obviously."

It was as though Eris knew what her reservation would be. Brad's voice telling her to take the leap echoed in her mind. "I'd love to. Do I need anything in particular?"

"I don't suppose you have motorcycle clothes and a helmet?"

Grace grinned. "As a matter of fact, I do."

"Fantastic. We'll be by to pick you up in about half an hour. Text me your address." The roar of engines grew louder. "See you soon."

Grace had to go into her tiny attic and dig out the box with her old riding gear in it. As she shook it out, she prayed it still fit. As the years went by, despite her diet of coffee and workaholism, she seemed to grow curvier.

The pants were a little snug around the waist, and the jacket pushed her boobs up, but that wasn't a bad thing. She liked the way it looked with the white tank top underneath. She'd just finished braiding her hair so it didn't tangle in the wind when she heard the rumble of Harley Davidsons coming up the street, along with car alarms going off.

She stepped out, holding her helmet in one hand, and the sight of the gaggle of riders coming down the street made her heart race. Eris pulled up first and waved, and Grace nearly skipped to meet her.

"Hey there," Eris said, her eyes hidden behind sunglasses, but the tone of her voice suggested she liked what she saw.

Grace climbed on, not as easily as she would have liked, and felt the muscles of Eris's waist tighten under her hold.

"You good?" Eris asked.

Grace squeezed her waist. "Very."

Eris revved the bike and received answering revs, and the group set off. Once they were out of the city and on Highway 2, the ride became peaceful. Scrub brush and tall, rocky cliffs soon gave way to pines and cedar trees, and they left the smog behind. Grace's back began to ache a little from sitting so upright and eventually she relaxed into Eris, who leaned back against her slightly.

With nothing else to concentrate on, she enjoyed not only the stunning surroundings but the way Eris felt in front of her. She was tall and strong, her muscles defined even under the riding clothes. Her hands lightly gripped the handlebars, and she was clearly at one with the giant machine she rode so expertly.

They pulled into a dirt parking lot in front of a building made of giant rocks, the Rock House sign swinging in the wind out front. She waited until Eris nodded, and then slowly slid from the bike. Another passenger on someone else's bike also slid off and came to stand next to Grace.

She pulled off her helmet and quickly unworked the braid so her hair fell in waves around her face. Although it didn't matter, of course, she still wanted to look presentable when Eris came over.

"Hi, I'm Chris."

She smiled at the person who'd taken off their helmet. Short dark hair framed an androgynous face, and sparkling eyes smiled at her.

"Grace. Nice to meet you."

Chris's eyes went wide. "You're Eris's attorney."

So much for the feeling of being out for a day of sexy fun. The reminder was a blast of cold air. "That I am."

The bikes were all parked, and she and Chris walked over to the group. Eris took her helmet off, and Grace's knees went weak. Her thick dark hair fell over her eyes, and her biceps bunched as she took off her jacket.

She stepped closer to Grace and bent her head low. "If you keep looking at me like that, we're going to have to find somewhere private so I can do something about it."

Grace flushed and took a step back. "It's not my fault you look like something out of *Hot Butch* magazine."

One of the other riders snorted as she walked past. "Maybe *Hot Old Butch* magazine."

The ensuing laughter broke the tension between them, and Eris grinned.

"Hungry?"

Grace nodded and didn't pull away when Eris took her hand, and they followed the group inside. They settled at a large, battered round table and Eris made introductions. Aside from Chris, who was softer, the rest were all old-school butch, and it made Grace's inner femme swoon to be sitting at a table among them.

Eris handed her a menu and swatted DK's hand away when she went to take it. "This is why your relationships don't last."

"You're the one who always says chivalry is dead," Deb pointed out as she flipped open the menu.

There was more banter as they decided what they were ordering, and Grace took in the dynamic. Like her, Chris seemed to be on the outside. "How long have you all known each other," she asked.

That started a new round of friendly arguing.

"Since I was born," DK said. "The muse of love was always meant to be in my life."

The others booed her, even though she insisted it was true.

"Five of us met on a ride," Eris finally chimed in, motioning at DK, Ebie, and Deb. "You haven't met Sue. She's running a farm somewhere in the middle of nowhere, but one day, I'll introduce you. Anyway, twenty-five years ago, we were doing the Sturgis run. Deb hit on the wrong woman in a bar, and it ended up being a bar fight to end all bar fights. We ended up in a square fighting people off, and we've been friends ever since."

"And I ended up going home with the woman Deb messed up with." DK raised her glass and the others laughed.

"And you?" she asked Chris.

"Um, I'm just Eris's house manager. For her beach house."

"Just?" Eris said. "Chris is amazing at keeping everything organized. And this morning, they made us the most amazing breakfast."

Chris blushed a cute pink and fiddled with their napkin. "It was no big deal."

Sian shook her head. "Anyone who shows up and cooks breakfast like that with no notice at all, is not *just* anything."

Grace smiled at the way they were supporting the quiet member of the group and couldn't help but notice the way Eris's eyes shifted between Chris and Sian, like she was watching something none of the rest of them could see. But as far as she could tell, there wasn't anything there.

"She saved my life," Sian said, thumbing the condensation on her glass. "I was in a plane crash, and I was dying. She and Prom rescued us. And after, when my heart was broken, she took me under her wing and showed me that life is still great, even when it feels really bleak."

The moment turned somber, and everyone seemed to take that in.

"Prom?" Grace asked.

Sian laughed. "Prometheus. The Titan god who gave fire to humanity."

That broke the tension, and there was teasing about her having been saved by a man on a reindeer, which then turned into her being saved by Santa.

She jumped slightly when Eris touched her leg, and Eris gave her a small smile. "Tell us why you have riding gear if you don't have a bike of your own."

Grace rolled her eyes and sipped the lemonade put down in front of her. "I've always been a sucker for a woman with a motorcycle. My ex rode with the Dykes on Bikes at LA Pride every year, and we'd go out for rides most weekends, so I got my own stuff. We split up about two months after I invested a hefty sum in gear that didn't feel too bulky."

There were supportive groans all around.

"So you're single?" Ebie asked, leaning forward, her gray eyes innocent.

"Back right on up there, cowboy." Eris put her arm out as though to physically block her. "Grace didn't come out with us today to get hit on."

Ebie shrugged. "But you never know when lightning will strike."

Grace laughed along with the others when they started teasing Ebie about her celibate status. She didn't miss the protective nature of Eris's words, nor the way her thigh had pressed against Grace's from that moment forward. Lightning, indeed.

Eris had been right; she did get to know her better, but it wasn't from Eris herself. Her friends had no problem sharing plenty of stories, some embarrassing, others revealing. At some point, they'd all dealt with heartbreak they'd brought to Eris's doorstep, and she'd gladly helped them through the emotional rollercoaster. Whenever they needed her, she was there, whether it was to take a ride, to help them move, to be their wingman, or to go to a family funeral so they didn't have to go alone. She was always there for them.

Two hours passed too quickly, and it was soon time to get back on the road. Grace could have listened to their stories all night long, and she hoped this wasn't the only time she'd get to hang out with them. This time, as they were headed for the bikes, she noticed the way Chris looked at Sian, and how they seemed as nervous as a teenager with a crush. Sian, on the other hand, looked completely oblivious.

"Did you and Chris want to switch?" Sian asked. "They got the backrest on the way here, you could have it on the way back."

Grace felt Eris stiffen next to her, but she didn't say anything. "Actually, I'm really comfortable with Eris. But thanks for the offer." There was no mistaking the relief in Chris's eyes, nor the slight relaxing of Eris beside her. Her breathing hitched at the notion that Eris liked having her behind her as much as she enjoyed being there.

This time when she got on, she allowed herself to slip close so that their bodies were pressed together, and Eris reached back and squeezed her leg. On long stretches of road, Eris let go of the handlebar and put her hand on Grace's calf. By the time they were nearing the city once again, Grace was on fire even though the air had cooled considerably. The other riders peeled away so it was just Eris and Grace when they pulled up at Grace's cottage.

She slid off. The moment was ripe with possibility, and gods knew Grace wanted to ask Eris inside, but professional alarm bells kept ringing in her head.

Eris pulled off her helmet and met Grace's gaze, and there was no question what was in her eyes. Grace turned and headed for the cottage, and Eris followed.

The door had barely shut when Eris pushed Grace up against it, and once again they were all over each other. Eris's lips were hot and soft, insistent as her hands slid up Grace's tank top. She pushed away from the door and shoved off the motorcycle jacket, leaving it where it dropped. Backing up, she put her hands in Eris's pockets and pulled her forward, still kissing her, until she bumped into the edge of the bed. Eris followed her down, her strong, hard thigh pressed against Grace's crotch, making her moan against Eris's lips.

Eris went to pull up her top, and a shiver of self-doubt coursed through her. "Wait."

She froze, her eyes full of lust, her breathing hard. "Is something wrong?"

"I…" Damn. What a time to be self-conscious. "I don't have time to work out, not that I would if I did, but—"

Eris silenced her with another hot, deep kiss, her tongue demanding entrance. "You're the hottest fucking thing I've seen in the last thousand years." She trailed kisses down the side of Grace's neck, nipping a little, sucking a little, as she went over her collarbone and down the center of her chest. "I want to taste every inch of you so nothing ever tastes as good as you do, ever again."

"God, yes." Grace pressed into her, thoughts of work and boundaries abandoned to the flames racing through her.

Eris pulled her tank top down and sucked on her breast through the lace bra, much as she'd done the first time, and it was no less erotic now. Then she went to the other breast, and Grace nearly sobbed with need. "Please," she whispered.

Eris undid her pants and thrust into her, and Grace noticed that Eris's eyes didn't leave her face as she started fucking her, slow and deep at first, and then harder and faster as Grace begged and writhed beneath her.

"Come, baby. Let go. Let me see your soul," Eris said, driving deeper, twisting her fingers just right.

Grace cried out, arching hard, bearing down on Eris's hand and begging her not to stop.

And she didn't. Not for a long time and several more orgasms in various positions, until Grace giggled and pushed feebly at her arm. "No more. You're going to kill me."

Eris gently pulled out and rolled onto her back, then pulled Grace to her. At some point their clothes had come off, though Eris remained in a sports bra and boxer briefs, whereas Grace was completely naked. She tugged at the sheet to cover herself, and Eris gently stopped her.

"You're beautiful in every way. Please don't hide yourself from me."

Grace hesitated, and Eris let go of her hand.

"Maybe we'll build up to that."

Eris smiled and pulled the sheet up, and Grace relaxed against her. She drifted off to the sound of Eris's heartbeat.

When she woke, Eris was still at her side, sleeping. Grace took the opportunity to study her high cheekbones, the way her short hair framed her face, and the way her muscles looked against the pillow, where her arm was crooked under her head. She ran her fingertips along Eris's leg, over the hard thigh muscle, to her stomach, which rippled under her touch.

"You're looking at me that way again." Eris's voice was husky and low.

"Can I?" Grace asked. She'd been with butch women who didn't want to be touched sexually or wanted it in certain ways. She never assumed.

"Definitely." Eris shoved the sheet away and rested both arms under her head.

Grace knelt on the bed, less self-conscious in the fading light. She ran her hands over Eris's legs, from her feet to the vee of her thighs, along her stomach, and over her small, high breasts. Eris's breathing quickened, and she made small sounds of pleasure as Grace explored a body that was most definitely not mortal. It had no blemishes, no scars, no marks. Eris could have been made of marble, if it weren't for the way she was responding to Grace's touch.

Grace slid off the bed and tugged Eris over. Kneeling put her in a perfect position to pull off Eris's boxers and then place her mouth where she wanted it most. Eris bucked and gripped the sheets, and

Grace took her time, figuring out whether she liked harder strokes or softer ones, faster or slower. Eris's hand tangled in her hair, and Grace thought she might get off again just from how good that felt.

It wasn't long before Eris jerked and cried out, her hand hard in Grace's hair, holding her in place until she stopped moving and sank back into the bed.

Grace made her way up Eris's body and snuggled back into her, and Eris wrapped her arm around her. They didn't say anything else, and Grace was glad. It was perfect, just the way it was. She didn't want to think about the realizations the following day would bring.

Chapter Eleven

Eris woke to the sound of something walking outside the window. A skunk, if she had to guess. It was still dark out, and she put her hand over her watch so the glow wouldn't wake Grace, who lay on her side, curled up under the comforter. Two thirty.

She willed herself to go back to sleep, but her mind jump-started and was soon in the fast lane going nowhere. Sex with Grace had been incredible. Probably the best sex she'd had in many, many years. Hell, even the nymphs of Olympus didn't really compare. Grace's open, intense sexuality was balanced by her sweet vulnerability. It was intoxicating and beautiful.

It was also problematic.

Eris hadn't wanted something real with someone in nearly two hundred years. She'd had plenty of lovers, but only one she could see spending a lifetime with. But when she'd enjoyed Grace last night, she'd felt the old song singing through her blood, setting fire to her soul. And that was why she needed to leave.

She edged out of bed and slowly gathered her things, thankful that the moonlight gave her a way to see. Once she was dressed, she stopped at the front door and looked over her shoulder at Grace, still sleeping soundly, lit by the moon like a goddess. She forced herself out the door, and she pushed her bike down the street without starting it to make sure she didn't wake Grace.

When she was on the road, she pushed the throttle until she was flying down the highway that had virtually no traffic at this hour. Although, with it being LA, there was always some. She took the curves leading to her home far too fast, but she needed to ride hard, let the adrenaline flood through her system and drown the possibility of potential.

❖

Unable to sleep when she'd gotten home, Eris had taken her camera out and done some night photography. A particularly attentive and curious owlet had posed for quite some time before its parent had shooed it back into the tree. The mountain lion stayed at her side, bumping against her and occasionally sighing like it was giving voice to what she felt. When she could finally barely keep her eyes open, she'd flopped onto the couch and slept, not caring that the mountain lion was lying on the floor next to her.

When she woke, it was mid-morning. The back door was open, clearly where the mountain lion had let itself out. Her phone buzzed, and she glanced at it to see she had two missed calls from Grace, as well as a couple of texts. She didn't respond.

Instead, she got up and showered, though she was sad to wash Grace's scent from her body. The hot water wasn't enough to wash away the feeling she'd been a coward and a jerk. She threw on sweats and a T-shirt and went to make coffee. Her appetite had deserted her. How had Grace felt when she woke alone?

She finally picked up her phone and read the texts, which were at least an hour apart.

Hey, missed you this morning.

Is everything okay?

Are you ghosting me?

Okay. Well, at least let me know you're okay.

She turned her phone over and over in her hands. What could she possibly say, when she didn't understand it herself? Some fucking muse of love she was. A little emotion and she ran for the hills. The phone rang, and she almost dropped it. But it wasn't Grace.

"Hey." She sounded as empty as she felt.

"You haven't been to play with Cerberus in quite some time, and he's getting rather frisky. He bit the heads off two children who'd come to sell cookies for their ghost troop. They're both extremely upset."

Hades sounded unperturbed, as usual. "Perhaps you could come down and have a drink with me. I've got a new chef."

Eris stood and grabbed the keys to her truck. "What happened to your last one?"

"He ran off with one of the death workers and they're starting a happy little dead family in the Deadlands. There was a time no one would dare leave my domain."

She got in the truck and started toward Afterlife. Hades, the place, not the person, was a perfect area for her to wallow in her inadequacy. "Yeah, well, life is a lot more complicated now. I'll be there in about half an hour."

She hung up and blasted the radio to drown out the noise in her head, but it didn't work. By the time she got to Afterlife she had a headache and was no clearer on why she was running. She took the elevator to level minus two, and as soon as she cleared the hall she was met by Cerb, all three of his massive heads swiveling toward her and licking her from every angle. She scratched each head in turn. "Hey, buddy. Sorry I've been away."

He flopped onto his back, the sound echoing off the obsidian black walls, and she gave him a good tummy rub, making his back leg shake when she found his ticklish spot. Hades came in, his black leather pants and black, lace-up top making him blend into the walls. "Lunch?"

She stopped rubbing Cerb, and he sat up with a grumble. "No more biting the heads off people here to sell stuff. I'll take you out to play later, okay?"

He snuffled and lay down, all his heads facing the door. It used to be a gateway of carved stone and menacing figures but now, even those coming to Hades for their afterlife arrived by elevator. It took some of the magic out of it, for sure.

She followed Hades along the river Styx, where the ferryman in his black cloak waved to her, his bony hand brilliant white in the darkness. She waved back and side-stepped a soul waiting to be picked up on the shoreline. Then they were in a clean, well-lit corridor that led to the restaurant. They took a seat and were quickly served.

"You look like one of the souls who belong here. What's wrong?" he asked as he blew on some soup.

She ripped off a chunk of bread. "Do you ever feel like being immortal sucks?"

He tsked at her. "You're the muse of love and erotic poetry. Surely you can come up with something better than 'sucks.'"

She sighed and closed her eyes as she chewed the best sourdough bread she'd ever had. "Do you ever feel like the world is spinning on an axis you can't see, and the longer and more it spins, the further you get left behind, orbiting alone?"

"Better, but stilted. You need to get the poetry back in your soul." He continued to eat his soup, daintily dipping his bread in it. "Explain."

It took her a minute to get started, but once she had, it all spilled out. How she'd met Grace, the lawsuit, sex with Grace, and how she'd run off like a snake in the night.

"Unlike you," he said, pushing his soup bowl aside. "A rather human thing to do, really. Perhaps you've been too long among them."

"Yeah." She wasn't sure what else to say.

"This lawsuit. Does it make you angry?"

She frowned. "Of course it does. I'm being blamed when it isn't even my fault. They're not even creatives. They're disenchanted people who want love. That's not my area."

He tilted his head and waved to the server to put down their next course. "That's not strictly true and you know it. You can lie to yourself and those on the surface, but never to me."

"What do you mean? This is delicious, by the way." The Asian fusion dish filled with vegetables and some kind of meat was truly divine.

"You know we all cross over one another. You can't have Hades without Olympus, you can't have Heaven without Hell. And since the Merge, we all overlap. My chef can run off and live in the Deadlands, children from the Christian heaven can come knocking to sell us cookies in Greek Hell. Love deities have always overlapped. You and your sisters worked under Apollo, which I never understood. It would have made more sense for you to be under Artemis."

Eris slurped a noodle, earning her a withering look. "She's too hot-tempered. She's a great protector, but when she blows, she's all about killing people off. We work with creative people who are naturally already ephemeral in temper. It would have been a bad mix."

He gave a small shrug. "Perhaps. Why did you run from the woman you were in bed with?"

She thought about it, and he gave her the time to think. "I don't want to go back, Hade. I don't want to fall in love again, not until the world finds its heart and remembers what it is to really love."

"And how do you know she wouldn't love you the way you wish to be loved? Though the concept of love baffles me, as you know. Everyone dies in the end, and just as they come into the world alone, they leave it that way too."

"I just know." She shrugged. "We might be together for a while, but then she'd grow bored, or jealous, or she'd find someone new. Or she'd grow old and die. And I'm not going to use what I am to get a woman to stay with me. It has to be real, and I can't be sure it would be. Too many women now want to be with an immortal for bragging rights or out of some morbid curiosity. Not because they want someone as an equal to intertwine their souls with." Their plates were taken away, and the most decadent dessert she'd ever seen was placed in front of her. "What is this?

He tapped his fork on the top, cracking the lace-thin chocolate shell to expose the dense chocolate cake inside. "Death by chocolate. It has a white chocolate cherry mouse in the middle."

Eris focused on the dessert, letting it melt in her mouth. She felt better. At least, a little better.

"I'm clearly not the right person to discuss this with," he finally said. "There was a time when I would have let Cerb bite off my feet rather than admit I don't have all the answers, but I like to think I've evolved." He sipped at his espresso, which was in a tiny mug with an image of Cerb on it. "I think you need to discuss this with Aphrodite."

Eris groaned. "No way."

"Your lack of eloquence bothers me deeply. However, I do believe it's true. She's the one who can explain why you've developed an aversion to the very essence of what you are."

"But she's so...so..."

He nodded. "Yes. But that's who she is, and she must adhere to that no less than you should." Leaning back, his expression turned even more serious. "Eris, the lawsuit is absurd. And you should know, if it goes against you, the primary gods won't stand for it. We will set humans on the right path if necessary."

She stared at him, trying to comprehend his meaning. "Are you saying you'd punish the humans?"

He nodded, his black eyes even blacker. "Gods are meant to be all-powerful. If humans start to believe we aren't, if they start to treat us like they'd treat their fellow man, which is what this lawsuit is suggesting, then we lose our power. We become less-than, obedient to their whims and inherent egotistical narcissism. They'll no longer see us as protectors or punishers but as slaves to their inane desires." His grip tightened on the cup until it cracked under his fingers. "It can't be allowed."

Her stomach sank, and the food she'd eaten threatened to return. "Jesus, H. You can't be serious."

He simply stared at her without saying anything.

She dropped her head into her hands. "So, if we lose this case, if the people suing me win, then the main gods are going to go all vengeful and red-line biblical?"

"That's a rather plebian way to state it, but yes. You've been immortal long enough to understand this, Eris." He sounded almost disappointed in her.

"And you've known me long enough to know that I'm more human than god, and I've always protected the humans around me."

His laugh was soft, more like a hiss. "You have. But now you have sex with them and run away like a frightened rabbit chased by hounds." He stood, smoothing down his shirt. "I wanted to warn you because I know how you feel about humans. I hope you win, child. But if you don't, I hope you understand that they brought this on themselves. Please go play with my dog before you leave."

He left her sitting there, alone. The ghostly servers came and went, her dishes floating away. Not only had she royally screwed up with Grace, now she had to face her with the knowledge that if they didn't win, the literal fate of humanity was on the line. That kind of pressure wasn't good for anyone.

She made her way back to the gate and rested against Cerb, who seemed to sense her mood. One of his huge heads rested next to her leg, one pressed against her back, and the other kept an eye on the elevator. "What am I going to do, boy?"

One of his heads nudged a large round skull toward her. Probably dinosaur, if she had to guess. It was good that she was supernaturally strong. She pushed to her feet and started a strange game of fetch until her arm ached too much to keep going.

When she eventually got home, she sighed when she saw Grace's car in the driveway. It figured she wouldn't accept silence as an answer. Of course, she was still in her car, given the mountain lion lying beside her door, lips pulled back in a snarl.

Eris walked over and scratched behind the lion's ears. "It's okay, girl."

Grace got out, glancing from the lion to Eris. "I'm not going to raise my voice and upset your death cat, but I'd like answers, please."

Eris nodded and turned away, knowing Grace would follow. The mountain lion ran ahead and went straight into the house when Eris opened the door.

"You've got a pet mountain lion?" Grace asked, leaning against the kitchen island.

"I didn't, but I guess I do now. She's been fine outside, but apparently she's decided to keep me."

"What's her name?"

"I haven't given her one." She didn't go into the explanation she'd given her friends. Grace wouldn't find it acceptable.

"Power like that deserves a powerful name. A Viking name."

"Hilda means fighter." It felt strange to be having such a mundane conversation, but anything that put off the inevitable was fine.

"Hilda it is." Grace turned away from the big cat who'd found a place in the sun by the window. "Now. Explain, please."

It was the second time she'd been asked to do so, and she still didn't have the right words. "I'm sorry. Let's start there." She motioned toward the deck, and they went out and sat at the table. "I freaked out."

"You freaked out." Grace pursed her lips as she stared off into the distance. "The muse of love freaked out after sex."

"No. I mean, yes. But it wasn't the sex."

Grace raised her eyebrows in a clear indication for her to continue.

She sighed and wiped her sweaty palms on her jeans. Hades was right. She used to know exactly what to say, and how. Now she sounded like she'd forgotten how to use words. "You know how I feel about love—"

"Whoa now. No one was saying anything about love."

Eris held her hands up in surrender. "I know. I'm not saying that. I'm just saying…well, last night was amazing. It was more than amazing. It was divine, something that touched a part of me that's been dormant for a really long time. And the thing is, I've been happy with it that way."

Grace nodded, still looking into the distance.

"This world, Grace. It's too complicated. Too surface, too sad. And when I let it touch the part of me born to help, born to inspire, it burns. It turns desire to ash and romance to dust. It damages me, taking chunks of who I am and blackening it."

"And?"

"And touching you opened that part of me again. And I can't allow that. I have to protect myself until the world changes, until it begins to feel on a more authentic level again." She took a chance and reached out for Grace's hand. She didn't pull away. "I freaked out because you're beautiful in ways that speak to the reason I was born, and I'm not ready for it."

Grace held her hand for a moment, then slowly pulled it away. "I've never gotten such a beautiful compliment and a brush-off at the same time."

Eris went to protest, but Grace waved her off and stood.

"I can accept what you're saying. It's sad, and if I'm honest, I think it's pretty twisted and jaded, and really, pretty much wrong. But it's what you feel, and I'll respect that, even though I think you might be throwing away something special because you can't see that special still exists. If you want to wait for some apocalypse that takes us back to pre-industrial ways of living, well, good luck." She turned toward the stairs leading off the deck. "We'll go back to being professional, client and attorney. Hopefully, you can handle that."

Eris watched as she got into her car and drove off and was glad when Hilda bumped her head against her leg. "I've really screwed this one up, haven't I?"

Chapter Twelve

Grace slammed her hand on the stapler, taking great pleasure in the sound of metal thumping into the paper. Brad reached over and held her mug still, as he'd been doing for the last hour, while she took out her frustration on inanimate objects. The first depositions started in an hour, and she was regretting taking the case. Not just because it had turned out that the muse of love was a heart-breaking sex demon wearing the disguise of a super-hot butch woman, but because Zane had buried them in paperwork.

She'd told Brad to let Eris know she didn't need to be there for the depositions, as she'd just be in the way. He probably hadn't done so in those exact words. In the other room, the team they'd assembled, including a litigation manager, a strategist, a document lead, the witness specialist, and a legal issues specialist, were already pulling apart Zane's pile of documentation. Among them were also three more paralegals who took their orders from Brad. They were all eager to help with the high-profile case. At least, they had been until they'd seen the boxes and boxes of files.

There were a minimum of thirty depositions to do, and there'd likely be more as further witnesses were added to the list. Figuring out who to use to support Eris had been daunting as well as frustrating. Her sisters were spread all over the country, they couldn't call her father because he was as likely to throw a lightning bolt and fry someone like a stick of cheese as he was to charm the jury, and Eris had refused to give any names of friends who would act as character witnesses. The ones she'd met on the ride up to the Rock Café would have been perfect, but

Eris refused to let her talk to them about it, saying she didn't want them involved. It didn't help that she wasn't in a relationship, and Grace most definitely wasn't in a position to speak up for her in that regard.

She slammed the stapler again, and Brad gently slid it away from her.

"That's enough stationery abuse, darling."

She sighed and slumped back in her seat. "She asked me, when I offered to help her, if I could still defend her if I thought she was guilty."

He raised his perfectly waxed eyebrows. "And?"

"And part of me wants to throw her to wolves. The other part of me wants to clear her name just to prove...prove...something."

"That you're a damn good attorney who does her job no matter what?" He gathered the files, placing them in order as he stacked them. "You'll definitely prove that." He left to hand out the stacks of files to their team.

She'd called him after she'd gotten home from Eris's place, and they'd met for drinks. Over margaritas she'd told him and his husband, Craig, the whole story, much to their drama-filled delight. The hangover had been worth the night of unloading her frustration.

She wasn't heartbroken. She'd been heartbroken before, and that had taken her to her knees. This ache was different. It was deep, like a stone settled on her soul, keeping it down like an evil paperweight. There were moments when she thought of their night together and she couldn't breathe. She could still see the way Eris's blue eyes stared down at her so intensely as she'd taken her, over and over again. The way she'd felt so seen, so truly appreciated.

But that was due to Eris's fundamental nature, wasn't it? The muse of love wasn't about to be mediocre and inattentive in the sack, no matter who she was with. How silly Grace had been to think she could measure up to the phenomenal women Eris had likely been with over the years. But that thing she'd said, about Grace touching a part of her soul...was it true? And if it was, that somehow made the rejection worse.

Brad knocked on the door. "It's time."

She accepted the mug of coffee from him on her way past, and he followed her to the large conference room used for depositions. Inside, a woman in flip-flops, a ripped T-shirt with varying shades of stains on it, and jeans three sizes too small that failed to contain her ample, thong-eating bottom, was tapping her foot like she had somewhere better to be. Beside her, Zane looked like a polished statue. The court reporter, sitting behind his little machine, looked decidedly uncomfortable.

Grace and Brad entered, and the woman blatantly looked Grace over.

"I can see why you're defending the bitch who screwed me over. Don't imagine you've had trouble getting away with someone." Her British accent was high-pitched and grating.

Well, that was a new way to be insulted. "Nice to meet you, Ms. Carter." Grace held out her hand and received a limp touch in return.

"Can we get on with this?" She popped her gum. "I've got to pick up the kid at my mum's before she has to go to her parole hearing."

Grace looked at Zane, whose expression was unreadable. "Sure. Let's begin."

The court reporter looked relieved and started tapping as Grace started talking.

"This is the deposition of Karen Carter in the case People vs. Love, deposition held at the offices of Kline and Associates. Zane Shaw for plaintiffs, Grace Gordon for the defense." She paused and the court reporter nodded to indicate he was caught up. "Ms. Carter, can you explain to us today what you're suing the defendant for?"

She frowned and turned to Zane. "It's all in writing. Is she not right in the head?"

He smiled, but it didn't reach his eyes. "Remember, I told you we'd be going over everything and she was going to ask you questions about what you have to say?"

She rolled her eyes. "Yeah, right. Whatever." She turned to Grace. "If she wasn't being lazy, I'd have been with that guy at the club."

Grace very much doubted it. "Can you tell me about the night you're speaking of?"

She leaned back, her arms crossed. "I was there with my girlfriends. We were out on the piss, having a good time. This guy comes up, offers to buy me a drink. He looks all right, bit of a prat, maybe, in his suit and nice shoes, but I figure I'll go with it. He goes on about what he does for work, some kind of finance guy. I'm getting vibes, right? We're hitting it off well good. The ugly lights go on, and we walk out to the parking lot together. I figure he's in, and if I play my cards right, I could be sitting pretty. And I've been at the club owned by that lezzer muse, right? So I'm bound to get what I want."

She paused for breath, and Grace nodded, though she'd have been more than happy for the woman to stop speaking. Possibly forever. "Go on."

"So, I walk him to his car and offer him a little hand wank, as a way to say thanks for the drinks and so he'll take me out again. Hell, maybe even home that night." Her face turned red, and her eyes narrowed. "What does he do? He gets all squirrely, tells me that's okay, he's not in the mood." She scoffed, spittle landing on the table. "What bloke isn't in the mood for a little hand play?"

Grace could feel the tension of Brad's body next to her as he tried not to laugh. How Zane was keeping a straight face she couldn't imagine. "And you're holding Eris Ardalides responsible for that?"

She nodded, tapping the table hard. "That's right. If she'd been doing her job, then I would have known what to say to that bloke to make things right. I'd have known what words turned him on, like." She glanced at Zane and then back at Grace, her chin lifted. "I would have known the words to express my feelings so that I started walking the path of love, instead of going home alone. It's been right hard on my mental health."

Grace looked at Zane. "Coaching, much?"

He smiled. "You know how practice sessions work. Or maybe you don't since you haven't done this before."

She ignored him and turned back to the plaintiff. "How many relationships have you had prior to the night at the club you're referring to?"

"Objection. Relevance," Zane said, writing on his notepad.

"You can't possibly think it's not relevant," Grace snapped. "They're suing the muse of love for failed relationships. Their relationship histories are fair game, and I'll bet any judge anywhere would agree."

He pursed his lips. "Very well." He waved at Ms. Carter. "You can answer."

She shrugged. "Lots, I guess. Never any of them amounted to much or lasted very long." She paused, a hard glint in her eye. "But see, that's why I needed the muse bitch to be on her game. All that could have changed if she'd just sent her magic or whatever out that night. It's her fault."

The rest of the deposition went much the same, with the woman answering Grace's question but always circling back to what might have happened if Eris had only done her job. When she left, Grace turned to Zane.

"People can't sue for what-ifs, Zane. These cases will get thrown out in bellwether trials. There's simply no way to prove that Eris's involvement would have changed the outcomes of any of these situations. You can't prove a negative." She motioned to the door with her thumb. "If that's an example of what you've got, then you're wasting everyone's time."

He held up the file with the next plaintiff's name. "Let's see what you think after this one."

Arthur Doyal looked a little like a postman from a kid's cartoon. Stocky and with thick glasses, he was also balding and had sad, doleful eyes, as though he expected whatever came next to be as equally as disappointing as the rest of his life had been thus far.

Grace's heart almost immediately went out to him. Brad shifted uncomfortably in his seat. "Mr. Doyal, thank you for coming."

His handshake was gentle but firm. "I'm a little nervous, to be honest."

"Nothing to worry about, Art," Zane said, still reclining in his chair. "Just tell her what we've already discussed."

Doyal nodded and slid into the seat, perching on the edge like he might get up and run off at any moment.

"Honestly, Mr. Doyal, this is simply for us to find out your part in the lawsuit, in your own words. We won't bite." Grace smiled at him, hoping to put him at ease. "So along those lines, can you tell me why you're suing Eris Ardalides?"

His protruding Adam's apple bobbed nervously as he nodded. "I met Louisa Leckie when she started coming to my bakery. At first, she only came on Fridays, but as we got to talking more, she started coming more often, until she started coming almost every day."

Grace nodded, prompting him to go on.

"She was single, and so am I." He blushed and fiddled with the end of his paisley tie. "You should have seen her, Ms. Gordon. Her hair was blond, streaked with just enough gray to make her look like a movie star. And she was so kind, so sweet. She always asked how I was doing."

Grace noted the use of the past tense, and a growing feeling of dread made it hard not to rush him. "And then?"

"I wanted to ask her on a date. Women like her don't usually have any interest in a guy like me, but she was different." This time he crumpled his tie in his hand, his knuckles turning white. "But I couldn't bring myself to do it. Any time I decided to, I couldn't find the words."

"And was this a usual thing, you being unable to find the words to communicate your feelings to people?" she asked, keeping her tone neutral.

"Not exactly." He took out his phone with his free hand, the other still choking his tie. "I do this." He pressed play on a video already loaded.

Arthur Doyal had a surprisingly exquisite voice. He played guitar and sang so deeply that Grace had tears well in her eyes. When the song ended, she slid the phone back to him.

"See, I don't look like much, but music has always been my way of expressing myself. But when it came to Louisa, there were never any words, no matter how hard I tried. One day, a customer told me about this big dance club owned by the muse of love. I just knew that if she could help me, if she could inspire me, that I could tell Louisa how I felt."

"And what happened then?" Grace asked, trying to ignore Zane's smug expression.

"I went to the club, Ms. Gordon. It wasn't my thing at all, all the noise and people. And I waited until Ms. Ardalides was off to the side, talking to one of her employees. I begged her pardon and asked if she could spare a moment."

"But she was busy running her business."

He inclined his head. "A little. She was mostly dancing." His tie was now twisted around his hand, which must have been in danger of choking the life out of him. "But I explained my situation, and to be fair to her, she listened to my whole story, even though there were a lot of people who wanted her attention."

"Were you aware that she had retired from her role?" Grace asked.

He nodded, his eyes downcast. "Yes, I'd heard that too. But can an immortal really retire? Especially when they're needed?" He shrugged his sloping shoulders. "She told me just that, essentially. That she'd retired and couldn't help me, and if I needed someone's help, then I should ask one of the other love gods."

"And did you?"

His eyes filled with tears which quickly slid down his pudgy cheeks. He released the death grip on his tie, which stayed crumpled. "I tried, but it wasn't enough. You can't just walk up and talk to them, and then it was too late. Louisa was killed crossing the street to my bakery the following week."

Brad's soft blow out of air wasn't terribly professional, but Grace agreed with the sentiment. "And what is it you're suing Ms. Ardalides for?"

"If she'd have helped me that night, or even the next day, maybe Louisa wouldn't have been crossing the street that morning at that time. Maybe we would have been together, or she would have slept in because we'd have been up late talking." He brushed ineffectually at the tears. "At the very least, she would have known how I felt about her before she died. I don't even care about the money, really. I just don't want other people to go through what I have. She shouldn't be able to turn away like that." His shoulders hunched, and he hiccupped as tears continued to fall. "We need help. Aren't they supposed to help us?"

Grace tapped her pen against her notepad. "Why don't we take a five-minute break?"

He nodded and blew his nose on an old cloth-style handkerchief.

Grace and Brad left the room and went to her office. He closed the door behind him, and she leaned on her desk. "If we only had this case up against us, we'd be in trouble," Brad said.

"It's a sad story, I agree. But he can't blame her for not being able to say what he wanted to, especially when he's so gifted at singing. People die all the time without knowing how others feel about them. It isn't unusual, sadly."

"But he specifically asked for her help."

Grace nodded. "Hence his involvement in the case and why Zane looks so smug I want to punch his oily head." She rolled her neck and winced at the cracking. "I can't even think of other questions to ask him that won't make us look like assholes."

Brad reopened the door so they could head back. "That's why they pay you the big bucks."

❖

The rest of the day had been much of the same, with the cases balanced between ludicrous and heart-breaking. She'd never worked on a case before where the question was so intangible: was the muse of love responsible for helping anyone and everyone who wanted her to, for whatever reason? Had Louisa been fated to die without knowing how Arthur felt about her?

At the idea of fate, she struck on an idea for a line of defense, and she picked up the phone. When Eris's husky, smooth voice answered, Grace was irritated that her body automatically twitched like someone had flipped a switch. "I was wondering if we could meet tomorrow. I have a couple questions of a more existential nature."

"Yeah, of course." She hesitated. "Do you want to come to my place? Or do you want to meet at Afterlife? Or should I come there?"

"You know, most people ask one question and wait for an answer instead of asking three at once." Grace couldn't help but smile.

"I think you'll find lawyers tend to ask one at a time. Most people ask a lot without even knowing what they're asking."

Was that true? She'd have to pay more attention. "Let's meet at your place, the one at the beach. And then if you can't answer my questions, we'll head to Afterlife. Does that work?" The idea of going to Eris's home, her special place in the mountains guarded by her own mountain lion, didn't work for her. At least she knew the beach house was used solely for the other part of Eris's life.

"That works fine. Ten?"

"See you there." She hung up, both irked and excited at the prospect of seeing her again. Looking forward to seeing someone who had told you she didn't have the emotional capacity for love was about as smart as hoping to cuddle with an angry walrus, but there it was, a flutter deep inside. And that was extremely irksome.

CHAPTER THIRTEEN

Eris stood on the deck, her forearms resting on the rail as she looked at the hazy horizon. Grace had been on her mind almost nonstop. Mostly, Eris thought of the deep look of disappointment Grace had given her before she'd left. This was exactly why she didn't do relationships. There was no way they wouldn't be as disappointing as a sand sandwich.

Chris came out and stood beside her. "Need anything?"

Eris needed a whole lot of things, but she couldn't put a single one into words. "No, thanks. It'll just be me and Grace, I think. Maybe Brad."

Chris leaned against the railing beside her. "You know, I've always looked up to you."

Eris grimaced. "Why? I'm a mess."

"Yeah, absolutely. I don't actually know anyone quite as messy."

Eris glanced at them and gave a wry smile in response to Chris's teasing one.

"But, as messy as you are, you're really great. You never want to hurt anyone's feelings. You take really good care of the people who work for you, and your friends adore you. And they all know you'd do anything in your power for them."

"Speaking of my friends," Eris said, Chris's words almost too much to bear, "how did things go with Sian the other day?"

Chris frowned slightly. "It's complicated."

Eris turned toward them, arms crossed. "Messy understands complicated. What's going on?"

"She says I'm cute, but I'm not her type. She's all about the girly girls and doesn't really get the nonbinary thing. Plus, she says she's too old for me." They shrugged again, and the hurt was clear in their eyes. "But I can't be anything other than what I am, even if I think Sian is amazing. If she can't handle me as me, then…" They straightened, and their expression once again became neutral. "Anyway. If you need me, just give me a shout."

Eris turned back to stare at the water. She shouldn't have asked. It wasn't as if she could do anything about it. If Sian had a type and Chris wasn't it, then she couldn't help even if she wasn't retired. No matter what Chris said, changing Sian's mind about what she was attracted to wasn't possible, not to mention ethical. Sometimes people simply weren't meant to be together, no matter which love deity they appealed to.

The doorbell rang and her heart began to pound. She'd been desperate to call Grace but didn't want to give any mixed signals. Sex the second time around had been a mistake, one she was trying to regret to no avail. There'd been something between them, something special, and she couldn't go there. Never again.

Chris walked ahead of Grace into the kitchen, and Eris stood there with her hands in her pockets, doing her best not to move forward and wrap Grace in her arms. The look of wariness and detachment was like a physical splinter lodged in her chest. "Deck or living room?" she asked.

"Living room. Silk isn't great in the salt air."

Eris took in the emerald green silk blouse that hugged Grace's breasts in the most perfect way possible. "No, I guess it isn't." She led the way to the living room and took the armchair, leaving the couch to Grace. If she sat beside her, she'd want to touch her. And touching her again was out of the question.

"So," Grace said, kicking off her shoes, black with shiny metal four-inch heels. "We had a chunk of depositions yesterday."

Eris nodded, but she didn't really want to hear all the ways people felt she'd failed. "How did they go?"

"They were…interesting." Grace opened her notebook and flipped to a blank page. "One thing they did was raise a question I could use an answer to."

Eris raised her eyebrows, then nodded her thanks to Chris, who came in with a tray of orange juice and bagels.

"If two people aren't meant to be together, will anything you say, or however your special brand of goddishness works, change that?"

"You're asking about fate." Eris hadn't given that any thought in a very long time, for good reason, and now it had come up twice in one day. Did that mean anything? She noticed Chris hovering just outside the door, waiting for the answer.

"I suppose. But then we get into territory that makes my head hurt. Is everyone's life already planned out? And if it is, then why bother asking for you to help them at all? Because they'll end up with the person they were meant to be with, right? But then, you're not about people getting together, you're just about getting them to express how they feel, and that's where your responsibility ends?" Grace already sounded baffled.

Eris sighed and picked up a glass of orange juice, if only to have something to do with her hands. "The fates aren't exactly forthcoming about how things work. Even the gods don't know. They're entities unto themselves. We have our roles, and we play them, and we pretty much don't think about whether what we're doing matters or not when it comes to destiny."

Grace stared at her, her brow furrowed in thought. "You're going about your lives and jobs based on your own job descriptions, and even the gods who think they control things don't know if that's true. You're essentially humans with more power but equally as clueless."

The barb hurt but Eris didn't blink. "When it comes to fate and destiny, there are only three beings who have those answers, and trust me when I say you don't want to meet them. They terrify every single person at Afterlife. Zeus literally ducks into another office if he sees one of them coming down the hall. What I can say is that if two people aren't meant to be together, then nothing I personally do will help. They can say the most beautiful things but ultimately, it won't matter. So I guess the opposite holds true as well. If they're meant to be, then they can bumble their way through a conversation and still end up in happy fucking ever after. Maybe that's where the other love gods come in. If things aren't going to plan but you're meant to be together, then the love gods can help smooth the way." What Hades had said about overlap rang true and Eris wondered if anything any of them did mattered. Only the Fates knew.

Grace rested her head on the back of the sofa. "Okay. I'll take your word for that, for now. Second question. If we needed a god or goddess of love to speak for you, to explain that they're the ones responsible for relationships and whether or not they work out, who would we talk to?"

When Eris started to shake her head, Grace held up her hand.

"Eris, you need to let me do my job. I'm sure you understand that this case is high stakes, well beyond you personally. If there are people, human or otherwise, who can testify to your character and how things work, then we need to use them. What's your objection to that?"

Eris nearly dropped the orange juice as she turned and turned the glass around in her hands. She wasn't about to tell Grace about her conversation with Hades and how the primary gods were going to tear up the world if this didn't go to plan. "I don't want to impose on anyone else. I don't want to drag them into my mess and put them in front of the human legal system. Gods aren't good at being challenged, in case you don't know that, Grace. If you do some reading in any of the religious texts, you'll find a whole lot of corpses when it comes to humans questioning the gods. If you want a last resort, trust me, that's it."

Grace was silent for a moment, and then she jerked forward and started spreading cream cheese on a bagel, still without saying anything. Then she sat back and motioned at Eris with the bagel. "Last resort. No burned corpses in the courtroom. I get it." She took a bite, clearly still thinking. "In that case, we need character witnesses. People you've helped or loved. Hell, you must have been in a relationship or ten in the last few decades? Women who can talk about how great you are?" She took another bite and waited. "Or have you told them all you're not worthy?"

Eris flinched and anger started to rise. "You can talk to my sisters. If Sappho were still around, you could talk to her about the women she loved and the erotic poetry she wrote, although not a lot of that survived, at least not in the public domain. You could talk to Shakespeare, or Byron, or Oscar Wilde, or Frida Kahlo, or Beethoven."

Grace set down her plate. "Fantastic. Anyone still living?"

Deflated, she slumped back. "I retired in the early nineteen hundreds. I haven't been around."

"You've been retired for more than a hundred years?" Grace's exasperation showed as she nearly flung the cream cheese off her bagel.

"Is there anyone who *truly* knows you? Who can testify to the kind of person you are? DK, Ebie, Deb, Sian? They seem to know you better than anyone else."

Eris considered and finally gave in. "You've met my only friends. And you know I wanted to leave them out of this."

Grace continued to eat and make notes, the scratching of her pen the only sound. When she finished, she licked her fingers and Eris had to look away. It shouldn't be erotic, but it was.

"Can I ask you something personal? But relevant."

Eris shrugged. "Seems like you have to know just about everything."

"When was the last time you loved someone? When was the last real relationship you were in?" Grace's gaze was probing, holding Eris in place.

The question couldn't have hurt more if Grace had poured gasoline into an open wound. A wound she thought long scarred over. "It doesn't matter. She's long gone, and you can't talk to her. I retired from inspiring everyone, including myself." Eris got up and moved to the window, not wanting Grace to see the hurt she knew would show in her eyes.

"Okay. We'll shelve that one, but I'm going to want to talk to your friends to see if we want them on the witness list, whether you like it or not. I assume Themis can put me in touch with your sisters?"

Eris gave a half shrug, still not turning around. Memories were invading, and she didn't have the fortitude to fight them off.

"I'm sorry, Eris." Grace's touch on her shoulder made her shiver. "I know this is painful for you, and incredibly invasive. If it's any consolation, I wish it weren't happening to you, and I'm still going to do my best to make it go away."

Eris gave a quick nod, but still didn't turn around, and she gave a shaky sigh of relief when she heard the door close so she was alone with the memories that she thought she'd put to bed a very, very long time ago.

❖

Eris waited in the private room at the restaurant, her headache already firmly in place, pounding behind her eyes. She knew Grace liked Mexican food, and so did her friends. After Grace had left the beach house, she and Chris had talked over lunch. She'd explained her feelings about not dragging her friends into it, and Chris had deftly made the point that it wasn't up to her. It was up to them, and it wasn't fair of her to make the choice for them. Chris had suggested something informal where Eris could be present when Grace spoke to the group on a more formal basis. That way Eris wouldn't have to wonder what was said about her and could maybe keep the conversation on the rails. She'd asked Chris to be there too, but they'd declined, saying it would be too hard at the moment.

She'd called her friends first, the people who knew her best, and then she added two more guests to the list. Those two might be a little petty, but she couldn't help it. If Grace wanted more, she'd provide.

DK, Deb, and Ebie arrived together, turning heads as they made their way through the restaurant. They were imposing in their butch confidence, swagger in full view. It made Eris smile, and she gave them bro hugs when they arrived. As usual, there was plenty of banter, and Eris's stress level decreased somewhat.

Until Grace and Brad arrived. Grace wore skinny jeans tucked into knee-high leather boots, and a loose V-neck tank top giving a view of deep cleavage. Eris stayed sitting down, solely because she couldn't bring herself to stand.

"Damn, dude," Ebie muttered beside her. "If she were my attorney, I'd be living under her desk and I'd crawl out whenever she wanted me."

Grace smiled as she stopped at the table. "Hey there. Good to see you all again. I was hoping you were real and not actors she hired to go for a ride to convince me she had friends."

That set the tone, and the banter was swift and sharp. Grace and Brad took their seats, and pitchers of margaritas were soon being poured into glasses. Eris stayed quiet, letting the conversation whirl around her. After all, this wasn't about her, technically. It was about what they thought of her.

There was a yelp, and she focused on the moment. She stood respectfully for the figure who'd appeared out of thin air, wispy, silently screaming shadows swirling around him and then disappearing. Dressed all in black, he was enormous, dwarfing everyone there and looking like the god he was.

"Grace, this is Hades, god of the underworld. He's known me for a few thousand years, so I thought maybe you'd like to speak to him." To her credit, Grace was pale and her eyes were wide, but she managed to stay calm. Brad, on the other hand, looked like he might faint. He gripped the table like he was trying to stay upright.

Hades inclined his head and took a seat next to Sian, who scooted her chair over a little. "It's nice to meet you, Ms. Gordon. You have quite the weight on your shoulders with this case, don't you?"

Grace swallowed quite obviously, and it took her a try or two to answer. "Yes, I do. Thank you for coming tonight."

He inclined his head again, and then he frowned when a loud bark of laughter made its way back to the room. He looked at Eris. "Was that truly necessary?"

She grinned at him. "He's known me as long as you have, and we still ride together all the time."

Prometheus, his big white beard neatly trimmed and sporting a few beads, entered the room, filling it with the strength of his Titan presence. "Hades! Good to see you, cousin. I didn't know you'd be here too. What a party!" He laughed again and it boomed around the room, making everyone wince. He spotted Sian and pulled her into a big hug, dwarfing her. "My favorite muscley little human."

Sian laughed and hugged him back.

"Prom, this is Grace, my attorney, and her paralegal, Brad."

They looked a little less overwhelmed by Prometheus, even though he was one of the oldest gods and even bigger than the rest. He was friendly and kind, and he'd always had a soft spot for humans. Unlike Hades, Prom practically yanked Grace and Brad from their chairs and pulled them into a tight hug. "You've got our Eris all tied up in knots, pretty lady." He wiggled his eyebrows, and Grace shot Eris a questioning look as she managed to disentangle herself from him.

"Prom. Not tonight." Eris gave him a warning look and he laughed again.

He raised his hands in surrender and poured himself a margarita. "Where do we begin?"

Grace took a long drink and then smiled, looking like she was drawing on every ounce of public cool she had. "I think it was a great idea to meet here. What I'm looking for are stories about Eris. How you met, what you think of her, anything you have that shows what an amazing person she is. Think of it as what you might say if I put you on the stand and asked you how she'd changed your life. Which, incidentally, I might do." She held up her glass. "To Eris."

They toasted, and she shook her head. "This is going to be a huge mistake."

Deb grinned and dug into the chips and salsa. "For you, maybe. It's going to be a lot of fun for us."

Grace smirked at Eris, but quickly flinched when Hades reached across her for the bowl of chips. Eris smirked back at her and got a dirty look in return.

"Okay, Hades. Hit us with your best story of Eris."

Brad put his phone on the table, the voice recorder clearly on. It was a good reminder, for her at least, that this wasn't a friendly social outing, no matter how it appeared.

Hades cocked his head, his void black eyes managing to look thoughtful instead of terrifying. "When Eris was a child, she liked to spend time with Cerberus, who was still a puppy then."

"The three-headed dog? It's hard to imagine him as a puppy, especially when he's dropping tree trunks at your feet." Grace said it innocently, but Eris caught the glint in her eye.

Hades turned to Eris. "When was this?"

She popped a chip in her mouth. "Doesn't matter. Go on."

He grunted and a spiral of black mist rose from the top of his head, then dissipated. "Yes, anyway. She enjoyed playing with him, but her sisters would never come to my realm. They were worried they'd be trapped. Eris had no such concerns. One day she came to visit me at the river, and there were two souls waiting to cross." His smile grew, mitigating some of his natural sternness. "She saw how sad they were, and she began talking to them. She got them to speak of their deepest desires, their love and loss. She helped create a bond that they took into the river with them. I still see them float by holding hands."

"Aw, she was a romantic little tyke, wasn't she?" DK said, laughing. "And then she grew up to be the woman everyone in the club wants to be under or on top of."

"She helped heal my heart," Sian said, interrupting the banter. "I was hurting over the loss of her sister, who chose someone else. I thought for sure we'd end up together at some point, but it didn't work out. When we got back, Eris helped get me back on my feet."

Eris tipped her glass at Sian, who looked embarrassed at her admission.

"You mean she helped you get back onto your back," Deb said and promptly ducked the chip Sian sent flying her way.

"I'm never the one on my back, I'll have you know."

"Hey, do you remember the vomit couple?" Ebie said and got a round of laughs. She turned to Grace and Brad. "It was several years ago now. This couple were right in the middle of the dance floor, having a full-on argument. The guy burps right in the middle of saying something about how she never cooks for him anymore, and it sets her off. She starts gagging, and then vomits right in his face. Obviously, he returns the favor. It looks like we're about to have a full house drowning in puke, and then Eris slides up next to them. Starts talking all low and quiet. He's still gagging, she's crying. But they both calm down, and then suddenly they're back in each other's arms, all smoochy and apologetic, and totally not caring in the least that they're both covered in slime."

Eris groaned. "I still think about that smell sometimes."

Grace's gaze was sharp. "That was you working, wasn't it?"

"I did what I needed to do in order to keep the peace and get them out of the club." She tried to keep her tone even, but it came out defensive anyway.

"My turn!" Prometheus said, pounding the table with his massive fist and making all the glasses bounce. "I bet none of you have heard this one."

Eris winced. Of all of them, Prom probably had the most embarrassing stories.

"We were in Greece. It must have been the late thirteen hundreds."

"AD or BC?" asked Hades. "They were very different times."

"BC. The best times." Prometheus nodded with certainty. "Anyway, we're in Athens, and Eris is the muse everyone wants. It was the age of heroic poets, of men who wanted to profess their love to every woman who crossed their paths. One day, Cupid shows up. At that point he was a real brat. His mother overindulged his every whim, and it made him a real pain in the ass. He was aiming his arrow at a queen of renowned beauty, because he was irritated she was married to someone he considered ugly." He took a slug of margarita and waved the pitcher in the air at a server waiting by the door, who quickly took off for more. "But Eris was there, working with some of the poets at the time. And she knew that the love between the king and queen was true." He snorted and started laughing. "Cupid let the arrow go, but Eris caught it midair, then jabbed it in his fat behind and turned him to face a statue of a centaur. He fell in love with it, and it took about a year for the spell to wear off."

Eris couldn't help but laugh with the others. "He couldn't stay away from it. Kept telling it how much he loved it, and he even mounted it a couple times, much to the horror of the nymphs who lived nearby and could see him. He's never forgiven me for that."

Although it was strange to be the focus of the stories, they served to lighten her soul a little. It was good to revisit some memories and to know that the people she cared for so deeply had been touched by her in some way. She managed to shut down any conversations about her sex life, though a few got through, making her unable to meet Grace's eyes.

Food was ordered and cleared away, more drinks were brought in, and the tales became a little harder to follow. The one thing she noticed, though, was that Grace's drink went down slowly, and she remained sharp. It almost hurt, the way Grace fit so easily into the group of people who mattered most to her. Brad, too, was holding his own and seemed happy to be snuggled up against Hades.

It was late and the stories had drifted into side conversations, when Prometheus looked up, bleary-eyed as he drained the pitcher that looked like a regular size glass in his hand. "And then," he said, apropos of nothing, "Eris met Kathleen. And our poor Eris—"

"Prom," Eris said sharply. "Not here."

He shook his head dolefully but nodded. "Okay, niece. Okay." He knocked over several empty glasses and a bowl of salsa as he reached across the table to take her hand. "But I haven't forgotten."

Having long since switched to water, she wasn't nearly as tipsy as the others, and she caught Grace's look of interest. She shook her head, her jaw set, and saw Grace looking thoughtful. She stood. "Okay, folks. Let's let the nice people who work here clean up and get home to their loved ones." When no one was paying attention, she'd ordered taxis for all of them.

They stood, and the owner and manager came in together, looking awestruck. "Forgive us, but could we have a photo for our wall and social media? To have guests like yourselves is such an honor."

The entire group managed to gather with Hades and Prometheus towering over them like monochrome monoliths. Eris jerked slightly when Grace took her hand.

"Thank you for doing this," she murmured as the owner took a number of photos from different angles. "We've got some really good stuff."

"Great." Eris squeezed her hand and let it go. "Glad I was useful for something." She ushered the group out and tried to look beyond Grace's injured expression. She made certain they all got in their cabs, and Prometheus and Hades decided to go back to the underworld to continue reminiscing about the old days. They puffed away in swirling clouds of black and white smoke that drifted into the pavement.

Grace was the last one in her taxi, and she hesitated before she got in. "Eris, I don't know what hurt you. I don't know why you're so frightened of love, of yourself. But I know every person in there loves you, and you've touched them in ways you don't seem to realize." She cupped Eris's cheek. "Maybe one day you'll see beauty in the world again."

She got into the taxi, and it pulled away, leaving Eris alone in an empty gray parking lot, Grace's touch lingering like a dancing flame on her cheek.

CHAPTER FOURTEEN

Grace sat in her little garden, debating what to do. She could, and should, go to the office. There was plenty to be done, and the whole team was already there. But after the night before, with all the stories she'd heard of Eris, her head was spinning, and she wanted some clarity.

She put on a sweatshirt and grabbed her keys, phone, and wallet as she headed out. The walk to the park took her past an array of houses, from little places like hers to apartment buildings and townhomes. A Korean man from the apartment building across the street waved to her as he threw bowls of rice to the pigeons. She wasn't sure why he did it, and the grandson who lived with him said it had something to do with their culture, but he didn't know what.

As she got closer to the park, she could hear the squawking and it made her smile. The wild parrots were in full voice today, and the clamor matched the noise in her head. When she got there, she took a seat on her favorite bench under a giant oak tree. From there she could see the green gold flashes darting from palm tree to palm tree, well-camouflaged if it weren't for the racket. The yellow-headed Amazons were the descendants of some that had escaped a fire at a pet store in the sixties, and now they were everywhere.

"Excuse me, miss."

Grace turned to see a homeless man standing awkwardly a few feet away, his cart parked behind him. "Hello."

He looked surprised that she'd spoken to him. "Um, hello. I was wondering if I could draw your portrait? Or if you have a picture of someone you care about, I could draw that?"

He had kind eyes, red-rimmed and sad, and Grace found she very much wanted to know his story. "On one condition."

His eyebrows twitched and he looked wary. "Okay?"

"You talk to me while you do it."

He frowned, holding his sketchpad to his chest. "What about?"

"Anything. Everything. Tell me about you."

He blinked hard. "It would be nice to do that." He moved a little closer, looking around her. "Do you think you could turn sideways a little? The light coming in from that side is better."

She turned until he motioned for her to stop, then he went and got a little stool. He sat on it, farther than necessary from her, and she had a feeling it was so he didn't bother the people he was talking to. Or maybe it was for his own safety.

"What's your name?" she asked.

"Patrick Reyes, ma'am." His pencil began to move swiftly.

"Yikes. Don't ma'am me, please. It's Grace."

He nodded, glancing from her to his pad. "Nice to meet you. Here to enjoy the parrots?"

She laughed. "I love the color, but the noise can get a little much."

"Tell me about it. They don't even go totally quiet when they sleep." He tilted his head one way, then the other. "What do you do for fun, Grace?"

"I don't have a whole lot of that, I'm afraid. I'm a lawyer, so I don't have much time for fun." She'd had more fun with Eris than she'd had in a long time, but that also came with feelings not nearly as pleasant.

"Shame. I see so many people whose lives revolve around work. Work, work, work. And they spend most of their lives working, only to enjoy the last ten or fifteen years they've got on this planet. Seems backward." He shifted slightly, moving his stool.

"I suppose you're right. And how about you? Tell me about you."

"Well," he said, scratching away, "I was an artist. Or, I wanted to be. But we were poor, and the military was really my only way out. Went and did a few tours, fell in love, came back, lost my way. Ended up out here." His laugh held little humor. "That's the short version, anyway."

It wasn't an unusual story. "But what about the Merge? Did that help at all?"

He stared at her for a moment, like he was visually tracing the lines of her face. "It might have. But I've never been a big believer, and after all I saw on tour, well...doesn't seem right to give any of them the time of day. Even if they could help me."

A couple walked past holding hands and walking a beautiful copper Chow. They stopped and watched over Patrick's shoulder as his pencil flew over the page, and Grace could tell by their expressions how impressed they were. "Patrick, could you stop for just a second?"

He stopped, a fleeting look of disappointment in his eyes. "Sorry, I didn't mean to burden you—"

"No, no! I just need to make a quick call. Don't move!" She smiled and watched him relax a little.

She pressed redial on her phone. "Can you come down to Loma Alta Park, right now? And bring lunch for three." When she got confirmation, she hung up. "Okay, sorry. Go ahead."

He began again, a little slower this time. "What about you? Have you been changed by the Merge?"

She nearly laughed out loud. Telling him she was defending the muse of love and having meetings and drinks with the gods didn't seem to be the right road. But then... "Actually, lately it's barged right into my world and turned it upside down. Last night I had margaritas with a Titan and the ruler of the underworld."

He stopped drawing and gaped at her. "That must have been some night." His eyes narrowed. "You're not one of them, are you?"

This time she did laugh. "Gods, no. And I wouldn't want to be. But I have learned that some of them are pretty okay." She considered the conversations she'd had recently. "In fact, I'd go so far as to say they're not all that different from us in a lot of ways."

He turned his pad upside down. "Don't see many homeless gods, though."

She thought about what she'd learned about pre-faders and wondered if that were true. It wasn't like anyone would know. "No, I suppose not."

They sat in silence for a while, the sound of the parrots and children playing, dogs barking and people laughing surrounding them.

A shadow fell over her and she looked up. "Hey, you found us."

Eris set the brown bags down on the bench behind Grace. "I never turn down lunch in a park full of noisy birds."

"This is Patrick. He asked if he could draw my portrait, and I wanted you to meet him."

He looked at Eris, his gaze appraising. "Now, you *are* one of them."

She picked up a bag and handed it to him, grease stains already showing through. He took it gently and set his sketchpad down facing him so the picture didn't show.

"What makes you say so?"

He tucked his pencil behind his ear and opened the bag. "Orean's. Haven't had that in ages." He pulled out the giant veggie burger and then looked at Eris. "It's in the eyes. I mean, the flawless skin and height, too, but it's always in the eyes. They're different."

She looked at Grace. "Do you think so?"

Grace opened her bag and took out a vegetarian burrito. Orean's was a fast-food drive-through that made being vegetarian a gift. "I think you have beautiful eyes, but I wouldn't have known you were immortal by that alone." She moaned around a giant bite of beans and rice. "I think Patrick sees more than we do."

He didn't deny it and seemed to savor his food. Eris sat beside Grace and took out a tray of dirty chips covered in chili and cheese.

Once Grace was satisfied, she turned to Eris. "He was about to tell me about the woman he fell in love with."

It quite obviously took plenty of control for Eris not to roll her eyes at Grace's unsubtle ploy, but she turned her attention to Patrick. "I adore a good love story. Tell us about it."

He crumpled the wrapper and put it back in the bag. "Thank you for that." He pulled his sketchpad back onto his lap. "Her name was Jackie. She was an English teacher in Saudi Arabia, at the American school. She was something else. Long, dark hair, and these brown eyes that you could get lost in. And kind. Man, was she kind. The kids loved her, the moms loved her."

"You loved her," Grace prompted her when he drifted off.

"Yeah." He sighed softly. "I did. And we got married, came back here. I tried to make it as an artist, but the PTSD kept getting me, making me reckless and unpredictable. It wasn't long before she couldn't take it, and I couldn't take the way I was hurting her. So I left."

There was no mistaking the tears in Eris's eyes, nor the way she was leaning toward him. She seemed to get a handle on herself and moved toward him. "Do you mind if I have a look?"

He gave a little half shrug. "Long as Grace doesn't mind you seeing it before she does."

Eris moved to stand behind him and her reaction was almost palpable. She jerked forward, staring intently at the sketchpad. "God's boxers, that's amazing."

He side glanced at her. "You don't need to say that."

"Can I touch you?" It was an odd response, and he looked wary.

"I don't want to be turned into no mushroom or blade of grass or whatever. If you don't like it, I can just be on my way."

"I promise, no transformations." Her hand hovered over his shoulder like she was almost desperate to touch him.

"Okay, I guess."

The moment her hand landed on his shoulder, his eyes grew wide and his breathing quickened. His pencil became a blur, his concentration so intense it almost looked painful.

"What is it you're doing, Eris?" Grace asked, entranced at what was happening.

"Just what I do."

It was hardly an answer, but one Grace would have to accept as Eris looked almost as intense as Patrick did.

He stopped and dropped his pencil into the grass beside him. He let out a long exhale and looked up at Eris. "That's really something. I haven't felt that way…ever. Which one are you?"

Eris didn't look away from the sketchpad, and she didn't wipe away the tears streaming down her cheeks. "I'm the muse of love. Retired."

"If that's what you can do when you're retired, you must have been something else at your peak." He grinned, breaking the strange tension, and she laughed.

Wiping away her tears, she said, "How much did you want for this, Patrick?"

"Ten dollars, if that's okay?" The wariness came back into his eyes, the light of creation dimming. "That will go a long way toward getting me into the shelter tonight."

Eris squatted in the grass, still looking at the sketch. "Patrick, when I say I'm a muse, you have to understand that I know what art is worth. And I don't mean just the monetary side. I mean the part of your soul that goes into it. The part you leave there, in every pencil stroke that might as well be a signature. The love you put into your art is priceless."

He seemed lost for words and looked to Grace like she could help clarify.

"Can I see it?"

For some reason, he looked at Eris, who slowly shook her head. "I don't think so." She pulled out her wallet and took out a wad of cash. "I'm paying for it, so I get to decide who sees it."

He shook his head, holding up his palms. "No way. Thank you, but I can't accept that. Really."

In response, Eris gently took his hand in hers and pressed the money into his palm. "Please, Patrick. This is going to mean the world to me, and it's worth every penny."

Grace figured there must be at least a hundred dollars there, if not more. But like Eris said, she knew the worth. And judging by her reaction, she truly was awed.

His hands shaking, he tucked the money into his jacket pocket without even looking at it. "That's very kind, thank you." His eyes welled with tears. "I wish I'd had you with me when my wife and I were splitting up. Maybe I could have explained. Told her that she was the only thing holding me together, the glue keeping my pieces from shattering."

Eris looked almost like she'd been punched, and she rocked back on her heels. "I'm sorry I wasn't there for that." She tapped the sketchbook. "Maybe you could draw those feelings. Get them out." She took his hands in hers and said, "Close your eyes."

He did as she said, and they sat that way for several minutes. When he reopened them, he looked like he'd caught a glimpse of something sublime. "Thank you," he whispered.

She let go of his hands. "Take care of yourself."

He carefully tore the sketch of Grace from the pad, got a spray out of his cart, and sprayed it down. "You want to let this dry for a bit before you roll it." He put his things back in his cart and looked at the two of them. "This has been the best day I've had in a long time." With that, he pushed his cart away and began to whistle.

Eris sat back down next to Grace, holding the portrait away from her. "Why did you call me? How did you know it would turn out that way?"

"It's hard to explain. I could see something in his eyes, and I just knew deep down that you needed to see what I saw." She winced. "That doesn't make a lot of sense, does it?"

Eris took her hand. "It makes plenty of sense. Thank you. I haven't had the chance to do that in years, and I admit, I forgot how good it feels."

"Can you explain it?" Grace asked. "I'd really like to understand." Eris leaned forward, her chin resting on her hands. "When I'm using my gift, it flows through me. Like warm water from the Mediterranean Sea, soothing every nerve ending, every fiber of who I am. It's sugar-coated electricity, and when I touch someone who already has a gift like Patrick's, it takes it up another level. It's the best kind of intoxication, the highest of highs, the purest emotion you can have. And I get to feel it, and then let the person I'm touching feel it, and it takes their gift and magnifies the emotions they're feeling so it comes out in their creation. Our combined desire for and understanding of love helps create the kind of beauty that transcends everyday words, that takes emotions and makes them into something you can feed someone else's soul."

It was a beautiful description, and Grace wished she was a creative type person if only so she could feel what Eris was describing. "That sounds amazing. You must miss the feeling."

"Yeah. Yeah, I guess I do." She sighed and stood. "It was nice to feel it for a minute."

"But you haven't changed your mind? Even after remembering what it is to be what you are?"

Eris's brow creased. "It doesn't change anything. His wife left him, a man who'd given up his sanity for his country. They promised forever, and she didn't stick it out. That's love now. A temporary, shallow declaration made by evolved apes who smell pheromones and jump the next ape, or who leave their partners when things get hard and confusing. If anything, the situation proves my point, Grace. They loved each other, but not enough." She shoved her hands in her pockets and backed away. "I'm sorry I can't be what you, what everyone, wants me to be." She turned and walked away, her shoulders hunched, her head bowed.

Grace remained on the bench for a long time, her heart aching. Though running after Eris would be a mistake, she desperately wanted to. She wanted to wrap her in her arms and tell her that love was still beautiful. What she'd seen was divine, and somehow, she had to find a way to show Eris that she was still needed in the world.

CHAPTER FIFTEEN

Eris propped her feet on the coffee table and stroked Hilda's head. The mountain lion was lying on the couch beside her, taking up the majority of it, but Eris was happy to have the company. A rare thunderstorm was passing over, sending sheets of rain sliding down the windows. Every time a rumble of thunder shook the house, Hilda raised her head and bared her teeth, like she'd gladly take a bite out of the shapeless threat if she could.

An evening news talk show came on, and she was about to flip the channel when she saw Grace. She hadn't heard from her in the last two days, and it hurt to think maybe she'd gotten through, and that Grace now understood she was a lost cause. She turned up the volume and took in the perfectly tailored black blouse and silver necklace that looked made for her skin. Her hair was picture-perfect, as was her makeup, which highlighted her beautiful eyes.

"I'm here tonight with Grace Gordon, lead counsel for the defense in the trial of People vs. Love. Thank you for joining us, Grace."

Grace smiled sweetly. "My pleasure."

"Let's get right down to it, Grace. This is the first time in history that one of the immortal set has been sued, and there's plenty of talk about the ramifications of this. Can you explain what this case is really about?"

Grace looked at the camera instead of at the news anchor. "This case is about a group of people who want to blame someone else for their shortcomings. It's about people who have forgotten how to communicate with one another, and because of that, they're attacking a kind, gentle immortal who wants to live her life without complication."

The anchor smiled, a predatory gleam in his eyes. "Surely you don't completely disagree with the plaintiffs, do you? If the gods stop doing their jobs, then what use are they?"

"You can't hold the immortals to the same standards as you do humans. They do things their own way, and if we're going to respect them and ask for their help, then insulting them and saying they're useless if they don't answer your specific needs isn't the way to do it."

Grace's tone had an edge now, and Eris smiled a little.

"If Eris Ardalides had helped any of the plaintiffs speak from the heart, mightn't they have had a chance at love? And isn't that what we all want? To be loved?"

Eris seriously doubted the anchor had ever desired real love in his entire life, the smug mud flap.

"If you spoke from your heart to me right now, told me you loved me and wanted me forever, who's to say you and I wouldn't develop something meaningful? And that's *without* Ms. Ardalides here. That's down to you and me having an honest, heartfelt conversation. Not down to a retired deity who never promised us, nor owes us, anything."

He sighed patronizingly. "Grace, the gods need us. They want us to worship them, as indicated by the many advertisements for the different religions that we're now surrounded by on a regular basis. And if you've seen Ms. Ardalides recently, I think you'll find she likes her share of worship just like the rest of them."

A montage of pictures of Eris flashed across the screen and she groaned. Her with her arms around different women, her in the DJ box as she responded to the crowd, her in a fancy car with several barely dressed women in it, including what appeared to be one between her legs. Sadly, she didn't even remember that night.

"She seems to be doing just fine in the love department. But she's unwilling to help other people do the same." The anchor's smirk suggested he thought he had her.

"Do you know what else she's the muse of?" She waited a moment. "Erotic poetry. Ms. Ardalides isn't a nun. She's the muse of love and eroticism. Do you know what a muse is? It's someone who inspires creative thinking. She isn't a dating service. Should she become celibate because you can't get a date or keep a relationship going? Sex-shaming isn't going to work in this instance. Sorry."

Eris nearly stood up and cheered. And then her heart dropped, and she sank onto the couch. "Oh shit."

Between Grace and the anchor, a pinkish red mist appeared and quickly solidified into none other than Aphrodite, dressed in a sharply tailored black suit with an apple red silk blouse beneath it, and equally red four-inch heels. Beside her was Cupid, looking strangely sober and most definitely out of sorts. He, too, was in a suit, but his pulled tight over his protruding tummy.

"Jesus Christ," the anchor said, jumping from his chair and yanking out his microphone so it dangled like a thread from his suit. "Who the hell are you?"

Aphrodite brushed at her little blond pixie cut. "I'm not from that department, although I was associated with it at one time." She went to Grace and squeezed her shoulder as Cupid hopped up on the coffee table, his bow and arrows glinting in the spotlights. "I'm the goddess of love. And I've had enough of this charade."

The anchor slowly replaced his mic, but he didn't sit back down. "Can you elucidate, please?"

She rolled her eyes. "You can't put *love* on trial. Eris isn't in my department. She never has been. We deal with different aspects of love. If those people who are whining about her not doing her job had been praying to actual love gods, then maybe we would have helped." She laughed, a tinkling sound that should have been pleasant but wasn't. "Instead, you go after a *muse*. She can't even protect herself. She's using a mortal to defend her, and she's practically a mortal herself. It's like choosing the slowest kid in class and making them race the fastest."

Eris's jaw clenched as she saw Grace flinch a little when Aphrodite's grip clearly grew tighter on her shoulder. Her expression remained impassive, but her hands were clasped tightly in her lap.

"And although Eris isn't one of my employees, love is *my* domain. And I refuse to stand by and watch this farce any longer." She turned to the camera and Cupid stood as tall as he could beside her, his wings looking slightly yellowed and ragged under the harsh lights. "If this case isn't dismissed, I and the other gods of love have come together to say we will stop working in the human world. There will be no more love, no more compassion, no more passion. We will take it away so you then see what your pitiful mortal lives would be without us."

Eris could barely breathe, and Hilda shook her head and jumped off the couch, shaking out her fur like she could shake off the negative energy. Eris's phone rang and she fumbled for it, not looking away from the TV.

"What the hell is she thinking?" Calliope's voice was sharp. "Did you know about this?"

"Yeah, of course I did. I knew the love gods were going to take a stand on my behalf, but not my behalf, and insult me in the process, while also nearly breaking my attorney's shoulder. What do you think?"

"This is disastrous, Eris. Zeus has already shot two lightning bolts through his office ceiling. He's saying he's going to have the Fates throw all of them into the void. I should have stayed in Scotland."

Eris shuddered. Everyone knew the story of the Fates forcing Dis, the goddess of creation, into the cosmic void, where she couldn't do any more damage. "They won't really do it, will they?"

Calliope was quiet for a moment. "I think they might, you know. Aphrodite has always had a vengeful side, and the other love gods can be just as bad. Of all of them, you're the only one who has never enjoyed hurting people."

"What do we do?" She finally took a deep breath when Aphrodite released Grace's shoulder.

"You have two days, mortal simpletons. If you haven't come to understand your error in two days, the love gods will leave you to your own stupidity. See how quickly you turn into cannibalistic vipers without us." Aphrodite waved, and she and Cupid were gone in that same sickly pink smoke. It wasn't necessary, of course. Aphrodite, like all the gods, could come and go unseen if she wanted to. But she did like to make a splash.

The show cut to a commercial, and Eris sank into the couch. "Should I talk to her? Or to any of them?"

"No," Calliope said after a moment. "Let Themis, Zeus, and I try first. She's going to take this out on you. I've heard her complain before that you shouldn't be allowed to retire and that you should answer to her. I think she's jealous, deep down. But then, she never knows what she really wants."

"Okay. I'm going to call Grace and make sure she's not hurt. If Aphrodite did hurt her..." Eris trailed off, unsure how to finish the sentence. The goddess of love was beauty personified. She was also a hard, cruel woman who didn't pull her powers if she felt threatened. And Eris was a lover, not a fighter. But for Grace, that might change.

"Okay. Then tell Grace to call Themis. We'll work this out." The show started again, with a different anchor in place, and Grace wasn't there. Eris hit her name and prayed she'd answer.

"I've decided being your attorney is bad for my physical and mental health. I quit."

Eris sighed and smiled. "I warned you."

"I was just attacked by the goddess of love on national television and you're saying I told you so?" Grace's laugh sounded shaky. "Classy."

"Seriously, are you okay, Grace? Her nails are sharp." Eris had felt them down her back more than once, but she didn't need to tell Grace that. Few people knew that she and Aphrodite had been lovers on and off through the centuries. Eris had always been a sucker for a feminine woman with an attitude, and Aphrodite was certainly that. It was also one of the reasons that Aphrodite chafed at the fact that Eris wasn't in her department. She might be a pillow queen, but she still wanted to be on top in every other way.

"Well, this blouse is trash, I can tell you that. And I'm going to have claw marks in my shoulder for a while, I imagine. But I'm okay, I think. I don't know. It's surreal that the ancient goddess of love and her…son? Is that pudgy little thing with wings her kid? Anyway, it's surreal that they just popped in and threatened all of humanity."

Grace saying she was okay was definitely at odds with the tone of her voice as it got higher.

"Want me to come get you? Or meet you somewhere?"

"Hold on," Grace said, and then, "Themis is calling. I should take it. Let me call you back."

"Sure. Let me know—"

But Grace was already gone.

Eris slid onto the couch and dropped her head into her hands. Hades had said the primary gods would get involved if it came down to it, but Aphrodite wasn't a primary god, even if love was universal. She was still a god who took orders from a higher god. Taking love away from the world was just about as bad as what the primary gods would do, and it would have quick, dire consequences. She groaned and flopped backward. She missed her days of DJing and drinking with friends.

❖

The Ancient College of the Arts, or the ACA, was in Northern California, in the beautiful coastal town of Big Sur. Clio, Eris's sister, was the director, and Calliope worked there as a teacher of music and justice. Normally, it was a place of calm and peace as the people studying there followed their chosen creative profession.

Right then, it was anything but calm.

Eris ducked a short lightning bolt and then a mug, which shattered against the blackened wall. She made certain to keep Grace and Brad behind her as much as she could.

Themis had called her from the airport. She, Grace, and Brad were on their way to the ACA, which had been declared neutral ground when the other departments at Afterlife had complained about Zeus messing up their offices with his tantrum. Zeus had demanded a meeting with Aphrodite and the other love gods who were standing together, and they wanted Eris there.

As she jerked Grace to her, out of the way of a flying snake, she wondered why.

"We were staying out of it!" Zeus thundered, making the windows rattle.

"No, *you* were staying out of it. We weren't asked how we felt, and we made a decision. Not everything has to go through you anymore. The world is bigger now." Aphrodite stood face-to-face with him, and Eris had to admire her hutzpah.

Parvati, Hathor, and Frigg sat at the table, watching the family squabble. None of the goddesses seemed particularly perturbed. They'd certainly had plenty of altercations with the male members of their families in the past, so this probably wasn't anything new.

"If I may, Zeus," Frigg said, the authority in her tone making both Zeus and Aphrodite turn to her, "what Aphrodite says is true. We weren't consulted."

He ran his hand over his beard. "There was a board meeting, and everyone agreed. Freya was there, and even she agreed, and you know how much she likes to start a fight."

Hathor, wearing her crown that featured two small horns and a small sun disk that sat on her forehead, held up her hand. "The board speak for the gods, it's true. But this wasn't about the gods or global policy. This was about a specific topic: love. Your board had no right to not consult us."

Parvati nodded her agreement. "As usual, we were being spoken for and not to. We decided it was necessary to do what we needed to do, and just as you thought it unnecessary to speak with us about your decision, so too did we decide it unnecessary to speak to you of ours."

"And you," Aphrodite said, swinging her attention like a scythe toward Eris. "You didn't think to contact me for help? You didn't want my assistance?"

Eris blanched, and when she felt Grace move forward like she was going to respond, she put her hand behind her to pull Grace back. "It wasn't that I didn't want to bother you, Aph. I didn't think it was worth your time. I assumed it would die off quickly."

She looked only slightly mollified. "But it hasn't died off quickly, and people everywhere are complaining, aren't they?" She looked at the other three goddesses, who nodded. "Prayers for help finding love have quadrupled, and now they're not just requests, they're threats. People are saying they're going to move to other sectors and stop devoting themselves to us if we don't grant them what they want. They have no concept of the suitability of the match, or that we don't just match up everyone who wants someone. They have no idea what's good for them."

Themis, undaunted by the displays of emotion, tapped on the table. "You're right. All four of you are right. You should have been consulted, and that's my fault. As Eris said, we thought it would blow over quickly, and it didn't occur to me that you would want to trouble yourselves with such a human affair."

Eris heard Grace's soft gasp and Brad's unique swearing as Parvati's necklace of shrunken severed heads disappeared, to be replaced by a parrot sitting on her shoulder. It was a good sign. She was usually a fairly benevolent goddess, and the skulls only appeared when she was well and truly pissed off.

"However," Themis said, "I'm still not certain it's a good idea to take love from the world. It might be destructive."

Aphrodite ran her hand through her short hair. "That's the point." She motioned at the others. "Humans have forgotten that we're not just love goddesses, and they've forgotten that we're not servants. We all have dark sides, and that's what they've brought out."

"And they're not going to follow through now, are they?" Hathor asked. "We won't need to make good on our threat. They'll be too frightened to continue down this path."

There was an awkward silence, and Grace hesitantly stepped partially out from behind Eris. "I spoke with Zane Shaw on our way here. He said that not only does he not want to drop the case, but he's calling your bluff. He's had more people request to be made part of the case."

Eris looked at Zeus and tugged Grace behind her once again, fully expecting an explosion, but he sat down, looking thoughtful. That was far worse.

"Then they've asked for this." He nodded slowly. "We can't continue to have authority as gods if we allow humans to question our ways and reasoning. I didn't allow it in three thousand BC, and the Christian god won't allow it now. The Egyptian gods never allowed it either. There were consequences."

Although Frigg looked appeased, she didn't look happy, and she twisted the thick silver beads around the braid in her hair. "Then it's settled. We take love from the world. Anyone praying to us, anyone hoping to make connections, is ignored. Those already in love will find it greatly diminished."

Grace once again moved to Eris's side. "If you take love, you're going to create destruction. The rebuilding we'll have to do will be…" She shook her head, looking at the assembled gods. "I can't even find a word big enough for it."

This time, Aphrodite really seemed to focus on Grace, and her gaze shifted between her and Eris. Her small smile was knowing in a way that made Eris grimace down to her toes.

"It's not like that," Eris said softly.

Aphrodite's eyebrow twitched. "Of course not." Her head tilted and her expression grew sad. "If you'd been under me, so to speak, you wouldn't have drifted so far from what you were born to be. Love is still beautiful, muse." She turned her attention back to Grace, who pressed the back of her hand to Eris's thigh as though needing stability. "And if destruction ensues, Grace Gordon, then they'll have to pray to us to help them make things right again, won't they?"

"It just…" Brad's voice was shaky and soft. "It feels a little vindictive."

Hathor sighed and the scent of cinnamon filled the air. "Yes, it would to a human. But what is faith, Brad?"

He took a moment, then said, "Belief in what you can't see."

"Simplistic, but yes. And humans don't see much of what we do. They often ascribe what we do to their own actions, failing to take into account that we have our hands on all the threads of the world. If faith fails, if humans no longer have something to believe in, what will the world look like? If we respond to human quarrels, insecurities, desperation, and entitlement as any other human would, where does that leave them?"

He glanced at Grace, who shook her head a little.

"That's settled. Themis, I suggest you speak with this Zane Shaw personally, on behalf of Afterlife. As a goddess of justice, try to make him see reason. If you can't, you have two choices. You can let this take its course, or you can come to the board and we'll figure out how to punish him in a very public way." Electricity zapped around Zeus's fingertips.

Themis ignored Zeus altogether and took Eris's hand. "I know you well enough to know you're feeling guilty about this, and what's about to happen will make your heart break. But you have to understand, Eris." She motioned to the group of gods around the table. "You're a scapegoat, darling. If this isn't stopped now, the consequences will be much worse than what's about to happen."

Eris dashed the tears away with her free hand. Her buddies would give her shit no end for being this emotional all the time. "Just because I wanted to retire doesn't mean I want humans to suffer. They were doing just fine without me."

Aphrodite moved around the table, and Eris felt Grace and Brad take a step back. She placed her hand over Eris's heart. "I can feel you. I felt it when you were hurt so badly it took you to your knees, but you didn't reach out to me, and when I came to you, you pushed me away. I can feel you now, when the cracks in your heart are so full of grief and fear that it keeps it from healing." Her gaze flicked over Eris's shoulder. "And I can feel the little spring of hope bubbling away, begging to be allowed to become a tidal wave." She pressed a little harder. "You can run from what you are for as long as you want, child of love. But you can't escape it."

She turned away and Eris took a deep, silent breath. Being touched by a goddess was no small thing, even for another immortal who'd felt that touch intimately before. A little like a talking, breathing boulder weighing the pros and cons of crushing you, it got your blood racing, but not necessarily in a good way.

"I'll let the board know what we've decided here today." Zeus stood, looking troubled. "We'll project a united front, but at some point we'll need to have a limit as to how much destruction we allow them to create."

There was general assent, and in the blink of an eye, they were gone, leaving Themis, Eris, Grace, and Brad alone in the room. Eris slid into a chair and closed her eyes. The humans had gone to war with the gods of love, and life was about to get very, very ugly.

Chapter Sixteen

Every news channel, every radio station, every social media platform was awash with news of the impending crisis, unimaginatively dubbed Love Court. Grace shook her head and tried to slow her breathing as she drove to work, listening to the news anchor taking calls from people who seemed to be firmly ensconced on two sides of the nonexistent fence. There were those who had faith and felt that the gods were above having to answer to humans, and there were those who felt the gods needed to be held accountable by the people in much the same way a government would be.

The focus had shifted from Eris, though she was still mentioned as a by-product, and it was mostly directed at the gods of love. The commotion had become much worse when the Christian God's spokes-angels had declared that it was his all-holy intention to join the lesser pagan gods and remove his love from the world as well, should the humans fail to understand their place. Given that more than thirty percent of the world was still Christian, it was a dire promise.

Themis and Grace had gone to Zane Shaw, but all he could see was the payout. As far as he was concerned, the world had faced disasters before, and it would again. It wasn't his responsibility to care what happened to the whole world, just to his clients, the number of which had doubled.

She pulled up in front of the courthouse and smoothed her hands down her skirt. Before she got out of the car, her phone rang. At the name on the screen, she groaned but made certain it didn't come out in her tone when she answered. "Hi, Rob. I'm just about to go see Judge Canmore."

"Grace, I'm here with the partners. Given the state of play, we feel that it's time we step in. I'm sending Richard and Cheryl. When you see the judge today, please let her know we'll be amending the documentation to show a change in counsel."

It wasn't surprising. In fact, she'd been surprised she hadn't had this mountain of poo dropped on her sooner. It still pissed her off. "I understand the board's concern, but—"

"It's not a request, Grace." Richard's tone sounded as smug as his smile probably was. "We expect to be fully briefed by the end of the day."

As an associate, Grace really had no say in the matter. "Of course. My team is already at work. Brad can gather them and begin briefing you when you're ready." The thought of them being briefed without her there was both a relief and a worry.

"I've already reassigned your team to work on our floor with the team we have in place, Grace." Cheryl's calm, matter-of-fact voice came over the line. "Brad is busy moving your office to our floor as well, so that we're all in the same space."

She rested her head on the steering wheel. "Great. That's so great. Thanks for getting the jump on that." Tears of frustration were blinked back as she didn't want to mess up her makeup. "I need to get inside so I'm not late. See you soon." She hung up, even though she heard Rob start to say something more.

Damn it. She ran her hand through her hair and tried for some calming breaths, but all that did was make her dizzy. Slamming the car door made her feel a little better, and she headed inside with her head held high.

Judge Patricia Canmore had light streaks of gray in her hair, laugh lines around her deep brown eyes, and was known for being both fair and strict when it came to how she ran her courtroom. Grace had never argued in front of her, but she was glad it was this judge who had pulled the short straw for this case.

"Ms. Gordon. Have a seat."

Grace sank into one of the thick, plush chairs across from the judge's desk, and was surprised when she sat beside her instead of in her big leather chair.

"Before the others get here, I want to say something." The judge leaned forward slightly. "I don't envy your position one bit. Being a woman in this field is hard enough, but defending the gods in a case that could change the world?" She shook her head. "I thought being the first Black, queer judge in this city was hard, and it is. Together, we're going to be responsible for whether or not the entire world goes to hell in the proverbial handbasket, and that strikes me as being harder than anything we've been through to this point."

Mortified, Grace felt the tears she'd been holding back begin to fall. "It wasn't supposed to be like this," she whispered as she wiped at her cheeks with the back of her hand.

"It always had the potential to go this route," Canmore said, handing her a tissue. "We'll do what we can to mitigate the damage." There was a knock at the door, and she stood and went around her desk. "Come in."

Zane Shaw entered, looking like he'd fallen into a pot of gold and come out covered in diamonds. Garish and loud, his entire outfit begged people to pay attention to him.

"Mr. Shaw. Please sit." Canmore sat at her desk. "The reason for this meeting?"

Grace opened her briefcase and handed over a file, keeping her eyes down so Zane wouldn't see what a mess she was. "Defense is filing to force the prosecution to stop accepting plaintiffs in the case."

Zane shot out of his chair. "That's ludicrous."

"Sit down, Mr. Shaw." Canmore put her glasses on and read the brief. "Your position is that continuing to take on clients forces a delay in the actual proceedings, which has a knock-on effect with regard to public safety." She lowered her glasses and looked at Zane. "That sounds reasonable to me, especially in light of the statements made by the gods recently."

Zane shook his head vehemently. "You can't stop people from joining a case of this magnitude. There are potentially millions of plaintiffs—"

"Which proves Ms. Gordon's point." She folded her hands and looked at him, no emotion on her face. "Mr. Shaw, I have to say that I find your desire to proceed with this case extremely reckless, to the point of being grievous endangerment. The court could stop this case from proceeding on the grounds of public welfare, and I'm sorely tempted to do so."

He lost some of the luster beneath his spray tan. "If you did that, people would riot. They'd claim there was no justice, that you don't care about humans anymore, and that the gods have the justice system in their pockets."

"Spin doesn't work here, Shaw, and I'd appreciate it if you didn't spread the muck in my office." She looked at Grace. "Sadly, Ms. Gordon, I think it's true that we have no option but to proceed, as the lines have clearly been drawn at this point, and it could seem like a miscarriage of justice if we failed to follow this to its likely bitter end."

"If it's justice you want to discuss, I'd be happy to bring the goddess of justice in to speak to you. She'd be more than willing to help us understand how what's going on is far from just." Grace's temper was fraying by the second and her pulse beat hard in her neck. "And, thanks to Mr. Shaw's interference, the goddess has just passed the California Bar Exam, so she's now legally able to practice in this state. We're also filing to have her reinstated as co-counsel."

Zane shifted uneasily, but there wasn't really anything he could say.

"I'd very much like that opportunity, actually. I'll grant the new counsel statement. But I don't think it will influence this case." Canmore tapped on the file on her desk. "However, I'm going to grant your motion, Ms. Gordon. There needs to be a final sum so we can properly move forward with this case, and we need it over with as soon as possible."

Zane stuttered, his face red and puffed up, reminding Grace of a fish she'd once seen at the aquarium.

"My decision is final, Mr. Shaw."

Without a word, he got up and stormed from the office, leaving the door open behind him.

"I imagine he's adding up how much money that decision just cost him in the long run." Grace's pulse slowed to a more normal beat, but her stomach was still upset. "While I have you here, I've been told to let you know that we'll be adding more counsel. Richard Kline and Cheryl Stone will be taking over as lead counsel. I'll be co-counsel." How the words didn't come out covered in bile, she didn't know.

Judge Canmore leaned back in her chair, her fingers tapping the edge of the desk. "Having a bigger team and experienced colleagues on your side is a good thing with a case like this."

Grace nodded and made a noncommittal sound. Her tone would surely give her away if she said anything out loud.

"However…"

Grace had begun to stand to leave, but she stopped and looked at the judge quizzically.

"I have a personal bugbear about attorneys who only step in when the limelight is brightest. And although I respect Rob Kline, his son is a pompous porcupine of an ass. It seems to me you've been handling this case just fine on your own, Ms. Gordon, and so you can let your firm know that I'll be denying the change of counsel, except with regard to the goddess of justice, of course, as the case is already complicated enough without adding more bodies to the seats in a courtroom that may very well end up in literal flames."

Tears welled in Grace's eyes once again, and she quickly dabbed them away. "I understand, and I'll be sure to let them know." She went to the door and hesitated as she opened it. "Thank you. I'll do my best not to get the world burned to the ground."

The judge smiled sadly. "My dear, the world burns to the ground all the time. We're just really good at walking through the flames."

Grace walked out to the car, inhaling deeply. Judge Canmore's support was an utter surprise, and it couldn't have come at a better time. Although she needed to call the office, especially with all the changes happening, she couldn't bear the thought of the confrontation to come.

She toyed with her phone for a moment before hitting the button. When Eris's husky, sexy voice answered, Grace shivered involuntarily. "Hey. I don't suppose you're free?"

"Yeah, of course. Do you want to come to my place? Or meet somewhere?"

Grace rested her head against the side window. "I don't know. I need to breathe, and I need to be with someone. It just feels like you're the right person to call."

"That's the nicest thing anyone has said to me in a while. Why don't you meet me at the beach house? No one will bother us, and we can sit on the deck."

"I'll be there in forty-five minutes." She got on the road, and while stuck in traffic, let her mind wander. As so often happened these days, her thoughts came to a stop on Eris. She was so damn sexy, with her easy, lithe masculine of center swagger, those blue eyes that seemed to see right through her, and the grin that made Grace's knees weak.

But there was so much more to her. She was kind and vulnerable. She felt things deeply and wasn't ashamed to show her emotions.

Creative, sweet, funny, and intelligent, there wasn't anything she seemed to lack. And unlike some of the other immortals, she didn't seem to have much of an ego either, which was pretty surprising given the number of women dropping at her feet.

But there was more, and Grace wondered what it was. She'd caught hints of something, some happenstance that had occurred in Eris's past. In all her years of practicing law, Grace had endured her share of sob stories from spouses who'd been cheated on, who'd done the cheating, who had fallen out of love, who had simply given up. How much worse would it be for the muse of love who had endured centuries of those stories?

She pulled up at the beach house and was relieved to see Eris's truck in the driveway. Chris opened the door and gave her a quick smile, pointing toward the deck.

Grace moved quickly, the urge to be near Eris almost overwhelming. When she stepped onto the deck, Eris turned from the railing and looked at her. In an instant, she was in front of Grace, pulling her into a warm, comforting embrace.

And the tears finally spilled. Grace held onto Eris like a life preserver as the sobs made her gasp for air. Eventually, she mumbled against Eris's shirt, "I need a tissue."

Eris didn't move, but she pressed a tissue to Grace's cheek. Chris must have brought some over. Grace turned and blew her nose, then sagged against the wall. Eris took her hand and led her to the sofa on the deck. She sat beside her and wrapped her arm around Grace's shoulders.

"That's unquestionably the most unprofessional thing I've ever done." Grace stared at the sea, hoping the waves would drown her embarrassment.

"Nah. You slept with me, remember? That's got to be worse than crying." Eris's tone was light, and she caressed Grace's hair. "Want to talk about it?"

"How did you know?" Grace asked, finally chancing a look at Eris. All she saw in her expression was compassion. "Did I just look that bad?"

"You're always beautiful, even when you're blowing snot bubbles on my favorite T-shirt."

Grace winced and looked at the giant wet patch, then focused on the design. "Bert and Ernie?"

"A perfect example of love. Fights, apologies, and always at each other's side." She brushed a strand of Grace's hair away from her face. "And to answer your question, I felt you. Your soul was crying loud enough to be heard on Olympus."

Grace sighed and dropped her head back onto Eris's shoulder. "And I'm not the one on trial. I don't even know why I'm so upset, honestly. I just can't seem to stop being a Weepy Wendy today."

Chris came in and quietly set down a tray with glasses of water, a bottle of wine, and several types of muffins. There was also a fresh box of tissues.

"Thanks, Chris." Eris nodded at them and then handed Grace a glass of water. "I don't think you're taking into account the pressure you're under, Grace. People are used to the gods being around now, yeah. But not one-on-one, in your face, throwing lightning bolts at you kind of around. The gods of love have threatened chaos, and you're basically the one tasked with making all that go away." She kissed the top of Grace's head. "Forgive me, but I think you'd be weird if you weren't a little thrown by all of this."

There was no question she should leave. Or, at the very least, move out of the comfort of Eris's embrace. But a throng of mutant bulls wouldn't have been able to move her at that point. "I guess. But I shouldn't be crying on my client. That's bad form. I should have gone to Brad."

"Why did you come to me?" Eris's tone was soft.

"Like I said, you felt like the right person to be with." Grace traced the seam of Eris's jeans absently. "I wanted to be with someone…" She couldn't find the words, although there were some that she wouldn't, couldn't, say out loud. "Someone I trust. Someone kind."

Eris was silent, and Grace closed her eyes and let the sound of the ocean and the warmth of Eris's body soothe her.

"Did something happen today that made things worse?" Eris asked after a while.

"My boss wants to take me off lead counsel and replace me with two partners. He's already moved my team to the partners' floor, and they've moved my office, too." She felt Eris tense against her. "But the judge has denied their request to change counsel."

Eris relaxed. "Is that unusual?"

"Extremely. The judge doesn't usually care one way or another who is trying the case. But she said there was enough going on without the changes. And it threw me off balance. Rob told me when I took your case that this could happen. But…I don't want to share you. Your case, I mean." Grace tilted her head to look up at Eris, who was looking down at her. She swallowed hard and her breath caught.

Eris's eyes were hooded as she pulled Grace up and crushed her lips to Grace's. The kiss was hot and hard and without breaking it, Grace moved so she was straddling Eris's lap.

"This is a bad idea," she murmured against Eris's lips when they came up for air.

"Incredibly bad," Eris said, wrapping her hand around the back of Grace's neck and pulling her into another deep kiss. "I'm more than kind and trustworthy, Grace." She nipped at Grace's lips, then made her way down her jaw to her neck. "And you're so damn beautiful. You're sexy and smart and you're driving me insane. I can't stop thinking about you. I want you under me. I want you to scream my name and beg, even if you don't know if it's so I stop or keep going."

Grace moaned, eyes closed, as she felt every inch of skin that Eris sucked and bit. She was on fire, about to burst into a conflagration of wet lust. Eris's hands slid up her top, her strong, long fingers tracing the edge of her slacks and then making their way up her spine.

A discreet cough made them freeze. Eris groaned. "Can it wait?"

Chris's voice came from the doorway. "If it were anyone else I'd have told them where to go, but it's Prometheus and two of your sisters."

Eris rested her head against Grace's chest, and Grace took the moment to slow her breathing. Carefully, she slid off Eris's lap and straightened her blouse. Eris looked like she was considering shrugging off her guests and taking Grace right there on the floor. As desperate as she was to allow just that, she took a step back. "Those don't seem like the kind of guests you keep waiting."

Prometheus's booming voice came through before he did. "Don't get dressed on my account. I've seen it all, and I'm happy to see it again."

Eris's shoulders dropped in defeat. "Bald ass monkey shit." She stood, looking as shaky as Grace felt. "Maybe we can take a rain check?" She bent and kissed Grace's cheek, lingering for a second. "I need you," she whispered.

Grace was pretty sure she actually whimpered, but fortunately it was drowned out as Eris's guests arrived. Prometheus swept her into a hug that lifted her off her feet, and then he set her down and thumped Eris on the back.

"He's a menace." One of the women who came in held out her hand. "I'm Clio."

She wore a fuchsia sundress painted with sunflowers. It was a bold choice, but somehow, she pulled it off. "Nice to meet you. I really love your new show."

"Kit is something to watch, isn't she?" Clio winked and motioned toward Eris. "And you and I clearly share a type when it comes to the short-haired lesbians of the world."

If ever there had been a time when Grace wished the ground would swallow her, it was now.

"Ignore her." The other woman held out her hand. "I'm Mel, another sister. The normal one."

Grace tried to remember what she'd read about Eris's sisters, but this one didn't ring any bells. She wore a gray dress, gray shoes, and her hair was pulled into a tight bun. She looked less like a muse and more like a matron for a strict all-girls school.

"Pfft. Normal?" Clio shook her head and went to Eris, giving her a tight hug. "Mel is the muse of tragedy, Grace. She's all doom and gloom."

Eris returned their hugs, but she looked bothered. "Not that I don't appreciate you coming, Mel, but weren't you in Asia?"

Mel's gaze didn't waver as she looked at the small group. "I was. But given the state of your trial, and the nature of the threats made by the perfume gods, I've become extremely busy all of a sudden. Artists are turning to me for support as they try to work through their grief and worry."

Grace's legs went weak, and she leaned on the back of a chair. "People are expecting tragedy?"

Mel's frown deepened. "Aren't you?"

Eris moved to Grace's side and put her arm around her protectively. "We're hoping to avoid that, Mel."

That strange feeling came over her again. Pressed against Eris, Grace began to calm and her nerves steadied. The feel of Eris's body made other parts of her awaken again, but she could control that. It was the sense of something solid, something true, that was so confusing. Maybe it was simply an effect of being in Eris's orbit.

She pulled away gently. "I have to get back to the office to deal with everything. I'll call you later?"

Eris nodded and leaned down to kiss her cheek again. "Please do. I'd like to hear your voice tonight, even if we just talk about socks."

"Socks it is." Grace squeezed her hand and waved at the others. "See you soon."

Chris opened the door and waved her out. "If there's anything I can do, let me know?"

"I will, thanks." She stopped at the look of worry in Chris's eyes. "Why do you work for her?"

Chris leaned against the doorframe. "I had a few different jobs. But none of them stuck. Everyone was so determined to put me in a box, and the ones who didn't understand were cruel and shitty. I was about as down as I could get, and I was thinking of heading into the afterlife."

Grace touched Chris's arm. "I'm so sorry."

Chris gave a short nod. "I was sitting on the beach one night, razor in one hand, a bottle of vodka in the other, and Eris came and sat down beside me. Started talking about philosophy and the stars and got me talking about myself. Then she hired me, told me I never needed to be anything other than who I am, not for anyone." Chris pushed away from the doorframe. "I owe her my life. If she needs me, I'm there."

Unsure what to say to such a story, Grace simply squeezed Chris's arm again and headed to her car. Eris truly had no idea how she made people feel. Maybe, at some point, she could help change that.

If, of course, the world didn't come crashing down before that.

Chapter Seventeen

Eris ignored the phone, no matter how often it rang. She also ignored the ping of emails. She knew none of them were from Grace, since she'd been buried in work from the moment she'd left the beach house. They'd had virtually no time to talk at all, and the lack of communication made her feel even more alone. Eventually, she left the house with nothing but a water bottle and an apple and hiked up to the overlook. She sat on the large, flat rock and wondered where Hilda was. It had been two days since the gods had enacted their threat. Grace had requested an immediate dismissal of the case based on world welfare, but Shaw had argued that the legal system was based on people's right to demand justice. Take that away, and the whole system would fall apart. Arguments were being live-streamed over every social media platform and news network in the world and lines were clearly being drawn. People were choosing sides, with most coming down on the side of love.

It wasn't enough.

Eris looked at the black smoke in the distance, a cloud of escalating tension. The gods had taken love away from the world less than forty-eight hours ago, and the world was in a tight, spiraling nosedive. Violence had erupted everywhere. In Los Angeles, gang violence in particular was creating utter destruction. Fist fights were breaking out in government buildings. Customer service people were dumping hot food on rude customers instead of simply smiling and taking it.

At least that was one good thing, she thought.

But it was going to get so, so much worse. It wasn't just love as people thought of it, with hearts and chocolate and candlelight. It was everything that went with love. Compassion, kindness, empathy. Love encapsulated so many other things, and without them...humans were vile creatures.

She ate the apple without really tasting it, and then held it out to her side when she heard Hilda's soft steps move up beside her. The mountain lion sniffed it, gave it an exploratory lick, and then huffed and turned away.

"Picky." She threw it into the brush for some little critter to make a meal of.

There was a distant explosion and another cloud of black smoke billowed on the horizon.

A shadow fell over her and she glanced up. "Hey."

Prometheus dragged a boulder over and sat beside her. "Hey."

Hilda moved to lay her head on Prom's leg, and he scratched behind her ears, eliciting a rumbling purr.

They sat in silence that way for a long while, watching the smoke, listening to the siren's wails carrying on the wind.

"So much destruction," he finally said. "They can't seem to help finding ways to drag themselves under, no matter how much they have or how much help they get."

There didn't seem to be a response to that, so she didn't say anything.

"I'm going to help anyway," he said, still stroking Hilda. "I'm going to go down and try to talk sense into them. Or I'll knock them unconscious so they stop killing each other until this is over." He looked sideways at her. "You could help, you know. Use your gift to slow the chaos."

She closed her eyes and tilted her face to the sun. "It would last seconds. Without the fundamental feelings of love humans need to survive, what I would do would be a Band-Aid put on under water."

He stood. "I have to try. They've always been my weakness. I can't do nothing. I'm going to get some of the other gods who like the humans too and see what we can do on a street-by-street level." He squeezed her shoulder. "You're so lost, little daughter. I hope you find your way back to us soon."

He disappeared as silently as he'd arrived, and the mountain lion jumped onto his spot on the rock.

She admired his constant, unwavering love for the humans they were so intricately intwined with. She'd shared that feeling, once upon a time. And as much as she hated what was happening, the gods who'd made this decision outranked her in every way.

Hilda's head lifted and her ears twitched. Eris concentrated, and it wasn't so much that she could hear Grace's car as it was she could feel Grace herself. She'd become attuned to her energy, to the way she emoted. She debated staying there on her rock and letting Grace think she wasn't home. Their last encounter had been hot, and it seemed like there was no way they could keep their hands off each other. So she'd kept her distance, knowing full well that when things went to hell, as they were doing, Grace would grow angry. And it would be Eris she'd turn that anger on. The growing feelings between them would be gone, thanks to the love gods ripping that particular emotion away, and she couldn't bear the thought of seeing a void in Grace's gaze.

She heard the car clearly and forced herself up. Hilda stretched and trotted alongside her as she walked back to the house.

When Grace pulled up, the car had barely stopped moving when she was out and striding toward Eris.

"Grace, I'm sorry—"

Grace grabbed the front of her tank top in her hands and yanked her forward.

And then she kissed her. Hard.

When she let go and stepped back, they were both breathing heavily.

"Okay…" Eris didn't care that her tank top remained rumpled. "Not really what I expected."

Grace turned toward the house and marched up the stairs. "Iced tea?"

"Sure." Completely befuddled, Eris poured them both glasses, put down a bowl of fresh water for Hilda, and then led the way outside.

"The gods can't take away what isn't theirs to give," Grace said after she took a drink. "Belief plays such a huge part of our lives that we assume they have control over everything. But they don't. We could exist just fine without them. We'd still love, and hate, and have sex." She looked pointedly at Eris. "It's a mind fuck of chaos down there because people believe that the gods have taken away their ability to love and everything that goes with that. But I refuse to allow that bitch—"

Eris clamped her hand over Grace's mouth. "No, no, no. If you've learned nothing else from Greek mythology, you should know better than that."

Grace rolled her eyes but nodded, and Eris took her hand away. "I refuse to allow anyone to take away my right to love, to be kind, to be gentle." She grinned a little when Eris let out a relieved breath. "Now, let's talk about why you've been avoiding me. Because with the kind of scrutiny we're under, I need you available pretty much every second of the day."

Eris winced. "Sorry. I thought it had gone way beyond me."

"It has and it hasn't. You're still the lynchpin, even though a zillion other aspects are now at play." She reached across the table and held Eris's hand. "Don't shut me out, okay?"

The feel of Grace's small hand in hers was enough to make her melt. Such a minor thing that still made her want to scoop her into her arms and protect her from the entire world. Not that Grace needed protection. "I'm sorry. It's become my go-to behavior these days. I'll try to do better."

"Good." She let go of Eris's hand. "Now tell me why you're in hiding."

Eris plucked at a loose piece of wood on the tabletop, trying to formulate her thoughts. The answer that came to her wasn't one she wanted to use, but she could feel that it was the only way forward. "In the year 1714, I met Kathleen Bairnbridge in Derby, England. I'd been at a local castle helping a poet compose some new work for King George's German mistress, and Kathleen was at the castle providing the most beautifully sewn gowns. She had someone who sold her silk, and she was the only one in the region who could craft it so finely."

Eris fell into the memory, seeing Kathleen as clearly as she had that day. She took a drink of her iced tea and saw that Grace was watching her intently.

"Go on," she said, watching as Hilda jumped onto the table and curled up on it in the sun.

"Anyway. I don't understand it, but I knew from the moment I saw her that we were meant to be together. She made me laugh like I hadn't in centuries, and in her work I saw the beauty of creation. It wasn't long before I'd moved in with her on the pretense that I was a cousin who'd come to stay with her. It wasn't that odd, back in those days. We were happy. I had enough money to make things easy, but she insisted on working. She loved what she did and being with me inspired her to make things that she poured her emotion into. And the people who bought her dresses could feel that emotion in the stitching."

"That sounds amazing. I don't suppose you have any of those gowns still tucked away somewhere?" Grace asked. "Did you wear them? That's hard to picture."

Eris laughed. "I did wear them, yes. I've had plenty of gender presentations over the course of my lifetime. I even lived as a man in the sixteen hundreds, just for a change of pace. I'm extremely comfortable in the butch presentation I'm in now." Grateful for the light interruption, she felt she could breathe again. "Kathleen became extremely sought after, which was wonderful. I helped people write beautiful works expressing themselves and their love for each other, and she helped make them beautiful on the outside. It was idyllic."

"Until it wasn't."

Eris nodded slowly. "Until it wasn't. In 1715, the Lombe silk mill was born in Derby. She was fascinated by the new technology and the possibility of creating new gowns in a quicker way. She went to work in the factory, but it wasn't what she thought it would be. For all that it had possibilities, she couldn't put her emotion into it anymore. She lost the connection she had with creation, and it became monotonous."

"And?" Grace prodded her when Eris drifted off.

"Sorry. And, she lost herself. I begged her to stop. We had enough money to live on comfortably, but she refused, saying she wouldn't be dependent on anyone, even me. But the desire for hand-sewn gowns had nearly disappeared as people sank into the mire of industrially made things they could get faster and cheaper." She could still smell the acrid odor of the oil used for the machines on Kathleen's clothing when she came home. "She started working longer hours, desperately trying to reconnect with her passion, to find that part of her that flourished when she was designing. At night I'd hold her, and I could feel her getting thinner, weaker. Like she was being eaten away from the inside. I begged, I ordered, I cajoled, I used guilt. Anything I could think of to get her to stop the madness. I showed her how she could go back to crafting in the house, but she refused. She said the only way forward was with the machines, and she just had to figure out how to make them work with her gift. It was bizarre, but I couldn't break through."

Unable to sit with the memory, Eris got up and began to pace the deck, staring at the lines in the wood which blurred as she slid back into the past. "And then one day she told me she was leaving. She said that a new factory had opened, one with more colors and better materials. She became obsessed. I told her no, that it would break her, break us. I told her she was being unreasonable and ridiculous. And that's when she told me she didn't want me to go with her. That she wanted to be on her own, that I was holding her back, that I was jealous of her success." She blinked back the tears and leaned on the railing. "I begged her not to go, but by the next morning, she'd already taken a bag of her things and left. Six months later I received a letter from the factory letting me know she'd been crushed under a faulty machine. I loved her more deeply than I'd loved anyone in centuries, and she still walked away from me like what we had didn't matter. The Industrial Revolution changed everything, and it made love into something that crushed people."

The beautiful birdsong filling the air around them was incongruous with the horror of the tale she'd lived with for so long. The only other person she'd ever spoken about Kathleen to was Prometheus. Her sisters knew some of it, but no one really knew the extent to which she'd been decimated.

"Someone broke up with you and that stopped you from being in another relationship for more than two hundred years? That has to be the worst pity party in history."

Eris turned at the dry sarcasm in Grace's tone. "What?"

Grace shook her head, looking distinctly unimpressed. "That's really sad, Eris. It is. And I'm sorry you went through it. But for fuck's sake. I mean, we all get dumped sometimes. And it hurts, and we swear off love, and we say we'll never love again. But we do. We heal and move on. People aren't meant to be alone forever."

Eris leaned back on the railing, stung by Grace's lack of empathy. Maybe she was being affected by the gods' actions after all. Surely, that must be it. "I think you're making my point. Grace, what do you think love is? How will you know when you're in love with someone?"

Grace settled back in her seat and crossed her legs as she looked at the sky. "I know what it isn't. So I know what it is."

Eris shook her head. "You can't know what something is because of what it isn't. That's false logic. I heard it being spouted when it was being invented, and it hasn't changed since. But go on. Share your thoughts with me."

Grace seemed focused on the hawk circling high overhead. "It isn't shouting each other down whenever you have a feeling the other person doesn't want to understand. It isn't manipulating someone with gifts or kind words in order to get what you want. It isn't passive-aggressive silences, thrown dishes, affairs, or words meant to tear open pieces of your soul."

There was steel in Grace's words, the emotions covered in barbed wire. "I'm so sorry. I'm guessing you mean your parents, and that must have been hard to grow up with."

Grace shrugged. "But because of that, I know what love is. Or what it is to me, anyway." She pulled out her phone, tapped a few times, and handed it over. "This is what I'm looking for. And when I find the person who has most of those qualities, I'll know that love with them is possible."

Eris's eyebrow twitched as she took the phone. Grace truly had no idea that she was making Eris's case even stronger. She began reading the list on the screen.

1. Taller than me
2. Has strong hands
3. Is kind to animals
4. Likes deep conversations
5. Enjoys cuddling
6. REALLY likes sex
7. Wants to talk to me
8. I want to talk to them
9. Has a generous spirit
10. Wants to make the world a better place

She set Grace's phone down, though she really wanted to toss it into the forest. "That's it? That you want to *talk* to each other? Grace, this is the worst list of necessary qualities in history. Surely there must be thousands of women within a ten-mile radius of us *right now* who fit all ten of these. They're..." she couldn't find the right word to describe how awful the list was, "mundane, at best."

"Oh? And what would yours include?" Grace looked genuinely hurt by Eris's response.

She crossed her arms and leaned against the railing. "She'd have to love to laugh, at anything and everything. She'd have to be willing to cry and let me see her at her worst, so I could wrap her in my arms and protect her from the world as best I could. And she'd need to accept me, both at my best and at my lowest. She'd need to be open to adventure, to new experiences, and to letting me love her so deeply and so well that it hurt to breathe without me near. And I'd want to worship her, help her grow, support her so she could do and be anything in the world she wanted, and I'd cheer her on all the way and be there for her to lean on when things got hard. I'd want to give her my soul for safekeeping because it would never be safer than it would be pressed against her own. I'd want someone I could fight with because we're both passionate, intelligent creatures with our own minds, and someone who would be beside me at the end of the day, no matter how intense the fight. I'd want someone I could make love to, someone who would give herself over to me physically and allow the essence of who she is to spill from her and combine with my being so we tangle into a web that can't be pulled apart as we learn one another's bodies in every intimate way possible. I want someone I can bring to tears with the beauty of how well I love them, and who can make me cry in turn with the way they hold me and the soft kisses they press to my neck simply because they need to touch me. I want to be with someone who sees every tomorrow in my eyes and someone I can't imagine waking up to a single sunrise without. To me, love is all-consuming, all-encompassing, even as it gives you room to be the best version of yourself and to help the person you love to be the best person they can be, too."

She ran out of words and eased her hands from the railing she was gripping so hard splinters poked into her hands. She hadn't said so much about real emotion in ages.

Grace was staring at her, wide-eyed. She blinked as though coming out of a trance. "Okay, so yours is a little better than mine."

She began to laugh, and Eris soon joined her. The tension broken, she sat beside Grace and took her hand. "You deserve so much more than what you've got on that list, Grace. You deserve someone who can't wait to breathe you in, who wants to taste your skin, make you laugh, and who does things just for the gift of seeing you smile." Slowly, she slid her hand away. "And until you can understand that kind of desire, that kind of emotion, then you don't really know what love is, even if you know what it isn't."

Grace stood, smoothing down her skirt. "Maybe as the muse of love, you're the one who doesn't understand. You're out of touch with the world, Eris. The kind of love you're talking about doesn't exist. Like everything, the nature of it has evolved. Is my list a little practical and…mundane? Maybe. In fact, yeah, it probably is. It's simple because I want simplicity. I don't want complicated. And if you want more from a relationship than simplicity then you're probably asking for too much. Do I want all those things you so beautifully say love is? Of course I do. Who wouldn't? But those things are a one in a zillion lightning strike. They're not for everyday people. Maybe I'll rethink my mundane little list, thanks to you. But at least I'm not going to be wallowing alone in my beautiful houses, surrounded by beautiful people who don't give a damn about me. Eventually I'll find someone who ticks all my boxes, and it will be enough."

She turned abruptly and stomped down the stairs as well as she could in her high heels, which sank into the dirt as she headed for her car. Eris couldn't help but notice how perfectly the skirt stretched across her so perfect butt. Inappropriate for the moment, definitely, but it didn't matter. This baseline conversation was one they needed to have, and although the comment about her wallowing stung, it wasn't something she hadn't heard before, many times.

But somehow, coming from Grace, the arrow of judgment managed to nick the edge of her heart.

CHAPTER EIGHTEEN

I told you not to speak over me. Why don't you ever listen?" The female news anchor's face was splotchy with anger. She held up the clipboard she lifted off the desk, and before anyone could react, she brought it down on her co-anchor's head.

He yelped and a gash opened over his eye. He stood, clearly ready to give back as good as he'd gotten, and the news cut to a commercial.

Grace rubbed at her eyes and then rested her head on the desk in her room. The upscale hotel had suites that included small offices complete with floor to ceiling windows overlooking the Civic Center Plaza. All that did was allow her to look out over the city at the plumes of smoke, the ambulances that seemed in constant motion, and the helicopters circling the city as they reported on the vitriolic chaos teeming along the streets below.

"Mess, huh?"

She looked up to see Cheryl leaning against the doorframe. The last three days had been nonstop, and they'd all been in and out of one another's rooms when they weren't occupying the main conference room on the ground floor.

"I wish I'd never taken this case." It was probably too honest to be with a partner when that was the position she wanted, but it was true, and she didn't have the energy to play the game just now.

"You and the rest of the world, I think." Cheryl came in, her stocking feet not making a sound on the thick carpet. This time of night, ties had been loosened and shoes kicked off. "But if you hadn't, someone else would have. Hell, Themis would have taken the case by herself, and everything would be exactly as it is now."

It made Grace wonder if the Fates were as cruel as Eris suggested. Maybe all this destruction was meant to be for some reason. "That's a comforting thought, I guess."

Cheryl sat on the stiff chair beside the desk. "Take it where you can." She motioned at Grace's desk. "Are you ready for tomorrow?"

Grace dropped her head to the desk and groaned. "To argue a metaphysical case in front of the whole world? Sure, why not."

Cheryl laughed lightly. "We'll be there with you. Remember you've got a team." She dropped a piece of paper on Grace's desk as she stood. "I thought you might find this interesting. One of the team you put together did a social media poll. You never know when this kind of thing might come in handy." She moved gracefully out of the room but stopped at the door. "And you never know when something simple might give you a leg up in the firm you work for." She winked and left.

Grace studied the piece of paper. At the top was the question, "What would you ask the goddess or muse of love?" Below it was a list of questions.

1. Do you believe that being someone's soul mate is enough to keep love alive?

2. Why are you such a sadist?

3. Why does love hurt?

4. If there's an afterlife where lovers are reunited, what happens to those of us who've loved, lost, and find love again?

5. What's the purpose of heartbreak? Why not just skip that part and go straight to finding our soul mates? Wouldn't that just be easier and kinder in the long run?

6. Do we as humans feel the whole extent of love or is it muted to fit within our tiny human capacities? Is it bigger, better (more than human brains can comprehend) for gods?

7. Does the second law of thermodynamics apply to love?

What was she supposed to do with this list? She had a feeling it could be inflammatory if she put any of them to someone like Aphrodite, a goddess she didn't want to mess with. But obviously Cheryl had something in mind. She just had to figure it out.

Brad came in, yawning loudly. There were dark circles under his eyes, and he flopped onto the narrow couch, his eyes already closed. "Have you talked to her?"

Grace didn't need to ask who he meant. "I left a message for her with Themis. The press showed up at her house in the mountains, so she's taken refuge at Afterlife. She'll be on the six a.m. flight and will be here in plenty of time for court tomorrow." She didn't say that it hurt to know she couldn't just drive up to Eris's house, sit on the deck with her, and talk about things the way they'd been doing. Even after their fight and the deafening disparities in the way they saw love, she wanted to spend time with her. Instead, they were emailing as she prepped her for the hearing. The partners had wanted Eris at the hotel with them, but when Themis explained that they'd have to do it this way or not speak with her at all, they'd had no choice but to capitulate.

"I'm thinking Aphrodite is right."

Brad cracked one eye open and looked at her. "About which part? The part where she told the Pope he had no right to be the face of the Catholic god thanks to the fact that he doesn't think women are sexual beings?"

She laughed dryly. "If I'm honest, I have to give her that one. No, I mean the part about humans not deserving the gods." The press conference held outside the Vatican, which had only recently been rebuilt after its destruction during the fight between the gods during the Merge, had been a show of female power. All the female love gods had shown up, and throngs of women in the street chanted their names.

The Catholic god, however, was siding with the Christian god, and they'd pulled God's love from the world. Wars were breaking out everywhere and people were dying by the hundreds. It was expected that the president of the United States herself would step in and shut down the case altogether the following day. But the damage had been done, and there was no telling when the gods would back down.

She tried to concentrate, but the words on the page in front of her kept blurring no matter how often she rubbed her eyes or how many cups of coffee she drank.

"The question is, do we not deserve them in a good way, or in a bad way?"

Grace tossed down her pen and closed her eyes. "What do you mean?"

"I mean," Brad said, forcing himself upright on her couch once again, "are they a punishment or a blessing? Because right now, it seems as if they're a lot like having someone hand you a laxative drink instead of the piña colada you were expecting."

She wasn't sure what to say to that. After her first encounter with Eris, she'd have said there was no question the immortals were a gift. Now, though, the world had descended into the kind of chaos that hadn't been seen since the Merge six years ago. People had forgotten how much good the gods had done since they'd begun moving among them openly, and Aphrodite had said as much.

"I have no answers. Absolutely none." She stood and stretched, her muscles popping audibly. "And I won't find any more tonight. Get out of here, go to bed. Tomorrow is going to be something else."

He waved half-heartedly as he left her room. The moment he was gone, she put the do not disturb sign on her door, locked it, and shrugged out of her bra with a sigh of relief. As she got ready for bed, she couldn't help but wonder what Eris was doing. Was she fast asleep? Was she in bed with a trio of blondes? Somehow, she didn't think so. While it was certainly her modus operandi in the past, the case seemed to have sucked away her passion, leaving her a husk of disappointment and disillusionment.

Grace was doing her best to believe that she wasn't being impacted by the gods taking love away from the world, but she had to admit to a certain dark, jaded feeling, like the sand slipping away under her feet while she was standing in the ocean.

Madness. Absolute, utter madness.

Grace couldn't think of any other word as the car slowly pushed through the crowd of protesters. Placards begging the gods to return love to the world were far fewer than those demanding that the gods be held accountable for the disaster the world had become. People held up photos of the loved ones they'd lost, children cried and screamed as they got shoved and pushed in the melee, and pervading it all was the deepest, most intense rage Grace had ever experienced.

Beside her, Brad clenched the door handle, his knuckles white. They both jumped when something hit the roof, and the driver swore under his breath. When they made it to the military blockade holding back the crowd from the courthouse, Grace was nearly dizzy with relief. The noise subsided and Brad unclenched his hand, flexing it as he shook his head.

"This has to end," he said, not looking at her.

She didn't need to reply. The car pulled up in front of the courthouse, as did the one in front of them and the one behind, all carrying the team of Kline and Associates. Not one among them looked steady. Except, that is, for Richard, whose eyes were lit up with an almost fanatical gleam.

"You ready for this, Gordon?" he called to her. "You brought us the case that's burning down the world. Hope you have a fire extinguisher under that skirt."

Rob threw him a stern glance and made his way over to her as they all climbed the stairs. "You'll do fine, Grace. Whatever the outcome, it's out of your hands now. Do your best, and we'll be there to advise you every step of the way."

She didn't take her eyes off the pure white stairs. "You don't expect to win?"

He tutted. "There's no winning for anyone now, Grace. Things have gone too far. They'll shut it down and it'll be over. You'll be partner, the gods will go back to doing what they do, and we'll be done with it."

She tripped and he reached out to steady her. "Partner?"

He gave her a swift grin that disappeared quickly. "You've earned it."

There was no more time for that conversation as they entered hallowed legal ground. It was almost silent, and the chill air made her shiver. Although deeply unnerving, she couldn't deny the excitement running through her too.

As her eyes adjusted to the dim interior, she saw two figures sitting on a bench in the hallway. Themis and Eris stood when the group approached.

Themis scanned the group, and Grace smiled when they made eye contact. "Love your suit, Grace. And those heels are killer."

It felt like such an odd thing for the goddess of justice to say at such an important moment, and Grace laughed. "Thank you."

Themis smiled and took in the group once again. "It's a reminder, everyone. Life will go on, no matter what happens here today. Things are messy, and they'll be messy again. But I truly believe that justice will prevail." She gave them a warm smile, and there was a glint in her eye that suggested she had true faith in her statement.

Grace could have hugged her for the simple reassurance. But what she really wanted was to hug Eris, who looked damn sexy in her three-piece suit with her hair slicked back. The despair in her eyes as she looked at Grace, though, made her want to weep and hold her tight at the same time.

"Hey," she said, her gaze steady.

"You okay?" Grace asked. It was a stupid question, really, but she couldn't think of anything else to say in front of twenty other people.

"Not really, no." She shrugged one shoulder. "But it is what it is."

Before Grace could respond, a clerk opened the courtroom door. "You can come in and get settled."

The group filed in, and it wasn't long before Zane Shaw came in as well, only a few of his clients with him. The case itself wasn't being tried, not exactly. The merit of it was in question, and Zane would have to prove that his client's complaints were worth the people out there living and dying in suddenly war-torn countries. It seemed pretty clear-cut.

Grace ignored Zane altogether when he came over to say hello to Rob and Richard. Rob was barely polite, but Richard actually shared a joke with him over the chaos outside. She couldn't have disliked him more than she did right then. And from the look of it, Rob wasn't impressed either.

Themis, Eris, and Grace sat at the defendant's table, and she didn't pull away when Eris reached under the table and squeezed her hand briefly. "I'm so glad you're beside me right now," she whispered.

Grace took a deep breath and looked her in the eye. "Nowhere I'd rather be."

Eris chuckled and Themis leaned around her. "Frankly, there are so many places I'd rather be right now there isn't a number high enough."

Eris grinned a little and bumped her with her shoulder. "You can't tell me a part of you isn't enjoying this."

Themis tilted her head, a small smile on her lips. "I am, you're right. Taking the bar exam, getting sworn in, sitting at the table like this… I've seen it all from the other side. It's quite exhilarating to be in the thick of it."

"Can you make them see justice?" Grace asked. "The judges, I mean."

"I can." Themis's smile faltered. "And I will, if it comes to that. But I'd rather them see it on their own. People in powerful positions like this need to be able to come to the right conclusions without being led, if they can. If they can't…" She motioned toward the bench at the front. "Then I'll do what I need to do."

Satisfied and comforted, Grace's shoulders relaxed a millimeter. "Then we'll be fine."

The courtroom had been closed to the public due to the extreme nature of the case and the emotions running rampant in humans, so when the room was called to order and the judges took their seats, the only sound was the rustling of the people somehow involved.

It was then that Grace really took it in. She was sitting beside the muse of love. On the other side of her was the goddess of justice. She was in court surrounded by the people she worked with, while defending an immortal she'd slept with. Repeatedly. The world, already in chaos, was waiting with collectively held breath.

Her legs grew weak, and she held onto the table to keep from having to sit down. Eris gently placed her hand on the base of Grace's back, helping to steady her. Grace nodded slightly and Eris's hand slid away.

She could do this. The partnership was already hers. The case, whichever way it went, would have nothing to do with the outcome of her career. But then there was Eris. Could she protect her? Did she need to?

They were told to sit, and the proceedings began. The judge began by stating that the courtroom would remain closed to the public, and that everyone involved in the case was under strict orders not to discuss the case outside of the courtroom.

"Mr. Shaw," he began, "it's the court's position—"

Glass shattered as three of the side windows exploded into the room. Screams broke out as people were hit with flying shards. Smoke billowed from containers that landed on the floor, quickly engulfing the room in a sickly, acrid scent.

Eris yanked off her jacket and pulled it over Grace, pressing it to her face. Themis stood, growing taller and more luminescent by the second. Two more containers were thrown into the room, and Themis held out her arms, protecting those nearest her.

Eris wrapped herself around Grace just as the bombs went off.

CHAPTER NINETEEN

Being immortal had its benefits. One of those was not dying. Although, that theory had yet to be put to the ultimate test.

Eris held Grace tightly to her chest, which shielded her from most of the flying glass and debris. She looked over her shoulder at Themis, who was standing goddess-tall in front of a cowering group of humans. Acrid smoke continued to weave through the room, and even Eris's eyes were watering.

The bombs had done incredible damage, and all Eris wanted to do was get Grace to safety. She looked down when she felt a tug on her pant leg. Brad had crawled beyond the now broken gate leading to the front area.

"Get us the fuck out of here," he hissed. Blood dripped from a cut on the side of his face.

She let go of Grace with one arm and reached down to him, pulling him upright against her as well. "Themis!"

The goddess turned, her eyes pools of jet-black fury.

"We need to go."

Themis moved away from the little group she'd protected and toward Eris. She wrapped her arms around them, and there was a flash of light.

And just like that, they were back at Afterlife. Silence and stillness greeted them in the large courtyard, an almost deafening contrast to the chaos they'd left behind.

Eris became aware of pressure against her chest and looked down. Grace's hands were pressed hard against her, and she finally let go.

Grace stumbled back, her hair mussed and her makeup smudged. "Jesus Christ. I thought you were going to suffocate me." She leaned forward and took in deep breaths of air.

"I'm so sorry. All I could think about was keeping you safe."

Brad turned away and vomited in a potted plant. He slumped to the smooth concrete, wiping his mouth with the back of his dirty sleeve. "I'll never complain about how long a flight takes again."

Themis sat heavily on a bench. "I'm sorry. That can be quite traumatic on the human body, but it was the only way to move quickly. I haven't done that with a human in a long time."

Eris led Grace and Brad to a bench and then ran to the water cooler just inside the back door. She brought two little paper cups out and handed them over. "Best I can do quickly."

They nodded their thanks and it seemed to help, as they both began to breathe normally again.

"What the fuck happened?" Brad finally asked.

"They attacked the courthouse. Someone had the *audacity* to bomb the trial. How *dare* they?" Themis was growing, glowering.

"Hey. Let's try to stay calm, okay?" Eris knelt in front of Brad and examined his face. "We should get that cut dealt with." She turned to Grace and ran her hand over her cheek. "Are you okay?"

Grace shivered under her touch and pressed her face to Eris's palm. "Thanks to you. If it hadn't been for you shielding me…" She turned to Brad. "Did you see what happened to the rest of the team?"

He shook his head, wincing as he touched the cut. "I only knew I needed to get to you guys." He paled slightly and placed his hands flat on the bench. "But I know I crawled over a couple of people who weren't moving."

Themis stood, her chin lifted. "I'm going back. I'll see if I can help, and I'll let you know the damage."

"Why go back? The police and ambulances will be there to deal with it."

Themis's eyes went dark once again. "There's been a devastating miscarriage of justice. Today was supposed to be about answers and setting things right. Instead, someone took it into their own hands and defied the system. It's my place to be there right now."

She raised her hand and was gone, leaving only sparkling dust motes where she'd been.

Eris pushed up. "Come on. Let's get inside. We'll get Brad's face looked at and turn on the news."

They headed into the cool interior of the atrium. It was busy, but no more than usual. Eris looked around, having expected chaos, not normalcy. Maybe they hadn't heard yet? It wasn't her place to tell them. She held Grace's hand and was about to guide them to the area where the healing gods worked when the elevator doors opened.

Tisera and Megara Graves stepped out, both looking somber. When they spotted Eris, they waved and headed over. Tisera's white wings caught the sun streaming in from the skylight, making them look downy soft, while Meg's wings, red with hints of orange, looked like dancing fire. Both sets dragged slightly on the floor behind them, causing a whispering sound to echo through the hall.

"Well, that was just the cluster fuck of the century, wasn't it, handsome?" Meg stood on her tiptoes and kissed Eris's cheek. "Glad you're okay."

Grace stiffened beside her, and it would have made her smile if it weren't for the fact that she had two upset furies in front of her. An angry fury wasn't something anyone wanted to be faced with. Nightmares and screaming always ensued, and the snakes they used as punishment didn't mess around.

"Grace, Brad, this is Tisera and Megara. Tis is part of the legal human relations team, and Meg is—"

"Simply fabulous." Meg pulled Grace into a hug. "And you're Eris's attorney. I'm sorry we haven't had a chance to meet before this cluster-fuckedness, but it's definitely a good time for us to talk now."

Grace stepped back, clearly flustered. "It's nice to meet you."

It sounded more like a question than a statement. Eris put her hand against Grace's lower back to help steady her. At least the fury sisters didn't have their fangs out, and their eyes were normal. Not to mention the snakes that were part of their being were quite perfectly absent. "We were heading to the healing floor. Brad took a hit in the courtroom."

The sisters looked at him and he took a half step back, but the polite smile never faltered.

"We'll walk with you." Tisera turned and Eris fell in step beside her, leaving Grace and Brad to walk with Meg. "I'm really sorry about all this, Eris. If it weren't for us being so busy on so many fronts, I would've called you myself. It's not an excuse, though. As soon as this became something big, I should have been in touch. How are you holding up?"

Everyone knew that of the three sisters, Tisera was the calm, logical one. Alec, the butch one, had been a friend of Eris's many decades ago, and they'd enjoyed their share of escapades. But time was slippery, and they'd drifted apart, especially after Alec had married the daughter of the moon. Meg was the wild one, and she was also married to the goddess of death, Dani. She was in charge of the social media and marketing side of Afterlife, and now that Eris thought about it, it was strange that Meg hadn't been in touch.

"It's okay, Tis. We're all busy, and since I retired, I haven't really spoken to a whole lot of gods."

"Other than Hades and Prometheus." Meg giggled behind her. "You're the only muse with a dark side. I love it."

They arrived at a door with the caduceus engraved in the window. Tisera gave a quick knock and walked in. "Anyone here?"

Asclepius looked in from an adjoining room. "Be right with you."

The four of them entered and Eris motioned toward the bed. "Brad."

He boosted himself up and swung his legs like a kid. "This is so surreal. If my face didn't hurt, I'd swear it was a weird dream."

"Nightmare, more like." Eris slumped into a chair. "Tis, has there been word on casualties? Or who did this? Surely one of the gods must know."

"Aren't the gods all-seeing and all-knowing?" Grace asked. "Wouldn't they *all* know?"

Tis tilted her head. "In theory, yes. But it depends on who did it. If it's a group of atheists, then it's possible they managed to keep this from the gods, who would only find out after the fact. Anyone who prayed to someone specific would be found out, most assuredly." When it was clear Grace was about to ask more questions, she held up her hand. "But I can say for certain that every god was going to follow that trial today, and the people responsible will be found."

"And dealt with in a probably messy and fundamentally awful way." Meg didn't sound in the least perturbed by that, and her bright red feathers fluttered like they'd been caught in a breeze.

Asclepius came in and went straight to Brad, who immediately looked like he'd fallen in love. The Greek god of healing was beautiful to look at, no doubt. His trim goatee over his muscled jaw highlighted the beauty of his face, and his dark brown eyes were soft and kind. When he put his hand to Brad's face, Brad actually sighed softly.

"Not too bad. I can heal it for you, or I can give you stitches. You'll have a slight scar. Your choice."

Brad's brow furrowed. "You're giving me the choice between a scar and no scar?"

"In a way." Asclepius dabbed at the wound with a damp cotton ball. "I'm giving you a choice between a god healing and human healing. You should always have a choice."

Brad looked at Grace, who shrugged. "Okay, I'll take god healing. I mean, how many people can say that, right?"

"Most people don't know they've been touched by a god. The difference is that you will." The god of healing smiled and pressed his hand over Brad's cheek. Light flickered around his fingers, and everyone waited in respectful silence until he removed his hand. There wasn't even a mark left behind. "There you go. Good as new."

Brad touched his cheek, looking awestruck. "Thank you."

He waved it away and turned to the group. "I'm the only one here. My daughters have gone to the courthouse."

"Good," Tisera said. "We should be there helping in a time of crisis, even if it is human-on-human violence, as usual." She turned to Eris. "Why don't we go up to my office and talk?"

Eris nodded and took Grace's hand. "Is that okay with you?" She wondered how much self-restraint it took for Grace not to roll her eyes. As if they were going to say no to one of the furies helping run the entire world's religious network.

"Of course." She looked between Tis and Meg. "Do you think we could find out about casualties or injuries? There were so many people from my firm there."

Meg hooked her arm through Grace's and led the way out of the room. "Of course. We'll check the social media networks too."

They took the elevator up to Tisera's office, a huge room with two distinct sections. One had charts and white boards on the wall, and a desk covered with files and trinkets, and the other side was well organized and had shelves of important-looking books behind it.

"My wife is visiting her family in Haiti." Tis motioned at the messy side. "That looks better than it usually does." She sat on one of the couches placed between the two sides of the room. "Have a seat."

"Can we get Grace and Brad something to eat and drink?" When Grace went to protest, Eris took her hand. "You've both got to be in some amount of shock, and if I know you, you haven't eaten today because you were nervous about the trial. Please? For me?"

Grace's protest died on her lips. "Thank you. That would be nice."

Meg picked up the phone and rattled off an order that sounded like enough food to feed every religion at Afterlife. "Now, let's see what's going on." She turned on the wall-mounted TV.

The room was filled with the sound of sirens and pictures of carnage.

"The death toll continues to rise," the anchor said, turning sideways so the camera could shoot the building behind her. "Currently, we're told fourteen people were killed and at least seven more were injured and are in critical condition. While we haven't been given the names of the deceased, one name has been released. Rob Kline, the head partner of Kline and Associates, has been confirmed dead."

Grace gave a muffled cry, her hands over her mouth, her eyes wide. Eris put her arm around her shoulders, Grace's pain reverberating like a hammer against Eris's heart.

"As we reported minutes ago, although Eris Ardalides, her attorney Grace Gordon, and Themis, goddess of justice have disappeared, a number of other gods have come to help."

The camera zoomed in, and Eris identified Asclepius's daughters working among the injured.

"Is that Aphrodite?" Brad leaned in as though he could see better.

"It is." Tis tilted her head again, in that thoughtful way of hers. "It isn't entirely surprising. I'd expected her, and possibly the others, to make an appearance at the courthouse today, even though they'd been specifically asked by the board not to, so as not to taint the verdict. It's good that she's there. Hopefully she brought Empathy and Comfort with her."

It did, in fact, look like Aphrodite was helping. Dressed in jeans and a simple black T-shirt, she moved among crying people who soon settled after she'd been with them. Nearby, two other women did the same. Eris had spent plenty of time with Empathy and Comfort, but she found both of them a little too clingy. It was good they were there, though.

Tears were running down Grace's face, and Eris unlocked the part of her she kept hidden away and let it flow. Grace slumped against her, the tears slowing. Eris let the feeling of love surge through her veins like a waterfall let loose over the edge of a dry cliff. Her fingertips warmed and she pressed them to Grace's skin, letting the love that Grace deserved, that so many of the people around her felt for her, flow between them. It made her eyes well up as she let that part of her free.

Grace stared up at her, eyes wide, lips parted slightly. "It's so beautiful," she whispered.

Eris kissed her forehead. "Love is definitely that."

"Jesus. Is that Death? I remember her from the mess in Mexico, but damn…" Brad seemed to run out of air.

Dani walked among the carnage, touching a person here and another there. Sometimes they sat up, sometimes…they grew still.

Meg turned off the TV. "This is really, really bad. And we're going to find the person responsible." She glanced at Tis and showed her fangs. "I think this might be a job for us, actually."

Grace pressed against Eris, and she didn't blame her. The fangs were one thing, but when the snakes in Meg's wings began to take shape, that was something else. "Uh, Meg?" Eris said, getting her attention. "We've got a couple humans here who probably couldn't handle the full fury effect right now."

Immediately, the snakes and fangs disappeared. "So sorry." She looked at Tis, who simply shook her head. "But I'm not wrong."

"No, you're not," Tis said. "And I suggest we go ahead with that course of action. I'll call Alec and the three of us will go together, but we'll make sure to divulge who the person is and get their reasoning before we—"

"Before you do what you do." Eris stood and pulled Grace up with her. "In the meantime, we'll get an Uber to take Grace home."

Tis shook her head as she walked toward her desk. "I think that's a bad idea, Eris. Paps will be all over this, and they're probably already outside both your houses, and possibly Brad's. I suggest you stay at one of the guest houses here on the compound until things settle down a little."

"I can handle the press," Grace said, but it didn't sound like something she particularly wanted to do.

Tis's smile was kind. "I don't doubt that for a second. But it's not just them I'm concerned about."

Eris flinched as she understood what Tis was trying not to say, and it was only a moment before Brad stood quickly.

"Oh my god. Could they bomb our houses too? My husband is home. Oh my god. He's going to be worried sick about me. And what if they bomb my house?"

Eris reached out and took his hand, letting the same feelings she'd given to Grace flow into Brad, though the essence of them was a little different. He calmed and gave her a grateful look.

"We'll have someone pick up your husband and bring him here, if that's okay? We'll have more humans on site than we've had in ages, but I think we can make the exception."

Tis already had her phone to her ear and was giving someone instructions. The food arrived, and Meg asked the person delivering it to take it to guest cabin forty-two.

"I'll walk you over, and we'll get you settled. Grace, I'll bring you something to change into, since we're about the same size. I'll find some other things for the two of you to wear. A hot shower and godly food will help."

The group walked through the office, across the courtyard, down a tree-lined path, and past a few other cute houses, to the one marked Guest Cabin Forty-Two.

Grace turned to Meg. "The house numbers don't seem to make any sense. Are they actual addresses?"

Meg laughed. "Each number corresponds to a number that matters to someone in the compound. This one is Kera's. Can you guess the book?"

Brad waved his hand like a kid in school. "The answer to life, the universe, and everything is forty-two."

Meg gave him a high five that sent him off balance. "Kera will be impressed."

Brad seemed satisfied with that and turned to follow the person pushing the food cart ahead of them into the house.

Eris hesitated, a thought occurring to her that she didn't want to voice, but which she couldn't keep to herself. "Grace?"

Grace looked over her shoulder.

"I can stay at another guest cabin. There are only two rooms in this one."

Meg laughed and bumped her hip to Eris's. "Everyone in the room could feel the fizz between you two. You may as well get to it." Laughing, she walked away and called over her shoulder, "I'll come by later with news."

Eris turned back to Grace, who was shaking her head, a small smile on her lips. "She's right. Thank you for the offer, but I'd really like you next to me tonight, if you're willing."

Willing wasn't what Eris would call it. Desperate to have Grace in her arms? Definitely. She took Grace's hand and led her inside. Tonight, they'd be staying in the safe confines of Afterlife. Tomorrow? She couldn't bear to think about it.

CHAPTER TWENTY

Terror gripped her as the ceiling fell in, concrete crashing around her, screams and pleas for help making it hard to tell where the injured were. It hurt to breathe and there were bodies everywhere. Someone grabbed her ankle and when she looked down, the mangled corpse asked, "Why did you let this happen?"

Grace sat up with a cry, her thin T-shirt stuck to her as sweat made her shiver. Eris's arms encircled her, and she rubbed soothing circles on Grace's back.

"It's okay. Just a nightmare. Nothing more."

Grace settled back into the supernaturally comfortable bed and laid her head on Eris's chest. "That isn't true, is it? It really happened."

Eris kissed the top of her head. "It did. But you're safe. Brad and his husband, Craig, are in the other room, safe."

Dinner had been a quiet affair, and none of them had bothered to turn on the TV. Meg hadn't returned, which Eris said meant they didn't have anything new to share, but Grace could tell she wasn't sure that was true. But it didn't matter. She'd been grateful for the reprieve from the horror that had become her life.

"I had a weird thought. Is Chris okay?" Grace asked.

"They're fine. Sian went and picked them up. No one will have my friends' addresses, and Sian is serious about her privacy. She'll be safe too."

Grace turned onto her back. "What's going to happen, Eris?"

Eris turned onto her side and lightly ran her thumb over Grace's hip bone. "Honestly, I don't know. We were part of *this* bombing, but the truth is, things have gotten really bad, really fast, all over the world. Without love, human life is fragile."

"Will they put an end to it? The love gods?"

"I don't think they'll need to. After this, the president will shut down the case, and things can go back to the way they were."

Somehow, Grace doubted it would be that simple. Things with the gods rarely were, and this case proved that to the nth degree. "This is a logic problem though, isn't it? People sued the muse of love, and by proxy, the idea of love itself. The love gods got angry and took love away, creating a world of hatred and evil. That will make people even angrier with the gods, and the love gods in particular, so they won't want to back down. Even if the gods put things right, people will still have turned against them. So it doesn't end. It just becomes a cycle." Examining the problem out loud was depressing, and when Eris didn't respond, she knew her musings were right.

"I think I disagree," Eris said after a while. "People love their gods. This was a select group of humans who followed each other like sheep. And it's a select group of gods causing most of the damage. But those same gods were out there helping people. If the love gods give love back to the world, I think things will mostly go back to normal. You're right, there will still be angry people, especially those who have lost loved ones during all this. But their gods can give them comfort." She stroked Grace's side, moving to the underside of her breast before skimming her nipple. "Love is more powerful than most anything you can imagine."

There was an undercurrent to Eris's words, something unspoken, but Grace let it stay that way. This wasn't the time for conversations that might feel like white lies or obligatory emotions in the cold light of day. Instead, she gave herself over to Eris's touch, to the way she felt so cared for, cherished, and desired, whenever Eris touched her. The feelings that had swept through her when she was spinning out of control wouldn't be denied, though. In those feelings, she'd felt what unconditional love was, and the woman touching her had it in abundance.

Disoriented, Grace blinked against the sleep in her eyes and tried to figure out what had woken her. She reached out, but the other side of the bed was cold and empty. Another knock brought her around and she sat up, the sheet over her chest. "Come in."

Brad came in holding two cups of steaming coffee. "I wanted to let you sleep in, but it's nearly noon and we should probably be doing something. I don't know what, but something."

She sipped the coffee gratefully. "How could I have slept so long?"

He perched on the edge of the bed. In clothes a size too big for him, he looked a lot younger. She sometimes forgot that he wasn't even thirty yet.

"Oh, I don't know. Bombs, bodies, gods, sex. Take your pick, it's all exhausting."

"And Eris? Is she in the living room?" Somehow, she knew Eris wasn't even in the house. That was illogical, though, so she had to ask.

"Mmm. No. Meg came by and said she had an important message for Eris, and they left together about three hours ago."

What messages did immortals pass between themselves? She couldn't imagine this one would be anything good. "Let me get dressed. Is there any food? I'm starving."

"Is there food? If they were cannibal gods, I'd swear they were feeding us well just so we'd taste good later. Eating god-cooked food is going to ruin me for the outside world. Hurry up."

He left, and Grace lay back against the pillows, contemplating. She'd lost her phone in the explosion, and she didn't know anyone's number by heart. Except for the firm, and it would be a good idea to check in. The memory that Rob had died brought tears to her eyes and she wiped them away with the sheet. If she hadn't taken the case, he'd still be alive. If she'd somehow kept control of it, found a way to keep Aphrodite and her ilk out of human business…

She nearly laughed out loud at the absurdity of that thought. She was nothing, less than a fly in a wineglass to the gods. Nothing she could have done would have kept the love gods from having their fragile egos bruised by the idea of people taking issue with them and how they worked.

She blinked in surprise at the anger rising in her, but she felt the truth of it in her bones. The gods were ego-driven narcissists. They always had been. They demanded obedience, subservience, and adoration. And if any of those things were taken from the offering plate, the humans were punished. Just like Aphrodite and the others had punished the entire world for daring to say that love wasn't what it should be.

She dressed, yanking on her borrowed shirt and slightly too snug pants, then stomped into the living room. She was in the mood to fight, but she saw Brad and Craig curled up together on the couch, and her anger deflated like a tire that blew out on the freeway. All at once, it was gone, and she just wanted Eris there beside her.

"How is it you're still in love?" she asked, pouring herself a glass of iced tea from a large pitcher. "Aren't you supposed to be throwing bricks and insults at each other?"

Brad continued to run his hand through Craig's hair. "I was wondering about that too. I think Eris might be right. If it's real, like, really real, then you don't need the gods for it. It's the other stuff making people crazy. Love thy neighbor only goes so far when their dog keeps peeing on your rosebushes."

She pondered that. Eris had said that people didn't understand what love was anymore, not really. Was true love so rare, then? Or were people settling more often than they used to? Were platonic loving relationships still a thing? Or was that the crux of the violence? There weren't any answers, so she loaded a plate with various Greek foods and sank into the sofa opposite Brad and Craig.

"I need to call the office, but I don't have a phone or computer."

Craig reached toward the floor and fumbled around until he held up his phone. "Use mine." He tossed it over and she fumbled it, getting tzatziki dip on the edge.

She wiped it off as best she could without tipping her plate of insanely perfect food and dialed the office. It only took two rings before a chirpy receptionist answered.

"Hi, it's Grace Gordon. I need—" She didn't have a chance to finish as the telltale beep of her being transferred rang in her ear.

"Grace? Oh my god. Where the hell are you?"

Cheryl actually sounded genuinely concerned, which was interesting given the state of the world. "Hey, Cheryl. I'm at the Afterlife compound. Are you okay? Were you hurt? What about the others?"

"Hold on." There was the sound of a door shutting. "First of all, yes, I'm okay. Some cuts from debris, but nothing major. Five of the staff died, including Ron." She paused and took an audibly deep breath. "Richard is senior partner now, and you'd never know he just lost his father. He's planning strategies, figuring out next steps. Grace, do you have a plan? Or know what's going on?"

Grace set the plate of food on the floor, her appetite gone. "I wish I had better news, but there's nothing yet. If I hear anything at all, I'll let you know right away. Should I come in?"

Cheryl's answer was swift. "No. Definitely not. The press are swarming, and we're trying to get some sense of normalcy in the building. And Richard..."

Grace sighed. "And Richard is saying this is my fault and calling me incompetent."

"That's about the size of it. Fortunately, he's saying that to a bunch of lawyers who can see the faulty logic, so it won't stick. For now, consider me your main contact. Can I reach you on this number?"

"No." Grace rolled her neck, a headache coming on. "My phone was in the courtroom, and this is Brad's husband's phone. He's with me, by the way. I'll make it a priority to get another phone and I'll call with the number as soon as I have it."

There didn't seem to be anything more to say, and Grace hung up after promising she'd call the moment she had anything at all to share. She slid the phone back to the other sofa. Just as she was trying to figure out what to do next, the door opened and Eris came in. There were dark smudges under her beautiful eyes and her shoulders were hunched. She tried for a smile, but it fell short.

"What now?" Grace asked, the feeling of foreboding one she wanted to shove into a box and drop in the ocean.

Eris sat beside her on the couch and held her hand. "There are a few things. Remember the artist you introduced me to, in the park? Patrick?" When Grace nodded, Eris continued, but she stared at their hands instead of making eye contact. "He asked to see me, so I went with Meg to meet him."

Grace frowned, confused. "I don't understand."

Eris's breath was shaky. "He was killed, Grace. A riot broke out in the park near your house, and he tried to help a woman who was on the ground. The mob turned on him."

Her stomach lurched, and she leapt to her feet and ran to the bathroom to rid herself of the few bits of food she'd managed to eat. He'd been so sweet, so lost, so gentle. He'd died helping someone. This world didn't deserve his kindness.

She shuffled back into the living room, and Eris held out her hand. Grace accepted it and curled into Eris on the sofa. "So what do you mean he wanted to see you?"

"Meg is married to Dani. When one of Dani's death workers picked up his soul, he asked if there was any way to get a message to me. The death worker took him to Dani, and he explained our connection. So Meg took me to the Deadlands, where I could talk to him one last time." She caressed Grace's hair. "I didn't think you'd want to go, and you wouldn't have been allowed to anyway. I thought it was best to let you sleep."

It was true. The last place she wanted to go was the land of the dead, the place where people were now living in-between afterlives because they hadn't yet decided where they wanted to go in the afterlife. "What did he tell you?"

"He asked me to go to his wife and tell her how much he loved her. He asked me to remind her of a few memories he held dear. That's where I've been for the last hour." She hugged Grace tighter, as though she too needed comfort. "I told her what had happened, and I held her hands and showed her his memories of their love, and how he still felt about her to the moment he died."

Brad gave a little sobbing hiccup from the other couch. "How awful."

"Knowing how much someone loved you is never awful." Eris smiled at him gently. "They'd been talking again, trying to see if they could find a way forward. I gave him some tools so he could express himself, and he painted her some things that allowed her to understand his pain on a deeper level. She loved him too."

"What else?" Grace asked. "You said there were other things."

"This is less personal but probably more serious on a global level. The board of directors at Afterlife are demanding that the love gods back down and return things to normal. Too many people are getting hurt and things are out of control. They're trying to protect their followers, as they should."

"And?" Grace pulled away and sat up but saw the lack of hope in Eris's eyes.

"And they're refusing. It could be another immortal civil war. Aphrodite has always liked a good fight with plenty of drama, and this is definitely providing her with that. There's the sweet side of love, and there's the scathing side. Right now, she and the other love gods are spurned bunny-boilers who can't be talked down. But the other gods won't allow it to continue."

Silence fell. The last time the gods had fought each other, they'd been fighting the goddess of chaos, Dis, who had a few deities on her side. A civil war between the primary deities existing in the world now would be catastrophic.

Brad sat up and ran his hands through his hair, then wiped the tears off his cheeks. "If that's the case, we're going home." He held up his hand to forestall Eris's argument. "If I've lived through all this just to die while the gods fight it out, then I'm dying clutching my husband and Betty."

Eris looked at Grace, who shook her head. "Betty is his houseplant."

"Hush your mouth," he said and accepted Craig's hand up from the couch. "Betty is a member of our family, the only child we'll ever have. Perfectly behaved, hardly needs food, and always makes us smile." They headed toward the bedroom. "We're going to shower. Eris, can you get us a ride?" He didn't wait for a reply and shut the door behind them.

"What now?" Grace asked. It felt like all she was doing was asking questions and hoping for an answer that would fix things.

"Now, I have a meeting with a few gods. You can stay here, or…" She shrugged. "Stay here, I guess. It isn't like anything has changed since last night."

If she stayed in the house she'd go stir crazy. "Can I see Themis? At least we could talk law."

Eris brightened and pulled out her phone. "Great idea." She made the call and was quickly told to bring Grace to Themis's temporary home in the compound.

"I'll walk you there, and then I'll go to my meeting and give Themis a call when it's over, okay?"

Grace studied Eris's face, trying to figure out what she was really feeling. "Are you okay? Honestly?"

Eris stood and moved away. She shoved her hands in her pockets. "Honestly? No. If I'd been doing my job instead of playing at being human, none of this would have happened. If I'd been helping artists like our friend in the park, if I'd been doing what I was literally born to do, then people wouldn't be out there dying. We wouldn't be on the brink of another war." Her expression wasn't just sad, it was stricken with grief and guilt. "This is all my fault."

Grace stood to take her in her arms, but Eris backed away.

"I'm not just damaged goods, Grace. I'm so lost that I've brought the world to destruction. I retired because I thought love was a joke, a throwaway emotion that didn't mean anything anymore. Because of that, I've proven that I don't deserve to be a muse. I don't deserve a place among my sisters or in whatever world will be left when this is over." She backed toward the door and reached behind her to open it, her gaze never leaving Grace's. "I'm sorry I'm not the woman you deserve. I'll have someone come over to take you to Themis's."

Before Grace could stop her, she was gone. Grace's knees gave way, and she crumpled to the floor. She'd never known it was possible to feel like someone had reached in and torn away a piece of her. Now it hurt to breathe. Her hands trembled as she moved them, but there wasn't anything to touch, nothing to grab. A silent sob wracked her body, and then the tears came.

Chapter Twenty-one

Eris walked down the long, dark corridor, grateful for the cessation of sound and light. She pulled open the obsidian door to Hades's domain and was met with three enormous tongues that lifted her off her feet. "Hey, Cerb." She scratched his heads for a few minutes, taking some small comfort in the way the guardian of hell's gates loved so sweetly. She had to force herself away toward the office, where Hades and Prometheus were waiting.

When she walked in, Prom took one look at her, then jumped up and pulled her into a crushing embrace. "It's not your fault, niece. It isn't."

She let go like a child. The fear, rejection of who she was, and guilt fueling the pain…she let them flow out of her like a toxic river. When she'd finally cried herself out and was only still standing thanks to Prom's arms around her, he finally lowered her into a chair across from Hades's desk.

"It is, in a way. Your fault, I mean." Hades sat ramrod straight behind his desk, his dark eyes like pits in his face.

"Hade!" Prom rested his huge hand on her shoulder.

"In a way, I said." He focused on Eris. "You were easy pickings, Eris, because you'd lost your way. And those lost in the woods are often the subjects of fairy tales, warnings about what it is to lose who you are."

She hunched forward, wrung out and hollow. "I know, H."

"However." He waited until she looked up at him. "We've all lost our way at some point, and had the humans had the audacity to complain to us, we would have dealt with them on the kind of level they're experiencing now. We often did so in Ancient Greece when we fought each other using humans as our pawns. The Merge has brought about extreme changes, among both gods and humans. There was bound to come a time when the humans overstepped. They always do, and then they're put back in their place. That's the nature of what it is to be a god, Eris. We are benevolent, and we are cruel. And they love us for both. They expect both. Not one of the major religions believes in a god of utopian sugary sweetness. All of us can give with one hand and take with the other."

She pondered that for a moment, and they let her think. "So we should just let the gods go to war?"

He harumphed and Prom shook his head, his big beard flowing like a wave. "Not what we're saying at all, Eris. That was Hade's way of saying what I said, in a way you might believe it. This isn't your fault. You might have been the way it got off the ground, but they would have found another way to insult the gods at some point. They're not all that smart, these humans of ours."

Hades tilted his head in agreement. "Now we must put a stop to this. The Deadlands are overflowing, and every department is getting an influx of souls. While we're used to that with war, this is coming from all over the world, and the paperwork and intake are a nightmare. I don't have time for that kind of nonsense and neither do the other gods, who should be acting godly, not squabbling like hens in a magnificent henhouse. At least, not over something as obviously necessary as love." He looked at his watch. "There's a board meeting in ten minutes. Are you two coming?"

Eris looked at Prom, who shook his head. "We're going to Eris's house in the canyon. If there are press there, I'll remove them. We need some quiet time."

Hades stood and ushered them out. "I'll call you after." He turned and strode down the hallway, stopping to give Cerberus a treat of what looked like someone's leg before he opened the door into the main building of Afterlife.

For a moment, she considered asking Prom to get Grace so they could go together, but she put a stop to the thought. No matter what Hades and Prom said, the fact remained that she'd left herself open to this, and if she hadn't, none of this would be happening. If she'd been meant to meet Grace, as she suspected was the case, then they would have met at some point anyway. Now, they were surrounded by death and destruction, and she wanted to keep that as far from Grace as possible.

"Let's go," she said, taking Prom's hand.

There were no reporters at Eris's house. Paper cups, empty cartons of fries, and other trash showed they'd definitely been there. When she hadn't shown up, they had probably figured she'd gone to Afterlife, a refuge for the immortals.

She and Prom appeared on her deck, startling Hilda, who was lounging on the table in the sun. She hissed, her hackles raised, until she saw it was Eris. Her ears flicked and she lay back down.

"Good to see you too." Eris gave her a scratch behind the ears and went inside. She'd never been so thankful for her mountain sanctuary as she was now. She poured them glasses of iced tea and joined Prom on the deck. Hilda was curled up in his lap, purring loudly as he rubbed her belly.

"Only you would have a mountain lion on your lap like a housecat." She handed him the drink and he laughed.

"For a god, a mountain lion is a lot like a house cat."

They sat in total silence for a long while, nothing but the sound of Hilda's purring and birdsong surrounding them. She let the thoughts whirl in her head, not trying to grab onto any one in particular, and only occasionally wiping the tears from her cheeks.

"I was a Titan," Prom said softly as he watched a pair of condors nuzzle each other in the tree. "Not the first of the gods, not really. There were plenty of ancient gods before the Greeks brought us to life. The Titans were all-powerful. Cruel, angry, and never satisfied with the humans we watched over. But I grew increasingly fond of them. I started to become something else, something more than just a Titan. I became a protector, and I've been trying to protect them ever since I brought them fire to help them evolve." His smile was sweet as he mused on the memory. "The question," Prom said, draining the last of his tea, "is who are you now? Who do you want to be, Eris Ardalides?

You know who you *don't* want to be anymore. But what does the future you look like?"

"You sound like a fortune teller," she said. The question was one of the ones caught in the tornado of her mind, though. "When I helped that artist in the park, I felt a part of me come back to life, and it felt good. When I opened up to Grace and Brad, it felt amazing. Like parts of me that had been dormant suddenly sparked into being." She glanced at him. "It hurts."

"Coming back to life often does. I've had to do it a time or two myself." He motioned at her. "Go on."

"I'm not sure I've got anything else yet."

He gently lifted Hilda off his lap and set her on the deck. Her tail snapped back and forth, and her ears were flat, a clear indication of how she felt about that. "Well, it's a damn good start. I want you to stay here and think about that question. No more blame. Muses weren't made to live in the past."

She gave a hoarse laugh. "How many people have I helped write or paint about the love they lost?"

He grinned. "Okay, maybe you and the muse of history are meant to look back a little too. But now isn't that time. Now you need to look forward, Eris." He put his hand on her shoulder and looked down at her from his great height. "Somehow, I believe you're still the key to fixing this."

"You're a god, Prom. You would know."

He leaned down and said in a mock whisper, "You'd be surprised how much we don't know." He stood and tapped the side of his nose. "But you didn't hear that from me. I'm heading back to the compound. I'll let you know if I hear anything, and I'll make sure Grace is okay."

She nodded, and he disappeared, leaving only shiny dust in the air behind him. She forced herself off the deck and into the house. Her bed was cool and soft and would have been perfect if only Grace had been beside her. But Prom was right. She needed to figure out who she wanted to be, and she couldn't be the person Grace needed until she figured that out. She grimaced when Hilda jumped onto the bed beside her. "We need to set some boundaries."

Hilda yawned and stretched, and Eris let the warmth of her unapproved bed fellow allow her to drift to sleep. The subconscious was often the best place to find answers in times like this, and if she was sleeping, then she wasn't hurting over the look of wounded fear in Grace's expression when Eris had left her.

Grace had waved off the person who'd shown up to lead her to Themis's house. She had to get out of there, away from the gods, away from talk of death and war. Away from the look of complete despair in Eris's eyes as she'd walked out.

She, Brad, and Craig shared an Uber, which dropped them off first. Grace gave the driver a new address and then texted her brother, who sent a handful of pissed-off emojis before saying he'd meet her there. As they made their way into Pasadena, her heart tore a little more at the evidence of destruction that littered the streets. Cars had been torched, graffiti covered normally pristine areas, and ambulances passed them, sirens blaring, almost constantly. By the time she got to her stop, she couldn't see how they could possibly fix the mess they were mired in.

Foothill Restaurant was quiet in the afternoon, and that was just what she needed. John was waiting outside and yanked her into a crushing hug.

"I didn't know if you were among the dead," he whispered against her hair. "What would I have done without you?"

Guilt added a fresh arrow to her already wounded heart. In truth, she hadn't thought of calling him at all, not until she needed a shoulder. But that had never happened before. He'd always been her rock, her go-to. And she'd been his. The understanding that she could be affected by the lack of love in the world, just like everyone else, hurt. It didn't have to be some big explosion. It could simply be…emptiness. Apathy. And that would be equally as awful.

"I'm so sorry, John." She hugged him tightly until he finally pulled back.

"Drink?" he asked, pulling open the door.

"All of them."

The server showed them to a booth at the back and gave her a lingering stare. "You're the attorney, aren't you?"

She gave him a weak smile. "Sadly. Please don't hold it against me."

He shrugged. "Good you're not dead, I guess."

She sighed and shook her head when John went to tell him off for his blasé comment. "Don't. People are out of control. We're going to need to be extra patient."

"Thank god Mom and Dad aren't still together. Can you imagine what they'd be doing to each other now?"

She shuddered at the thought, and when the server came over, she ordered a drink called Chaos is a Friend of Mine. It felt more appropriate than a mimosa. John ordered water.

"Water?"

He studied her face as though memorizing it. "I need to stay clear-headed or I'm going to head down the depressed rabbit hole with all the stuff happening."

She respected how much he'd grown to understand his mental health, and she wished she was in a similar place. But right now, numbness was begging for her attention.

"Nothing for me," she said when the server came to take their food order.

"She'll have the chilaquiles with no egg, and I'll have the chocolate chip pancakes." John handed over their menus.

"I'm not hungry. You'll have to take them to go." She took a long sip of the vodka and blackberry cocktail. "I'll have another of these, though."

"You'll eat because that's what we do. We bury our emotions in food and animated films. When was the last time you watched a Disney film?"

"The last time we watched one together. So, six years ago?"

He shook his head and flicked some water at her. "That's a travesty. After we eat, we're going back to your place and we're eating ice cream and watching *Brave*."

"Where magic gets people turned into animals? I've had enough of that world, thanks." She slurped the last of her drink through her straw and motioned to the server for another.

"Yeah, okay, fair enough. We'll watch some silly sitcom where everything turns out right at the end of an hour."

"Better."

He reached across and took her hand when she went to take another sip. "What's going on?"

His earnest question, one asked for no other reason than because he cared about her, broke open the dam. She spilled the story, from meeting Eris to her walking out and leaving her only hours earlier. "And the worst bit is, I think she's the one for me."

He pushed her plate of food at her. "Start eating this while I process this surreal cluster fuck."

Half-heartedly, she started in on the spicy tortilla chip dish which, without the eggs, was really just extra saucy nachos. As soon as it hit her tastebuds, though, she started to eat with more relish. Having unburdened herself to her brother, the one person on Earth she trusted, aside from Eris, lightened the heaviness in her soul.

"So, essentially, she walked away because she thinks she's protecting you, not just from this mess, but from herself." He raised his eyebrows for her agreement, and then continued. "It's not that she doesn't want you, it's that she's way damaged."

"But what do I do with that?" She slowed down eating, already feeling a stomach ache coming on.

"What you'd do with anyone who felt like they were too damaged for love. You prove them wrong. Patiently, I might add."

"I'm incredibly patient," she said, pushing the plate away and then snagging a bit of pancake off his.

"You buy pre-popped popcorn because the two minutes in the microwave feels like too long." He smacked the back of her hand with his fork when she went in for more pancake. "You're patient with your clients, but not with yourself or much of anything else." He grinned. "Except me. But I'm worth it."

"Speaking of which, we'll have to stop and get some popcorn for our movie night." She thought about what he'd said. "What if how patient I am doesn't matter? What if she's too far gone for me to reach her?"

He mopped up the last of his syrup with a final bite. "Then you let go. It isn't like you have a choice. You probably wouldn't want to stalk an immortal. Magic and animals and all that."

"It feels like we're all blaming ourselves. Me, Eris…but if Aphrodite hadn't made things worse, none of this would have happened." She stabbed her fork at the plate, making an ugly screeching sound. "I'm so damn angry, and I can't even bitch about any of them because…well, magic and animals, right?"

He motioned for her to keep going.

"And how is it the one person I've found who makes me feel incredible, is someone who will also bring me into this world of insanity?"

He sipped his water, looking thoughtful. "You know what I find kind of amazing? You're a romantic-at-heart divorce lawyer who has fallen for the muse of love. It's some kind of cosmic convergence, right? But I don't know if that means the universe is about to implode or you're part of some grand plan. Either one could be frustrating."

She set down the fork, perplexed and a little breathless. "You think we were meant to be? As in, all of this was meant to be?"

He shrugged. "You've spent a ton of time with them. What do you think?" He fanned himself with his napkin. "Surely Eris has ticked every box on your perfect woman list?"

"I didn't have immortal on it." She rolled her eyes at his raised eyebrows. "Yes, obviously she ticks all the boxes. And I've already admitted that I've fallen for her. What's your point?"

"My point, sister dear, is that maybe neither of you have any control over this, and you need to let go and see what happens."

His phone buzzed and he pulled it from his pocket. Frowning, he handed it to her. "I think it's for you."

She took it and looked at the screen to see her office's name. "Cheryl?" she said when she hit the accept button.

"Hey. I'm guessing you don't have a phone yet, and I saw your brother's name as next of kin in your file. I was hoping you'd be with him." There were voices raised in the background that diminished with the sound of a door closing. "I needed to speak to you right away. The board has voted, and we're offering you partner. We've outvoted Richard, and although he's pissed and saying we're disgracing his father's memory, the position is yours. If this case goes any further, or if we all die tomorrow, at least you'll do it as partner."

There was no question that Cheryl was waiting for Grace's excitement. For a reaction that Grace would have had not even three months ago. But instead, it was as though she was listening to her own breathing underwater.

"Grace? Have you passed out? Or been whisked away by a god?"

"Sorry. Sorry, Cheryl. That's…wow. I don't even know what to say."

"No need to say anything. But maybe stay out of the office today anyway so you don't have to deal with Richard. And remember to call me when you hear anything."

She hung up before Grace could respond, and she stared at the phone in her hand as though it could explain the heavy feeling in her chest. John gently withdrew it from her hand.

"More bad news?"

She thought she shook her head, but she wasn't sure. "They've offered me the partner position."

He raised his arms in victory. "At last, something good coming out of all this." When she didn't respond, he lowered his arms. "Right?"

"I…I don't know. I mean, that's what I've always wanted. But it seems so…so…trivial now. People everywhere are dying, and I'm worried about a better title?"

"And more money. There's that too." He took her hand and tugged on it to get her to look at him. "What's changed? Not catastrophically in the world. Inside you."

She gulped the last of her drink and choked on it as it fizzed up her nose. When she was done coughing and wiping away the tears streaking down her cheeks, she took a deep breath. "I'm not sure. I need to think. But I'll do it tomorrow. Right now I just want to close my eyes."

He paid the bill, and they walked out to his car. She hooked her arm through his and rested her head on his shoulder. "Thanks for coming when I called."

"You're stuck with me being awesome, sis. I've tried to be less amazing, but it's too much work." He kissed her cheek and opened the car door for her. "Popcorn, ice cream, movies. Everything will be fine."

But everything wasn't fine, and it was clear as they drove past people arguing in the street, past shops with broken windows, and gas stations that said they weren't selling any to be put in gas cans.

"Jesus." Brad pulled up in front of Grace's house and she let yet more tears fall. There was no press but scrawled across the pretty frontage in garish red paint was one word.

Traitor.

"We're not staying here." He put the car in drive and drove away, too quickly for her to protest.

"I need fresh clothes." It was all she could think to say. She couldn't imagine being inside, knowing that her beautiful home had been branded that way.

"We'll order everything you need online and have it delivered to my place tomorrow. You could do with some new clothes anyway."

She didn't say anything, and she didn't see any more of the scenes of destruction as they headed to her brother's place. All she could think about was how badly she wanted to call Eris. How she wanted to be wrapped up in her arms where she felt safe and cared for. But Eris seemed to think she had to fight this battle alone. Somehow, Grace needed to convince her otherwise.

Chapter Twenty-two

Eris woke to the sound of motorcycles coming up the driveway. Several, by the sound of it. Pulling the pillow over her head to dampen the sound didn't help. It wasn't long before there were voices calling her from the living room.

She groaned when someone threw open her bedroom door.

"She's in here, all curled up like a little kitten," DK said as she pulled open the curtains.

"Fuck off," Eris mumbled from under her pillow.

"Aw. How cute. Little wounded baby animal hiding from the world." Ebie's voice was too close.

"You fuck off too." Eris held onto the pillow as someone tried to yank it off. "Leave me alone."

"We need to hear how you're going to put the world back together," Deb said, swearing in Spanish when paws clattered through the room and Hilda jumped on the bed.

She finally lost the fight with the pillow, and it was flung away. Hilda jumped off the bed and went to lie on it, as though agreeing with Eris's group of annoyingly insistent friends.

"I'm so not in the mood." She struggled to sit up and grabbed the sweatshirt tossed to her.

"Your mood in the face of world destruction is largely irrelevant," Sian said. "You can be as moody-sexy as you want, but if we all die, there won't be anyone to appreciate it."

She struggled out of the tangled sheets. "The gods would just make new humans. You're all replaceable." There was silence for a second, and she looked around. "Not me, obviously. I'd miss you, mostly."

The tension dissipated and they herded her toward the kitchen, where Chris was already in place, setting dishes and various trays of food on the dining room table. When Sian went around the island and wrapped her arms around them, Eris blinked and tried to focus. "How has this happened when love doesn't exist in the world right now?"

Chris gave a shy smile. "You taught me that when it's real, nothing can stop it. This one just needed a push out of her little box of labels and ageist bullshit."

Sian huffed and kissed their cheek, then went over to the table to pick up a taco. "I think love being taken away from the world meant it had to be real. Like, really real. Nothing got in the way of me getting to see how amazing they are."

That was something Eris would ponder later. She picked up a taco and studied it. "Is this filled with guacamole?"

"Yup, in place of meat. There's also pork, beef, and chicken. But we couldn't pass up the option to have a mouthful of guac and chips topped with cheese and lettuce. It feels healthy."

Eris took a bite and decided it was anything but healthy, and also perfect. "Any news?"

"The press is saying that the gods have closed themselves off to continue discussions out of the public eye. So the world is going to shit, and they've abandoned us, essentially. And you can imagine how people are taking that." Ebie shook her head dolefully.

"I can't, actually. Are they praying more, or less?" Eris asked.

"Both. Sides are definitely being chosen, and there doesn't seem to be anyone in the middle." Deb grimaced at the guac taco and chose a pork one instead.

"Where's Grace, by the way?" Chris asked.

"At Afterlife, where she's safe." Eris winced at the thought of the way they'd parted. "Away from me."

"Dipshit," Sian mumbled around a mouthful of food.

There were nods of general agreement.

"What's that supposed to mean?" She put her taco down and stared at them, defiant. "If I'd been doing my job—"

"Yada, yada." Ebie waved her words away. "If, if, if. If doesn't cut the mustard, dude. Just fix it."

"How? How do I go about fixing the world?"

Chris leaned over and gathered a bowl of chips and salsa. "You're the muse of love, Eris. Do your job."

The sensation was a little like a jackhammer being rammed into her foot. Could it be that easy? "I need to make some calls."

They bumped tacos like they were cheering her on, but she didn't care about their teasing now. What had begun as tortured fragments of ideas in her subconscious was now an avalanche, and she could see the individual flakes as they became a wave to wash over the world. She called Afterlife, but Themis was in the board meeting with the gods. So where was Grace? She called reception and was told that Grace had left with Brad and Craig. So she called Brad, but he said she'd left them, and he didn't know where she'd gone next.

Where the hell was she? Was she safe? Had she been hurt by a mob? If anything happened to her... *Her brother.* But she didn't have his number. She hit speed dial on her phone and was relieved when Tisera answered. "Hey, Tis. I think I might be able to fix this. Or at least get the ball rolling. But I need Grace and I can't find her—"

"Hold on." There was the sound of keys tapping for a minute. "I'll text you her brother's number. She's at his place."

She wasn't sure how she wanted to know that Tisera knew that, but it didn't matter right now. "Thanks, Tis."

"Want to let me in on the plan?"

She debated but came down on the side of caution. "Not yet. I'm still working it out. But can you keep the gods in the boardroom and tell them to turn on the TV when I call you?"

"I can't really keep gods from doing anything at all, but I'll do my best. Good luck."

Eris hung up and hit the number Tis had sent. It rang and rang, and she nearly gave up.

"Hello?" a male voice asked.

"Hi, John? This is Eris. I'm trying to find Grace."

"Oh, hey. She's asleep. We went by her place, and someone had graffitied it, so we came here. She was drunk and upset so I put her to bed. Need me to wake her?"

Eris mentally ticked off the things she needed to do. "I've got a couple of calls to make, but I think she and I can make this right. Can you bring her to my place in an hour or so?"

"Sure. Need her to bring anything?"

"Nothing, thanks."

Her heart began to race as she made the next call. If this didn't work, she had no idea what the next move might be. But as her blood sang and her soul answered, she knew she was on the right track. All she had to do was listen.

Grace adjusted the sunglasses which weren't necessary at night but helped with the glare of the streetlights as they punctured her eyes. Their movie night had turned into a muddled blur of crying, snot, and mumbled opinions about love. When John woke her to say they needed to go to Eris's, she was far from enthusiastic. But as they drove up the winding canyon, she couldn't deny the anticipation rising at being able to see her again.

Her disappointment was quickly eclipsed by her curiosity when she saw not only the motorcycles she knew belonged to Eris's wonderful group of friends, but also a van marked Atoma in street art style.

She and John made their way up to the deck, where a floodlight lit up the area like a stadium. When they saw her, the group gave her a rousing welcome, and she wondered just how much they'd had to drink. Probably more than she had if she had to guess.

"Is that a god with a mountain lion in his lap?" John whispered in her ear, his gaze not leaving Prometheus.

"It is. Don't stare."

John looked away and Grace laughed. She went to Prom and received the kind of hug that made everything better. "What's going on, Prometheus?" she asked.

"We kicked her ass into gear, that's what's happening," Deb said. "Now she's bossy."

DK shook her head. "Not bossy. Determined. I don't think we've ever seen her this way. It suits her."

Grace looked inside and saw Eris seated at the dining table with a woman who looked strikingly similar. She started to go inside, then looked over her shoulder. "This is my brother, John. John, the brothers in arms. And the Titan god Prometheus." She left him standing there as they converged on him, already starting to tell stories.

She slid open the patio door, and her heart jumped when Eris looked up from what she was doing. When their eyes met, electricity shot through her in the best way.

"Hey."

"Hey." Eris came around the table and pulled Grace into a tight hug. "Thank you for coming," she said against her hair.

"I'm pretty sure I'll always come for you." The double entendre was unintentional, and she felt her face flame when Eris snort-laughed. "You know what I mean."

"Oh, I do. And I'll hold you to that in every way." She released her from the hug. "Grace, this is my sister Lyra. Lyra, my attorney and so much more, Grace."

She shook her hand, but her mind was whirling. "I'm so sorry, but in the list of Eris's sisters, I don't remember your name."

Thankfully, Lyra didn't seem offended. "My Greek name is Euterpe. Rather old-fashioned, and it doesn't suit me anymore. Like our Erato, I decided to go with something a little more modern. I'm glad you're here."

The sincerity in her tone and gaze made Grace want to sit on the couch and talk about life with her. She was tall, like all the muses, but her hair was long and braided down the back, with wisps framing her face. She was stunning in a way that made Grace extremely aware of her own short, dumpy frame.

"You're beautiful and perfect, and I'm going to do wonderful things to you," Eris murmured in her ear.

"Stay out of my head." She pressed closer. "What are you two up to?"

Eris pulled out a chair for her and pushed the notepad over. "Have a look."

Grace started reading and was quickly immersed in the beautifully crafted wording. Tears welled in her eyes, and she finished reading before she dashed them away. "Wow. Did you write that? And is it really the way you feel?"

Eris tilted her head toward Lyra. "We did it together. Lyra is the muse of epic poetry, and we needed to tell a story. Between the two of us, I think we nailed it. What do you think? Will it work?"

Grace picked up a pen and went into analytic mode. She scanned every line and changed a few words here and there, and then added a full sentence in between the last two paragraphs. "I think you need to take logic into account as well, for those less emotionally inclined." She pushed the pad back. "Is this why there's a spotlight to rival the sun on your deck?"

Eris nodded. "I've got an old friend coming over for an exclusive interview, and the moment we go live, it'll start showing up everywhere. Meg is already waiting for the social media aspects, and Tisera has told the gods they need to wait for the ten o'clock news."

She rubbed her hands together, and there was a beautiful lightness to her Grace hadn't seen before. She'd glimpsed it when she'd shared her gift in order to calm Grace down, but now it was like the moon shining through her skin. She was luminous. God-like.

"And your rambunctious Randys out there?"

"Part of that third paragraph."

Grace scanned it and saw where they'd fit in. "And me?" Her gaze met Eris's, and she hoped Eris saw that the question wasn't just about what was on the paper.

"There from beginning to end. Right beside me, all the way. In fact, I'm hoping you'll have something to add when you think the moment is right." Eris stood and held out her hand. "What do you say?"

Grace's hand shook as she accepted Eris's touch. "I say let's make the world right again."

Lyra took the notepad and clicked off photos of it on her phone. "I'll send the photos to Tis and Meg, and they'll do their thing the moment we start."

They went onto the deck and the conversation stopped as the group looked at them. Eris took a deep breath. "This is the play, guys." She held up the yellow notepad. "We're hoping it will work. But if it doesn't, it could seriously piss off some gods who have very inventive ways of making humans *very* sad." She looked around, meeting everyone's eyes. "If you want to go, you know I won't hold it against you. You'll have to buy every round at the bar for forever, but I won't be upset." No one moved, and she turned to Chris and Sian, who were practically wrapped around each other. "We could seriously piss off the goddess of love, guys. As she's quite dramatically shown, she can take as well as give."

"And as we've shown, we can find the real thing without her. Which means we can keep it too." Chris's chin lifted, making Eris smile.

"Let's not insult them before we even insult them, okay?" She turned to Grace. "You sure?"

Grace slipped her hand into Eris's. "I've been inside the compound. I know all about pointy teeth and snakes and far more nightmarish things. And I know you'll protect me." It was, without question, true. She felt it down to her bones. The fear and shame that had been in Eris's expression only the day before had been replaced with a kind of serenity usually reserved for monks living on remote mountaintops. "Okay. Let's do it." Eris and Grace read through the notes a few times as the lights were adjusted, and the microphones were set up. Gravel crunched, and they turned to see the news van pulling up.

Investigative journalist Madison Ford slowly moved up the steps as she looked around, her cameraman in tow. She stopped when she saw the odd assortment of people, and non-people, on the deck. "You know, I covered the Merge six years ago, and yet I still can't quite get used to seeing you all in one place." She rolled her shoulders. "Whatever it is, I'm in."

"We're going on together, and we've got a plan." Eris held up the notepad. "Your being here lends veracity to what we're saying, and I hope you'll ask questions when we're done."

Madison held out her hand. "Can I read it so I'm ready?"

Grace shook her head and lowered Eris's hand. "The most honest reactions are the ones that aren't prepped, and we need you to be fully present as you listen. The audience would know if you'd been informed beforehand. Everything about this needs to be authentic." She looked at Eris, who nodded, her eyes shining with emotions she had yet to voice. Hopefully there'd be time later.

"Fair enough. I'll introduce you and then you have the floor."

The cameraman got into position, and they rearranged the lights and fiddled with some other things. Grace leaned against Eris. "We have to talk after this."

Eris cupped Grace's face in her hands, ignoring the whistles and calls from her friends. "We're going to do more than talk."

The kiss was slow and deep, and Grace held onto Eris's shoulders as her knees grew weak.

Whatever was about to happen, however this turned out, she'd never regret taking this case again. Eris was worth it, whatever the cost.

CHAPTER TWENTY-THREE

Madison stood to the side of Eris and Grace, the camera focused on them, their audience out of the picture. "I'm here with Eris Ardalides, the defendant in the case of People vs. Love, and her attorney, Grace Gordon. For this exclusive interview, Eris has prepared a statement."

She turned and held out the mic, and Eris nodded. She didn't need the notepad. The words were already part of her. "The question has arisen—what is love? For a very long time, I'd forgotten. I lost sight of what love brings us, what it creates, what it allows for in our lives. I was deeply hurt by love myself and, like so many of you, I turned away from it so it couldn't happen again. But the chaos and destruction around us have reminded me of who I am. The people I've met, the people surrounding me, have forced me to see that I was lost, and that we can't turn away from the most fundamental emotion on Earth." She swallowed as the shame threatened to steal her breath, but Grace pressed their shoulders together and she steadied.

"Even as tragedy surrounds us, I've been surprised by the tenacity of love, by the way the real thing refuses to let go, the way it's as solid as granite and as stubborn as a tree in a hurricane. What is love? It's all that you think it is but so much more than you give it credit for. It's that flush of desire when they touch their face a certain way. It's the warmth of their smile, like a perfect summer day. It's wanting to see them even though you've hardly been apart. It's the deepest, maddest desire to help them succeed and watch them be the best version of themselves, no matter what, even if that means they have to leave you watching from the ground as they fly. It's holding them when they cry, it's being okay when they make decisions you don't agree with because you're different people who will explore the world in all your beautiful, impossible ways. It's forgiveness and acceptance."

She paused for breath, feeling the words burn through her. With the people she loved around her, she could do this. It would work. "But love is not unconditional." She laughed at Grace's surprised expression. "That's a fallacy, a product of Hallmark movies and romance novels. Love doesn't mean giving up who you are or what you need to feel whole. It doesn't mean accepting behavior that hurts, that makes your life less than the expanse of everything it could be. Love should lift you, never bury you. You can love someone and know they aren't right for you, that you're on journeys that need to take you down separate paths." She looked at Sian and Chris, and the camera panned to them. "Love is understanding that people don't fit into boxes, and if you can be open to someone else's soul without letting your preconceived notions get in the way, you can find something special, something divine."

The camera panned back to her, and she glanced at Grace. "Love is seeing someone's strength and finding it as awe-inspiring as the Grand Canyon at sunrise and as timeless as the beauty of a sunset over the ocean. It's allowing for flaws, and we're *all* flawed. It's allowing for change and growing together, helping each other feel so impossibly cared for, accepted, cherished, and desired that there can be no doubt you're going to be at their side as long as what you have lasts."

She looked at Ebie, DK, and John and smiled. "And sometimes the romantic love doesn't last. And that hurts. Our hearts break and mend, break and mend, until we decide to love in other ways. We love our true friends with devotion. We show up to cook them food and give them a hug, to pull them out of the emotional mire they may be sinking into. We help them by understanding who they are because we love them—not for what they give, but for what they provide to our souls, to the part of us that knows we need them as much as they need us."

DK nodded, and Ebie gave her a thumbs up. Once again, she turned to Grace and took her hands. "Love is passion of every permutation. Yes, it can be deeply sexual, and there's little else that compares to looking into a lover's eyes as they allow themselves to be vulnerable in the most intimate of ways, to see their body respond to your touch, your voice, your breath. There is a divine aspect to sharing your body with someone."

She cupped Grace's face in her hands. "Love is scary because that person sees all of you, and you want them to, while also worrying that you won't be good enough, deserving enough, for them to feel the same way about you. It's overwhelming and can make you feel like you're losing your mind. It can make you irrational, and it can make you find ways to make every one of their dreams come true."

The words had lit the fire that had created her, the reason she'd been born to the world, and love spilled from her, all the power in her filling the space and enveloping those around her. "Love isn't for gadgets or jobs, for material possessions or where we live. It's for the people around us who make us better and help us to see the divinity, the god-self, in each of us." She finally turned back to the camera. "Humans have a greater capacity for love than they know. As immortals, it's our job to help you see that, to help you express it. But it's your job to search for the *truth* of love, to delve deeper and to work at things that are hard. Love will save us. It will. Since the Merge, life has gotten better on this beautiful blue planet. But there are still things to work out, and obviously, we're still going to have problems. But if you give it a chance, love will be enough to get us through."

She paused, waiting to see if Madison or Grace wanted to step in, but both were watching her, wide-eyed. Madison blinked and motioned her to keep going. In truth, now it would be hard to stop.

"I'm asking you now to close your eyes and ask yourself what love is to you and how you can use it to heal your little section of the world. And then put that into practice. Help your elderly neighbor. Help the mom with kids with her groceries." She squeezed Grace's hand. "And tell the people you love that you love them. Right now. Not later when you have time. Not when all this is over. Because as we've seen, time can't be counted on. It's slippery and can melt away when you're not looking. Do it now and do it often. Take no one you love for granted. We will be here to help. The gods are here for you, and they're going to be among you soon to help put everything right again. Aphrodite and the other love gods will be making a statement shortly." She smiled at the camera, hoping her uncertainty around that sentence didn't show through. Speaking for what the gods might do next was never a good idea.

"Love is madness. It's a complex and messy concept that is more beautiful than we can ever imagine. You've seen what the world is without love, without all the elements that make up its grand design. Compassion, empathy, kindness, generosity, selflessness…these are all aspects of love that the world has lost in the last few weeks. And you can see how necessary they are." She finally began to run out of words, and she looked at Grace.

"We're not telling you how to deal with the gods you worship," Grace said, keeping hold of Eris's hand. "But what we *are* saying is that if you're a believer, then believe. Follow their guidelines. Because there isn't a single one who doesn't include love at the top of their doctrine. And respect not only the gods you believe in but the people around you. Stop blaming other people and look inside yourself. Find the part of you that is decent and aware and make that your focus. Work harder to fix your own lives and to better yourselves, and your world will be richer for it."

Madison stepped closer. "What you've said here today is beautiful. But how is it going to change things?"

"It will change things because people are born with the capacity to love. No one is born to be cruel and unkind." Eris saw Prometheus on the phone, his brows furrowed, and she had a feeling she knew why. "And now that their point has been made, that humans need to respect their gods and love as a whole, the gods will make things right."

As though called up out of a magic lamp, Aphrodite appeared in her pink mist in front of them. Beside her were Parvati, Hathor, and Frigg, who'd been on her side from the beginning. She turned her back to the camera and hissed, "You and I are going to have a talk about boundaries," before she pushed between Eris and Grace and put her arms around them.

"As you can imagine, it isn't often that a muse can speak for the gods. But we felt that Eris was a voice you could truly hear, given how similar she is to you humans."

Her hand was too tight on Eris's shoulder, but she wouldn't dare shrug it off. She could only hope that she was being more gentle with Grace.

"We have already released love back into the world, and you'll all be feeling the warm fuzzies once again. This time, make sure you appreciate the gift, and as Eris has so eloquently said, respect both the gods and each other."

Madison, who had been in the midst of the final battle at the Vatican just before the Merge and who'd also helped take down a vile organ trafficking gang, seemed to have no problem sticking the mic in Aphrodite's face. "And what about the destruction all over the world? Who will be held accountable for that?"

Eris winced and remembered in a flash the many stories of Aphrodite's wrath. Madison could easily be cursed with some form of sexual fetish, and not the good kind. She held up her hands. "*Humans* are accountable for *human* folly. They turned on each other. They killed and maimed and started wars...just like they did before the Merge made things better." Eris stared into the camera, needing to make her message crystal clear. "And if there's a lesson to be learned here, it's that the gods aren't to be held accountable to human standards. They're your gods for a reason. If they were human like you, then—"

"Then we wouldn't be the gods you depend on." Aphrodite smiled and fluttered her heavily mascaraed lashes. "From now on, you respect us, and we'll respect you." She sobered slightly and her grip on Eris's shoulder eased. "And you need to understand something. You need to hear this and take it in. There are things you don't understand. Things you can't comprehend. There are reasons for things that happen that you don't know, and you may never know. But if you believe, then you have to trust that we love you and truly have your best interests at heart."

"Was it in humanity's best interest to take love away from the world and create chaos?" Madison's tone was neutral, but the question had barbs.

"Yes, it was." Aphrodite's smile held a hint of malice. "Humans need to remember that benevolent gods have dark sides too. We're gods for a reason."

Before Madison could ask another question that would potentially get her turned into someone attracted to goats, Eris moved forward slightly to cut her off. "The horror is over, and the gods will help you create beauty once again. Turn to them now for help."

Madison moved away and the camera stayed with her, making it so the other three were no longer visible.

Aphrodite turned to Eris, fury in her eyes. "How dare you speak for me? How dare you say this is over without consulting us?"

"Stop being a drama queen, Aph. You know as well as I do that things had run their course, and someone had to step up and say so. But the gods are so fucking stubborn that none of you would take that step. You left me no choice, and frankly, I don't answer to you."

Aphrodite's lips were pursed, her eyes narrowed. "You're a minor deity. You shouldn't have spoken for us all."

"Minor?" Eris stepped closer, tired of the games and ego. "I've helped people sing your praises, lament your loss, call on you for inspiration, and beg for your forgiveness. For three thousand years, I've been the one who helps them express how you make them feel. Because of me, they've written love poems that speak to people's souls for generations. Because of me, they've danced with the kind of passion that makes gods jealous. You might be in charge of the emotion itself and for people finding, and losing, each other, but there's no way in hell you can call what I do minor. So back off."

If she weren't so surprised at the words she'd just spouted, she would have laughed at the shocked surprise in Aphrodite's expression. Everything she'd said was true. She'd simply forgotten who she was.

"Welcome back, I guess." Aphrodite stepped back and straightened her jacket. "I don't have time for this. We need to get the rebuilding underway."

The other love goddesses, who'd remained off camera next to Prometheus, joined her. They disappeared as a group, leaving a lighter atmosphere behind.

Madison came over. The camera had stopped rolling, and Eris wrapped her arm around Grace's shoulders. "That was a hell of an interview. Will they follow through?"

Eris looked at the place on her deck where Aph had been. A little puddle of glitter remained. "Yeah, I think they will. The other gods were ready for this to end, so now it's a matter of helping people back to their feet."

"Well, you've got my card. Be sure to give me a call if the world falls apart again." She waved, and she and her cameraman headed off, talking about the next place they'd stop to film.

There was a moment of silence as everyone still on the deck looked at each other. DK began to laugh, and soon the others joined in.

"I can't believe you told the goddess of love to back off," DK said, wiping at her eyes.

"Now that you're safe and she didn't turn anyone into anything they shouldn't be, I'm going to help with clean-up." Prometheus gave Hilda one last scratch behind the ears, and then he was gone.

"Damn," Sian said, shaking her head. "I'm still not used to that. I'm glad the muses can't just poof in and out."

"It isn't a pleasant sensation, I can tell you that." Grace shuddered. "I'll be quite happy never to do it again."

Eris tilted Grace's face up to hers. "I promise we'll fly economy and sit in traffic all you want." She kissed her lightly and waved off her friends' whistles and catcalls.

"You smooth talker. I can see why you're the muse of love." Grace pulled her down by the back of her neck.

The rest of the night held plenty of banter, and the news showed that the destruction had not only ceased, but the gods had also made good on their promise. Help was being given everywhere it was needed. The world had turned right side up again.

As Eris laughed with her friends and held Grace to her, life held more promise and meaning than it had in decades, and she couldn't wait to see what was around the corner.

CHAPTER TWENTY-FOUR

The first blush of dawn was showing over the treetops when everyone finally left Eris's place. Eris had woken Grace from where she'd curled up in an overstuffed chair and fallen sound asleep, despite the conversation flowing around her. She'd wanted to stay awake and involved, but she'd hardly slept the night before and that, combined with the alcohol, had done her in. John had left not long after the camera crew, saying he had somewhere he needed to be. She figured he'd tell her about it when he was ready.

Blearily, she followed Eris to her bedroom. "I really thought the first time I spent the night here would be different," she said, the final words part of a jaw-aching yawn.

"We've got plenty of time for you to make it up to me." Eris dug around in a drawer and pulled out pj's that would be too big. "Tonight, you'll sleep in my arms, and it will be perfect."

Grace took the clothing and set it on the dresser. "Maybe I don't need them."

Eris grinned. "I agree wholeheartedly." She slid Grace's sweater off, her fingertips trailing softly over her skin.

When she took off Grace's bra and her palms slid over Grace's breasts, sleep was the last thing on her mind. "More."

Eris took her time taking off Grace's jeans and underwear until she stood there naked, and doubt began to seep in. Eris had slept with goddesses and, no doubt, human women who looked like goddesses. What was she thinking? She crossed her arms over her stomach, but there was too much to hide with just her arms.

She gasped when Eris took her upper arms and pulled her close. Her mouth was hot and insistent, and Grace let herself sink into the feeling of being wanted in a way she'd never felt before.

Eris lifted her onto the massive bed and pulled a pillow under Grace's head, then she stood back and slowly, methodically, unbuttoned her shirt. She slid it from her shoulders and let it fall to the floor, leaving her in a black tank and jeans, which she unbuttoned before returning to the tank top, which soon joined the shirt on the floor.

By the time Eris was down to her sports bra and boxers, Grace was a wet mess, throbbing so hard she was sorely tempted to touch herself to relieve the pressure. But the look of lust in Eris's eyes promised breathtaking rewards if she played along. And god, did she want those rewards.

Eris slid onto her, her weight perfectly heavy, and Grace wrapped her legs around her. "I need you."

"Oh, baby, trust me. A meteor hitting the earth wouldn't keep me from fucking you comatose tonight."

They weren't words of rose petals and champagne. They were thorns and whiskey, and Grace was about to be reduced to begging. But she didn't have to.

Eris's hand slid over Grace's pussy, palm down, the pressure so, so perfect. She arched into it and groaned when Eris pulled away.

"Slow down, sexy. We've got all night. Let me show you what it is to be made love to the right way."

Grace settled back onto the bed. "You're going to kill me."

"No, sweetheart." Her palm once again pressed against her, just as she bent to take Grace's nipple in her mouth. "I'm going to make you feel exactly the way you should."

From that moment, Grace's world narrowed into nothing but sensation. Eris's words, alternately sweet and dirty, drove her mentally wild, as her touch alternated between soft and demanding and drove her physically insane.

Just when it was becoming too much, Eris drove two fingers inside her. She screamed and bucked, riding Eris's hand. Eris wrapped her arm around her and flipped them so Grace was on top, and she was too desperate to take Eris deeper to be in the least self-conscious. She rode her fingers, crying out for more, the feel of Eris's strong arm holding her in place making her feel like she was safe as she let go in the most primal way.

It was only later, when she was resting her head on Eris's shoulder, that she realized she was crying.

"Good tears?" Eris whispered, stroking her back.

"I'm not sure there's a word for it. Good definitely isn't it. Awe, maybe? What's the word for being overwhelmed by being fucked by a god?"

Eris laughed and kissed the top of her head. "Great, maybe?" She thumbed away Grace's tears. "I love you, Grace."

Grace raised up on her elbow. "I love you too. But what does that mean? You can't possibly want a relationship with a potato like me. How can I ever compete with the women you've been with? Won't you grow tired of watching me grow old? When I get warty and pass gas all the time and have wrinkles I could lose marbles in?"

Eris burst out laughing. "Are you done? I mean, you make it sound really appealing. But the fact is, it would be my greatest honor to be beside you for the rest of your time here, Grace. You're amazing. You're beautiful, intelligent, witty, sexy, stubborn, and you're most definitely divine in bed." She wiggled her eyebrows. "And I would know. You're better, I swear."

Grace rested her head back on Eris's shoulder. "You're probably going to have to tell me that a lot over the years."

"I like the sound of that." They lay in silence for a while. "Can I ask you something?"

Grace nodded, but she could barely keep her eyes open. "Maybe. If it requires a quick answer without any multisyllabic words."

Eris reached down and pulled the covers up over them. "It'll wait till morning. Sleep well." She pulled Grace in so they were spooning perfectly.

Eris loves me. The muse of love, who knew exactly what love was, what it required, what it demanded, was in love with her. She smiled as she drifted to sleep.

When Grace woke, even the blackout blinds couldn't keep the sun from slipping along the sides, showing it was late. Eris slept on her back, her arms over her head, leaving her upper body on full view, the sheets bunched around her hips.

She was flawless. And she was Grace's.

Carefully, she got to her knees and started at Eris's collarbone, lightly licking her way along it, before moving down her chest to her breasts. Eris's hand tangled in her hair, but she didn't say anything. Grace continued her exploration, tasting the salty sex they'd had the night before, breathing in the sandalwood forest kind of scent that was all her own. She traced each ab muscle with her fingers and tongue and delighted in the soft moan and tightening of Eris's hand in her hair.

She slowly pushed the sheets off the bed, exposing her completely, and moved to lie between her legs. She nipped and licked each thigh and then breathed lightly over her hot, wet center. Another moan and hair tug rewarded her. She flicked the tip of her clit with her tongue and Eris's hips jerked.

"Fuck. Yes. That."

She did it again and settled into a rhythm, moving in slow circles, then flicking, then back to circles. Now both of Eris's hands were in her hair and her thighs shook as Grace took her time, stopping when it seemed like Eris was getting too close.

"You're killing me, Grace." Eris's voice was husky and low, and it made Grace shiver.

"No, sweetheart, I'm making you feel exactly the way you should," she murmured and received a hard hair tug for her quip.

"Please," Eris said, her hips lifting, chasing Grace's mouth as she pulled away again.

Grace pressed her tongue to Eris's clit and didn't move away until Eris had come, bucking and swearing as she let go. Grace rested her head on Eris's thigh, content to be exactly where she was.

"If we're going to do any more of this, we should eat." Eris levered herself onto her elbows, and it looked like it took effort. "And we should hydrate. Because I plan to make love to you until you can't take anymore."

Grace slid from the bed and wrapped a sheet around herself. "I'm a fan of all three of those things. Lead on."

Eris pulled on her tank and boxers and held Grace's hand as she led the way to the kitchen. Grace sat on a stool and watched as Eris started pulling the makings of an omelet from the fridge.

"You wanted to ask me something last night," Grace said, her chin in her hands. "What was it?"

Eris cracked eggs into a bowl. "I wanted to ask you why you've never let yourself fall in love."

Grace blinked. "Good thing you didn't start that conversation last night."

Eris shrugged. "I'm curious. I know you have your list, and that I'm everything on it." She grinned and popped a piece of tomato in her mouth. "But really. Why?"

Grace thought about her answer. She owed Eris the truth. "I wanted to believe in love. I read romance novels when I was a teenager. My parents were awful to each other, but I had friends whose parents seemed to actually like one another. So, I knew it was possible. But then I got into law and saw all these relationships that failed, time after time. No one goes to a divorce lawyer because they're happy. But I couldn't give up the feeling that the real thing was out there if I just waited. Part of it was probably protecting myself, I guess. I couldn't fathom being in the kind of relationship my parents had, so I created my list and promised myself I wouldn't settle." She snagged a piece of tomato. "And it turns out, I was right. I was waiting for the perfect person to come along."

"I wouldn't say *perfect*. I mean, *you* can say it about me. That's cool." Eris laughed when Grace flicked a bit of mushroom at her. "I'm sorry you haven't had love before. And I'm sorry that you're self-conscious about your body. But I swear to you, you're fucking magnificent, and I'm going to worship at your feet until the sun stops rising."

"You do know how to melt a girl."

They ate their omelets on the deck, where Hilda lay on her back, sunbathing her belly.

"Penny for your thoughts."

Grace sighed, realizing her thoughts had gone where they usually did. To logical and practical places. "I'm thinking about work and my house."

"Your brother said something had happened at your house?" Eris said, handing her a glass of orange juice.

"Someone spray-painted *traitor* across the front." She winced at the pain it had felt to see it. "It's weird, but between that and Patrick's death, I can't imagine going back there."

"And work?" Eris said, propping her feet on the footstool.

"They offered me a partner position."

Eris looked sideways at her. "And isn't that what you've been working so hard for?"

"It is. And yet…" She closed her eyes and tilted her face to the sun. "It doesn't feel right. I…I think I want to leave. But I'm not sure what I'd do if I did."

There was the quiet of bird chatter and the call of a coyote, but nothing else as they sat in easy silence.

"Okay, so, I'm going to make a suggestion about one of those things. Why don't you move in here, with me?"

Grace's eyes flew open, and she looked over. "Wow. How lesbian cliché would that be? We've known each other for what, a month?"

"Who cares? We're in love. Why waste any more time if we know what we want?" Eris left her chair to kneel in front of Grace. "I want you here, with me, if that's what you want too. Sleeping with you in my arms last night was the most amazing thing, aside from making love to you and that thing you did with your tongue." She lifted Grace's hand to her lips. "What do you say?"

Tears welled in her eyes. "Yes. Definitely yes."

Eris kissed her then, slow and deep. "Perfect."

"Oh. Hello."

Hilda lay her head on Grace's lap, her big soulful eyes looking up at her.

"If she's staying, can we get her a bed so she doesn't keep trying to share ours?"

Eris laughed and pulled Grace from her chair, upsetting Hilda's resting place. "Ours. I like that." She swung her around in the air until Grace batted at her shoulders to get her to stop. "And as for your job, you shouldn't do anything that doesn't feel right. You can move in here and take time to resettle, figure out your next move."

And just like that, everything fell into place. She took Eris's hand and led her back to the bedroom. "I know what my next move is right now."

Hours later, as they snuggled on the couch and Eris's breath was slow and even on her neck because she'd drifted to sleep, Grace thought about how wonderfully strange life was. She'd found love with an immortal, faced down goddesses, and decided to quit the job she thought she'd loved. As she felt Eris's hand twitch where it rested on her stomach, she smiled and closed her eyes. Life was so wonderfully strange, and she was going to love every second of it from here on out.

EPILOGUE

Eris adjusted the microphone attached to her shirt and rolled her neck to ease the knots that always appeared before she went on stage. Music thumped through the auditorium, something she'd insisted on when she'd begun this journey. It increased endorphins, which meant the audience was more likely to listen when the music dropped and their attention needed something to focus on.

"Hey, handsome."

She turned and all her stress melted away. "Hey, beautiful. I thought you were at the clinic."

Grace pulled her down for a quick kiss and then rubbed away the smudge of lipstick she left behind. "The team can live without me today. There are enough therapists and lawyers to go around and Brad is loving being the boss. He'll keep everyone in line. Your idea to help young adults in the legal system learn what healthy relationships are was genius, and who knew that Cheryl would be so happy to start something new with me?"

Eris pulled Grace to her, and once again felt the Universe shift into perfect alignment as their souls touched. The last year had been full of ups and downs as the world put itself back together, and devotion rates among religions had spiked, proving Aphrodite right. People wanted gods with light and dark sides that reflected human nature. Now that they'd seen what the world turned into without divine interference, more people had become devout.

And that was likely what led to the sold-out shows featuring the muse of love.

"I'm so glad you're here. Are you going down to the seats or watching from backstage?"

Grace pulled up a stool and settled on it. She was in the shadows but could still see the stage. "I'll be right here, waiting. Always. And John and his fiancée are going to meet us for lunch after this."

"And now, humans of every variety, we welcome to today's TED talk, Eris Ardalides, daughter of Zeus and Mnemosyne, everyone's favorite DJ, the muse of love!" The disembodied announcer's voice boomed through the room when the music cut out.

"Guess that's my cue." Eris took a deep breath, kissed Grace quickly, and then stepped onto the stage. She waved and nodded her thanks at the audience's appreciation. As often as she'd been behind the turntables in the club and been the center of attention, she still had to get used to being the sole focus. The room radiated with expectation and rather than back down from it, she let it feed her desire to share what she knew.

"Thank you for coming tonight. I know you have a zillion other things you could be doing with your time, and the fact that you've come here to hear me speak is mind-boggling. It says a lot about you, that you're willing to sit through something like this instead of going out for your favorite meal or watching Cupid's new dating show, or even better, staying home and having amazing sex."

She waited for the laughter to die down and as she did so, she studied the audience. Over a thousand people had come to hear her discuss the open-ended topic of love. After the first few talks, she'd realized that preparing a topic wasn't useful. She needed to tailor it to the crowd, which often had a uniquely strange quality. She didn't understand how the fates worked—no one did—but in doing these talks, she'd come to understand that the audience needed to hear a message that would resonate with that particular group of people.

She looked at them and it grew quiet as she studied them. The power that made her divine let her know what it was they needed to hear. She made eye contact with many, who gave small smiles or looked away or gave a little wave. The longer the silence went on, the more uncomfortable it became. When it seemed almost unbearable, she said, "Hello."

And the ice was broken. There was laughter and sighs of relief.

"Isn't it strange how silence in the presence of strangers can make us want to start singing, if only to fill the space? There was a study done where people were put in a room with an electric shock machine and nothing else. Many resorted to shocking themselves rather than simply sitting in silence with nothing else to do. I think some of you were about to reach for the machine a minute ago." She smiled and noted the uncomfortable laughter. "Why does it make us feel so odd? And when we're with people we care about, why is it that silence can suggest so many emotions?"

She began to move, unable to stay still as she let the words flow through her. "Do you remember the last time you had a fight with someone you cared about where silence was used as a weapon? You both sat there, arms crossed, pulling back behind your walls." She mimicked the pose and facial expression. "And in the meantime, words are flying through your head like jet planes, crashing into each other, ready to fire from your mouth the moment the silence breaks.

"But when was the last time you used silence as a way to show someone how much you cared? When was the last time you held one another without any other interruption? No TV, no music, no phones. When you sat together in silence and simply listened to the beat of one another's hearts?" As she looked around the room, she could see the confusion and consternation in people's expressions. "A long time, I'm guessing."

She nodded and took a sip of water. "When was the last time you listened to the concerns of someone you care about, and then sat and silently considered their words? Without judgment, without defensiveness. You simply listened not only to what was said, but the emotion beneath it, the vulnerability that it took them to share with you. How fucking hard is it to do that, right?" She smiled and nodded at the laughter. "It's so hard to listen in a way that's genuine, in a way that allows you to really hear the person's soul speaking to yours."

She glanced at the area where she knew Grace was sitting, though she couldn't see her. Love filled her like a fountain, overflowing, moving from one piece of her to another. "When you learn to listen to not just what your heart needs, but what their heart needs too, you're going to find a way to love yourself as well as them. Silence is often the bridge between ego and heart, and when you learn how to cross that bridge, love becomes something truly divine."

She went on, and when her time was nearly up, she sat on the stool in the middle of the stage. "When I met the woman I'm deeply in love with, we both had misconceptions about love. I thought it was a waste of time." She paused and nodded as they laughed. "And she had a list of attributes that a perfect partner simply had to have in order for her to consider them as dating material, let alone long relationship material."

She smiled at Grace, who had moved out of the shadows enough for her to see her. "I couldn't stand silence because my heart had turned to leather and if there was silence, I had to feel the way my heart had shriveled. She didn't like silence because she was worried that if she didn't spend every second trying to make her mark on the world, then she was a failure."

The words slid from her and into the air, flowing around and through the audience, and she felt them land.

"We made each other better. We learned to be open, to be vulnerable. We learned to listen and let go of old hurts that were doing nothing more than poisoning our present and clouding our futures. Between us, we created a space where silence can mean safety and acceptance. My advice to you, the thing I want to leave you with, is this."

She stood and made plenty of eye contact once again, letting the quiet draw out. This time, it was far less uncomfortable.

"Find someone you can be silent with. Find someone who helps you fill the silence with love, with passion, with caring, with empathy. Find someone whose hand you can hold and whose touch conveys almost everything you could ever say with words alone. Learn to listen with your heart, not your ego. And when you do this, you will learn what love is. On my website, you'll find a list of great questions people asked about love, and you'll find my answers to them. Feel free to add your questions to the list. I'm Eris, the muse of love, and I'm here to help."

She left the stage to a standing ovation, and when she got to Grace she pulled her into her arms and swung her around. "You're so beautiful."

Grace laughed and smacked at her shoulder until she put her down. "Yeah? Well, after lunch, why don't you take me home and silently show me just how beautiful I am."

They walked arm in arm to the car waiting out back, and once they were in the back seat, she pulled Grace close. "As much as I like our silences, I like hearing you scream my name more." She nipped Grace's earlobe.

Grace shifted to look at her, and the love in her eyes made Eris's heart leap.

"I love you. You're truly my better half."

Eris brushed the hair from Grace's cheek. "No, love. We're both whole. No halves. We just create a picture of love better than any artist could ever imagine."

Grace sighed and rested her head on Eris's shoulder again. "That'll do."

Eris stroked Grace's hair, more content than she'd been in centuries. Love flowed freely, no boundaries, no lines. Love was truly something divine.

About the Author

Brey Willows is a longtime editor and writer. When she's not running a social enterprise working with marginalized communities on writing projects, she's editing other people's writing or doing her own.

She lives in the middle of England with her partner and fellow author and spends entirely too much time exploring castles and ancient ruins while bemoaning the rain.

Books Available from Bold Strokes Books

A Haven for the Wanderer by Jenny Frame. When Griffin Harris comes to Rosebrook village, the love she finds with Bronte de Lacey creates a safe haven and she finally finds her place in the world. But will she run again when their love is tested? (978-1-63679-291-0)

A Spark in the Air by Dena Blake. Internet executive Crystal Tucker is sure Wi-Fi could really help small-town residents, even if it means putting an internet café out of business, but her instant attraction to the owner's daughter, Janie Elliott, makes moving ahead with her plans complicated. (978-1-63679-293-4)

Between Takes by CJ Birch. Simone Lavoie is convinced her new job as an intimacy coordinator will give her a fresh perspective. Instead, problems on set and her growing attraction to actress Evelyn Harper only add to her worries. (978-1-63679-309-2)

Camp Lost and Found by Georgia Beers. Nobody knows better than Cassidy and Frankie that life doesn't always give you what you want. But sometimes, if you're lucky, life gives you exactly what you need. (978-1-63679-263-7)

Felix Navidad by 'Nathan Burgoine. After the wedding of a good friend, instead of Felix's Hawaii Christmas treat to himself, ice rain strands him in Ontario with fellow wedding-guest—and handsome ex of said friend—Kevin in a small cabin for the holiday Felix definitely didn't plan on. (978-1-63679-411-2)

Fire, Water, and Rock by Alaina Erdell. As Jess and Clare reveal more about themselves, and their hot summer fling tips over into true love, they must confront their pasts before they can contemplate a future together. (978-1-63679-274-3)

Lines of Love by Brey Willows. When even the Muse of Love doesn't believe in forever, we're all in trouble. (978-1-63555-458-8)

Manny Porter and The Yuletide Murder by D.C. Robeline. Manny only has the holiday season to discover who killed prominent research scientist Phillip Nikolaidis before the judicial system condemns an innocent man to lethal injection. (978-1-63679-313-9)

Only This Summer by Radclyffe. A fling with Lily promises to be exactly what Chase is looking for—short-term, hot as a forest fire, and one Chase can extinguish whenever she wants. After all, it's only one summer. (978-1-63679-390-0)

Picture-Perfect Christmas by Charlotte Greene. Two former rivals compete to capture the essence of their small mountain town at Christmas, all the while fighting old and new feelings. (978-1-63679-311-5)

Playing Love's Refrain by Lesley Davis. Drew Dawes had shied away from the world of music until Wren Banderas gave her a reason to play their love's refrain. (978-1-63679-286-6)

Profile by Jackie D. The scales of justice are weighted against FBI agents Cassidy Wolf and Alex Derby. Loyalty and love may be the only advantage they have. (978-1-63679-282-8)

Almost Perfect by Tagan Shepard. A shared love of queer TV brings Olivia and Riley together, but can they keep their real-life love as picture perfect as their on-screen counterparts? (978-1-63679-322-1)

Corpus Calvin by David Swatling. Cloverkist Inn may be haunted, but a ghost materializes from Jason Dekker's past and Calvin's canine instinct kicks in to protect a young boy from mortal danger. (978-1-62639-428-5)

Craving Cassie by Skye Rowan. Siobhan Carney and Cassie Townsend share an instant attraction, but are they brave enough to give up everything they have ever known to be together? (978-1-63679-062-6)

Drifting by Lyn Hemphill. When Tess jumps into the ocean after Jet, she thinks she's saving her life. Of course, she can't possibly know Jet is actually a mermaid desperate to fix her mistake before she causes her clan's demise. (978-1-63679-242-2)

Enigma by Suzie Clarke. Polly has taken an oath to protect and serve her country, but when the spy she's tasked with hunting becomes the love of her life, will she be the one to betray her country? (978-1-63555-999-6)

Finding Fault by Annie McDonald. Can environmental activist Dr. Evie O'Halloran and government investigator Merritt Shepherd set aside their conflicting ideas about saving the planet and risk their hearts enough to save their love? (978-1-63679-257-6)

Hot Keys by R.E. Ward. In 1920s New York City, Betty May Dewitt and her best friend, Jack Norval, are determined to make their Tin Pan Alley dreams come true and discover they will have to fight—not only for their hearts and dreams, but for their lives. (978-1-63679-259-0)

Securing Ava by Anne Shade. Private investigator Paige Richards takes a case to locate and bring back runaway heiress Ava Prescott. But ignoring her attraction may prove impossible when their hearts and lives are at stake. (978-1-63679-297-2)

The Amaranthine Law by Gun Brooke. Tristan Kelly is being hunted for who she is and her incomprehensible past, and despite her overwhelming feelings for Olivia Bryce, she has to reject her to keep her safe. (978-1-63679-235-4)

The Forever Factor by Melissa Brayden. When Bethany and Reid confront their past, they give new meaning to letting go, forgiveness, and a future worth fighting for. (978-1-63679-357-3)

The Frenemy Zone by Yolanda Wallace. Ollie Smith-Nakamura thinks relocating from San Francisco to her dad's rural hometown is the worst idea in the world, but after she meets her new classmate Ariel Hall, she might have a change of heart. (978-1-63679-249-1)

A Cutting Deceit by Cathy Dunnell. Undercover cop Athena takes a job at Valeria's hair salon to gather evidence to prove her husband's connections to organized crime. What starts as a tentative friendship quickly turns into a dangerous affair. (978-1-63679-208-8)

As Seen on TV! by CF Frizzell. Despite their objections, TV hosts Ronnie Sharp, a laid-back chef; and paranormal investigator Peyton Stanford, have to work together. The public is watching. But joining forces is risky, contemptuous, unnerving, provocative—and ridiculously perfect. (978-1-63679-272-9)

Blood Memory by Sandra Barret. Can vampire Jade Murphy protect her friend from a human stalker and keep her dates with the gorgeous Beth Jenssen without revealing her secrets? (978-1-63679-307-8)

Foolproof by Leigh Hays. For Martine Roberts and Elliot Tillman, friends with benefits isn't a foolproof way to hide from the truth at the heart of an affair. (978-1-63679-184-5)

Glass and Stone by Renee Roman. Jordan must accept that she can't control everything that happens in life, and that includes her wayward heart. (978-1-63679-162-3)

Hard Pressed by Aurora Rey. When rivals Mira Lavigne and Dylan Miller are tapped to co-chair Finger Lakes Cider Week, competition gives way to compromise. But will their sexual chemistry lead to love? (978-1-63679-210-1)

The Laws of Magic by M. Ullrich. Nothing is ever what it seems, especially not in the small town of Bender, Massachusetts, where a witch lives to save lives and avoid love. (978-1-63679-222-4)

The Lonely Hearts Rescue by Morgan Lee Miller, Nell Stark, Missouri Vaun. In this novella collection, a hurricane hits the Gulf Coast, and the animals at the Lonely Hearts Rescue Shelter need love, and so do the humans who adopt them. (978-1-63679-231-6)

The Mage and the Monster by Barbara Ann Wright. Two powerful mages, one committed to magic and one controlled by it, strive to free each other and be together while the countries they serve descend into war. (978-1-63679-190-6)

Truly Wanted by J.J. Hale. Sam must decide if she's willing to risk losing her found family to find her happily ever after. (978-1-63679-333-7)

A Good Chance by Ali Vali. Harry, Desi, and Desi's sister Rachel are so close to getting everything they've ever wanted, but Desi's ex-husband is coming back to get his revenge and rip apart their chance at happiness. (978-1-63679-023-7)

A Perfect Fifth by Jaycie Morrison. Streetwise pianist Zara Keller and Lady Jillian Stansfield couldn't be more different; yet their connection brings a new awareness of who they are and what they truly want in their lives—including each other. (978-1-63679-132-6)

Catching Feelings by Ana Hartnett Reichardt. Andrea Foster expected to catch a lot of pitches from the Alder Lion's star pitcher, Maya, but she didn't expect to catch feelings. (978-1-63679-227-9)

Defiant Hearts by Lee Lynch. In these stories, you'll find your lovers, friends, and lesbians you wish you knew—maybe even yourself. (978-1-63679-237-8)

Love and Duty by Catherine Young. All Princess Roseli wants is to marry her three lovers, but with war looming, she must instead marry Princess Lucia to establish a military alliance between their planets. (978-1-63679-256-9)

Murder at Union Station by David S. Pederson. Private Detective Mason Adler struggles to determine who killed a woman found in a trunk without getting himself killed in the process. (978-1-63679-269-9)

Serendipity by Kris Bryant. Serendipity brings jingle writer Annie Foster and celebrity pop star Bristol Baines together, and their undeniable attraction keeps them close, but will their different paths drive them apart? (978-1-63679-224-8)

The Haunted Heart by Jane Kolven. A ghost, a ring, and a quest to find a missing psychic—it's a spell for love. (978-1-63679-245-3)

The Rules of Forever by Nan Campbell. After reconnecting at their high school reunion, Cara and Lauren agree to embark on a textbook definition friends-with-benefits relationship, but trying to keep it uncomplicated is harder than it seems. (978-1-63679-248-4)

Vision of Virtue by Brey Willows. When virtue and desire come together, be prepared for sparks in this next installment of the Memory's Muses series. (978-1-63679-118-0)

Cherry on Top by Georgia Beers. A chance meeting leaves Cherry and Ellis longing for a different life, but when Ellis's search for truth crashes into Cherry's insta-filter world, do they have any hope at all of a happily ever after? (978-1-63679-158-6)

Love and Other Rare Birds by Angie Williams. Ornithologist Dr. Jamie Martin and park ranger Rowan Fleming are searching the Alaskan wilderness for a bird thought to be extinct and they're about to discover opposites really do attract. (978-1-63679-108-1)

Parallel Paradise by Mayapee Chowdhury. When their love affair is put to the test by the homophobia of their family, community, and culture, Bindi and Rimli will need to fight for a chance at love. (978-1-63679-204-0)

Perfectly Matched by Toni Logan. A beautiful Cupid named Hannah, a runaway arrow, and just seventy-two hours to fix a mishap that could be the best mistake she has ever made. (978-1-63679-120-3)

Royal Exposé by Jenny Frame. When they're grouped together for a class assignment, Poppy's enthusiasm for life and love may just save Casey's soul, but will she ever forgive Casey for using her to expose royal secrets? (978-1-63679-165-4)

Slow Burn by Missouri Vaun. A wounded wildland firefighter from California and a struggling artist find solace and love in a small southern town. (978-1-63679-098-5)

The Artist by Sheri Lewis Wohl. Detective Casey Wilson and reclusive artist Tula Crane are drawn together in a web of passion, intrigue, and art that might just hold the key to stopping a killer. (978-1-63679-150-0)

The Inconvenient Heiress by Jane Walsh. An unlikely heiress and a spinster evade the Marriage Mart only to discover true love together. (978-1-63679-173-9)